THE TRIALS OF DAPHNE HOLDFAST

Christopher Mitchell is the author of the epic fantasy series The Magelands. He studied in Edinburgh before living for several years in the Middle East and Greece, where he taught English. He returned to study classics and Greek tragedy and lives in Fife, Scotland with his wife and their four children.

By Christopher Mitchell

THE MAGELANDS ORIGINS

Retreat of the Kell
The Trials of Daphne Holdfast
From the Ashes

THE MAGELANDS EPIC

The Queen's Executioner
The Severed City
Needs of the Empire
Sacrifice
Fragile Empire
Storm Mage
Soulwitch Rises
Renegade Gods

THE MAGELANDS ETERNAL SIEGE

The Mortal Blade
The Dragon's Blade
The Prince's Blade
Falls of Iron
Paths of Fire
Gates of Ruin
City of Salve

For Graeme

ACKNOWLEDGEMENTS

I would like to thank the following for all their support during the writing of the Magelands - my wife, Lisa Mitchell, who read every chapter as soon as it was drafted and kept me going in the right direction; Graeme Innes for reading the manuscripts and sharing many discussions over whisky; my parents for their unstinting support; Amy Tavendale, Sandra and Donna Wheat and Vicky Williams for reading the books in their early stages; James Aitken for his encouragement; and the Film Club and Stef Karpa for their support.

Thanks also to my Magelanders ARC team, for all your help during the last few weeks before publication.

DRAMATIS PERSONAE

Holdings

Daphne Holdfast, Cavalry Captain
Jaimes, Sergeant and aide to Daphne
Chane, Lieutenant
Mink, Lieutenant
Dex, Lieutenant
Wilkom, Lieutenant
Manahan, Chief Doctor
Delia, Junior Doctor
Jonnas, Junior Doctor
Garrick, Junior Doctor
Dreff, Chief Engineer
Rijon, Priest
Billock, Quartermaster
Harrian, Sergeant of Company Battlers
Weir, Sergeant
Goldie, Sergeant
Ethan, Sugar Merchant
Jorge, Daphne's boyfriend
Holder Fast, Daphne's father
Sandy, scavenger
Mabel, scavenger
Howie, Holdings Field Marshal
Bruit, Archdeacon - Capital
Barker, Chief Justice - Capital
Lessing, Deacon - Capital
Summel, Captain of Household Cavalry
Ariel, Daphne's sister

Sanang

    Agang Garo, Chief of the Beechwoods
    B'Dang D'Bang, Tattooed Warlord
    Badalecht Nang, Beechwoods Hedgewitch
    Echtang Gabo, Agang's nephew
    Gadang Gabo, Agang's nephew

Rahain

    Douanna, Rahain Trader
    Jaioun, Douanna's Butler

THE PEOPLES OF THE STAR CONTINENT

There are five distinct peoples inhabiting the Star Continent. Three are descended from apes, one from reptiles, and one from amphibians. Their evolutionary trajectories have converged, and all five are clearly 'humanoid', though physical differences remain.

1. **The Holdings** – the closest to our own world's *Homo sapiens*. Excepting the one in ten of the population with mage powers, they are completely human. The Holdings sub-continent drifted south from the equator, and the people that inhabit the Realm are dark-skinned as a consequence. They are shorter than the Kellach Brigdomin, but taller than the Rakanese.

2. **The Rakanese** – descended from amphibians, but appear human, except for the fact that they have slightly larger eyes, and are generally shorter than Holdings people. They are descendants of a far larger population that once covered a vast area, and consequently their skin-colour ranges from pale to dark. Mothers gestate their young for only four months, before giving birth in warm spawn-pools, where the infants swim and feed for a further five months. A dozen are born in an average spawning.

3. **The Rahain** – descended from reptiles. Appear human, except for two differences. Firstly, their eyes have vertical pupils, and are often coloured yellow or green, and, secondly, their tongues have a vestigial fork or cleft at their tip. Their heights are comparable to the Holdings and the Sanang. Skin-colour tends to be pale, as the majority are cavern-dwellers. Their skin retains a slight appearance of scales, and they have no fingerprints. They are the furthest from our world's humans.

4. **The Kellach Brigdomin** – descended from apes, and very similar to the Holdings, they are the second closest to our world's humans. Their distinguishing traits are height (they are the tallest of the five peoples), pale skin (their sub-continent drifted north from a much colder region), and immunity to most diseases, toxins and illnesses. They are also marked by the fact that mothers give birth to twins in the majority of cases.

5. **The Sanang** – descended from apes, but evolved in the forest, rather than on the open plains that produced the Holdings. As a consequence, their upper arms and shoulders are wider and stronger than those of people from the Holdings or Rahain. They are pale-skinned, their sub-continent having arrived from colder climates in the south, and they occupy the same range of heights as the Holdings and Rahain. The males bear some traits of earlier *Homo sapiens*, such as a sloping forehead and a strong jaw-line, but the brains of the Sanang are as advanced as those of the other four peoples of the continent.

The Magelands
The Unknowable Ocean
Realm of the Holdings
Royston
Shield Mountains
Holdings City
Blackwater
River Holdings
Barrier Mountains
Plateau City
Arakhanah
Sanang
Twinth
Beechwoods
Broadwater
Mya
Tritos
Black Mountains
Inner Sea
Rainsby
The Plateau
Forbidden Mountains
Basalt Desert
Grey Mountains
Akhanawarah
Tahrana City
Jade Falls
Rahain Capital
Calcite City
Brig
Domm
Fire Mountain
Kell
Lach
Rahain Republic
N

CHAPTER 1
THE MASK

River Tritos, Sanang – 15th Day, First Third Summer 503

Daphne vomited into her bedside basin.

Kneeling by the campbed, she wiped her lips, and shuddered. Her shoulder length brown hair fell in morning tangles about her face, sticking to her clammy forehead. She closed her eyes, struggling to keep her nausea at bay. She tried to clear her mind, but was unable to ignore the rank odour of the stale sheets or stop the assault upon her ears by the alien sounds coming from the Sanang forest that surrounded the garrison. She gagged again, her face an inch from the mattress, but nothing came.

She tried to think of the wide open plains of home, but voices kept asking if this was the day she would be found out, if this was the day the garrison finally concluded she was unsuited to command. Her officers knew she was inexperienced, and the more some whispered that she had only obtained her commission through her father's influence, the more she was starting to believe it might be true. Her hands shook as she gripped the twisted, sweat-dampened sheets, a morning chill having removed all traces of the previous night's humidity, and raising goose-bumps on her dark skin.

It was taking longer each morning for her *normal* self, as she contrived to call it, to reappear. Her confident, smart young officer-self, who she would probably like if she hadn't been so painfully aware it was an act, a mask she had learned to put on at will.

She raised her eyes. The dirty grey canvas walls of her personal quarters hung sullenly in the dawn air. Patches of lighter grey spread up from the eastern side, dappling the room in patterns of mottled gloom.

She clenched and unclenched her fists, waiting for her stomach to settle. She knew the source of the debilitating nausea that she felt every morning, and understood the reason it was worsening: the expected orders from command to commence the withdrawal were late. Fifteen days had passed since Summer's Day, the date most had predicted they would begin dismantling the fort in preparation for the long march home.

This year's invasion of Sanang had gone smoothly, and the villages, farms and settlements they had swept through had been abandoned and derelict, left un-repaired from the previous year's attack. Of the enemy, she and her company of troopers had seen no sign, not a single Sanang had shown themselves on the route to their current position just south of a bend in the River Tritos, deep within the forest tribes' land. None had approached as her soldiers had felled trees and built their palisaded fort on a steep three sided rise twenty paces from the southern bank of the river. It didn't seem possible to invade a land for an entire season and not see a single inhabitant. They had occupied the fort for over a third and a half, how much longer would the Sanang remain out of sight?

She grimaced. Knowing the source of her anxiety did nothing to alleviate it. She felt herself slip on her mask, that of an unflappable Holdings cavalry captain, a look she hoped oozed the confidence she rarely felt. Looking back, she wondered at the comparative ease with which she had carried out her command before Summer's Day, when her dawn anxiety attacks had started. Now with her mask on, she could hide her fears, foremost of which was that her officers would realise she had no idea how to answer the question – what would they do if the orders never came? It was a question that devoured her every thought if she let it, if she didn't concentrate on what was going on around her. She was exhausted.

She retched painfully, but knew that morning's bout of nausea was starting to pass. Her breathing was back under control, and she smiled. She told herself there was nothing to worry about. This, her first proper command posting in Sanang, was as routine as could be. The previous year, the advanced fort companies had suffered barely one in forty casualties from any actual contact with the enemy. Three times as many had perished from disease or had been lost to accidents. Garrisoning had been boringly uneventful, and the retreat elegantly coordinated, with the entire army back behind the frontier wall a third and a half after the phased withdrawal had begun. She knew this to be true, because she had been there – posted to the southern fort directly adjoining the frontier wall as a lieutenant in the army staff, organising traffic through the great gates. Carts and wagons had passed through day after day, creating road jams miles long. Those heading west into Sanang were crammed with soldiers and army supplies, while the ones trundling east on their way back to the Holdings were laden with as much Sanang booty as could be hauled away as quickly as possible. And what was possible, Daphne learnt, had turned out to be quite a lot. Timber, coffee, chocolate, swine and a multitude of other treasures were being stripped from the forest in what the Holdings referred to in polite company as 'tribute', but which was in fact organised pillage on an unbelievable scale. Well, she thought, if the Sanang hadn't gone and massacred that Holdings trade delegation, then the two peoples could be happily rubbing along by now. Trading peacefully instead of, instead of *this*.

She rose to her feet, rubbing the knees of her tunic where the fraying cotton had picked up dirt from the packed soil floor. Her quarters were small, three paces by four, and she knew every detail from the many sleepless nights spent there. She stepped over to her dressing table, and washed in the clean water her aide Jaimes had brought when he had awoken her that dawn. Brushing her teeth, she turned to face her clothes stand. Dress uniform again today, she thought, glancing at her armour, fully wrapped in waterproof hides to keep it from rusting in the humid forest. She had worn it a total of five times during her command of the fort, for ceremonial or religious occasions. The troopers liked their officers to look smart on the Holy Days.

Pulling her uniform on, she gazed into the shimmering silvered mirror on her dressing table. She straightened her captain's shoulder insignia: a crown, and a star embossed with a rearing horse. Her dark grey dress jacket had once fitted her perfectly, having been made to size by the best tailors in Holdings City, a present from her father. That this was no longer the case, she could see in the mirror, her mother's gift. The jacket hung loose around her frame now, the weightloss caused by a continual niggle of petty ailments, no doubt due to the strange forest air, and the bites from the swarms of blood drinking insects that drove them all into their tents each dusk. Their field infirmary usually held upwards of twenty soldiers, groaning and retching and leaking from both ends, some fevered, and others who had succumbed to extreme fatigue following bites from the nasty little bloodflies.

While none had yet died of illness, she had lost two troopers. One, a recruit called Jek, barely out of boyhood, had fallen into the river and drowned. Swimming was not a common ability on the immense plains and grasslands where Daphne and her cavalry company had grown up. It was with an almost overwhelming sense of helplessness with which the soldiers on the riverside had watched Jek drown, his ankle caught in a fallen branch, which was preventing him from getting his head out of the water. Orders had been given for rope and poles to hook and pull him free, but by the time they had rigged it together he was already dead, and they dragged a corpse back to the bank. The priest said a few words at his burial, under a mound of soil to the south east, fifty paces from the fort. He told stories about how Jek had shown himself as brave, honourable, pious and loyal, all the things the dead are wise to be, while a couple of his squad, a male and female the same age as Jek, had sobbed, earning disapproving looks from the veterans.

The other fatality had been caused by a savage goring from a Sanang forest beast, a boar that had stood waist high, with nine inch horns and heavily muscled shoulders covered in thick black bristles.

The soldiers had hunted them for the first third after their arrival at the river, until they had driven the beasts from the vicinity, but this time the hunt had gone wrong. A corporal called Sadie had slipped and been gored and trampled, before the animal had been brought down by spears. The woman's battered body had been carried back, and the company had buried her next to Jek.

Daphne strapped on her sword belt and picked up her hairbrush, tugging the tangles into a semblance of order. Once smoothed, she pulled her hair back and tied it with a band. She noticed a few new worry lines marking her chestnut brown skin, especially around her dark green eyes, but her mask was on, and her face looked as calm as she wished she felt.

Smiling at her reflection, she unpegged the thick draw rope that secured the door, and stepped through into another canvas-enclosed space, several times larger than her own quarters. The meeting room was empty, excepting the presence of Sergeant Jaimes, who snapped to attention as she entered. He slept on a cot outside her door each night, and shadowed her during the day, always a pace behind her left shoulder, walking with a gait that told of a life spent more on horseback than on the ground. She nodded to him as she passed. He tipped his head in reply, and clapped his hands twice. Moments later two aproned aides entered from the opposite corner, and began to set pewter cups and plates onto the long table stretching along the back wall of the room. A large urn was carried in, along with silver spoons and bowls of sugar, and the scent of brewed leaves filled the air as tea was poured.

A large flap was opened in the north-east corner of the room to allow in sunlight and fresh air from the atrium in the centre of the command tent. Ashtrays, cigarettes, pipes and bowls of golden brown tobacco were arranged on the table next to the steaming cups of tea. A tiny brazier was set up on a stool by the opening, and an aide prepared a set of lighting tapers.

Daphne helped herself to a cup of liberally sugared tea, and took a cigarette from a dish. An aide offered her one of the long tapers, the end of which smouldered. She took the light and relaxed a little. Sweet tea and a smoke, like mother's milk to the Holdings army. Her staff and officers began to enter. In first were the company doctor, the chief engineer and one of her four lieutenants.

'Good morning, Captain,' Lieutenant Wilkom said, as she headed to the tea urn and began pouring for her and her companions.

'Good morning,'

'Indeed it is, Captain,' Doctor Manahan said. 'Another beautiful morning in the forest. I was fortunate enough to catch the sunrise from the top of the northern tower about half an hour ago. The pink haze of the dawn, and the lustrous and varied greens of the tree canopy combined to create a most marvellous vista, and for a moment it all seemed to turn to gold before my eyes.' He sighed.

Wilkom shared a sideways smile with Engineer Dreff.

'I'm glad someone here is enjoying themselves,' said the quartermaster as she entered, already smoking. She had another lieutenant in tow, and a further couple of paces behind trailed the company priest, Father Rijon. Good mornings were shared around the room, tea cups clinked, and cigarette smoke floated in slow twisting tendrils towards the open air, where the summer sky was a deep and cloudless blue. Her final two lieutenants, Mink and Chane, entered and all were now present.

Allowing the arrivals to refresh themselves, Daphne observed them. Of the staff, each had been on the invasion the previous year, and each had reacted in their own way to Daphne's evident inexperience. Of the officers, two of the lieutenants, Wilkom and Dex, were younger than she, having freshly graduated from the academy that spring. Both remembered Daphne from her time in training, though she had been a couple of years ahead of them, and looked up to her as if they really believed she knew what she was doing.

The other two were veterans, both having served as lieutenants in the previous year's invasion. One of them, Chane, was in her mid-twenties, a few years older than Daphne, and had a reputation as a formidable fighter. As she stepped forward to take a cup of tea, she looked the part of a Holdings officer, more than Daphne ever did. Her uniform was starched and immaculate, and, standing straight backed with her chin raised, she was also a good hand taller than Daphne. By rights, Daphne thought, Chane should have been the captain, not her. The camp rumours insinuated that Chane's fondness for illicit alcohol had held her back, rather than any lack of skill.

The other lieutenant, Mink, had served in both the first and second invasions, and here he was again, at the same rank, for the third year in a row. Despite being the most experienced officers present, Daphne had never heard either Chane or Mink talk about what had happened, or what they had witnessed on the previous invasions. And, as stupid as it now sounded to her, she had never asked, not wanting to appear naive. Compounding this, she wasn't sure she trusted either of them. She would catch them sharing looks when they thought she wasn't watching, looks that spoke of a cynicism bordering on contempt. She had noticed these looks increase over the past few days, usually when she reminded them that they would not be leaving without orders. She wondered how many soldiers felt the same way. Were they grumbling behind her back, well, of course they were, they were soldiers. But were they grumbling about why she hadn't yet ordered them home? She had felt the tensions rise in the fort. At what point would the soldiers demand to leave?

'Everyone,' she said, quietening the room. 'Father Rijon, if you would.'

The priest stepped forward into the rough semi-circle they had created. They closed their eyes and lowered their heads.

'O mighty Creator of the world,' he intoned, a serious voice for a serious man, Daphne thought as he paused for effect. Come on, get it over with, she cajoled him silently. She opened her eyes a fraction. All the others looked deep in prayer and reflection. Why, she thought, should she pray to a god she wasn't sure she believed in? Surely nobody was watching her from up there. She sighed. It was too ingrained. 'Always follow the rituals,' her father had repeatedly said to her. 'Even if you don't believe. Especially if you don't believe.'

'We give thee thanks for this new day,' the priest continued, 'and pledge to thee our faithful worship and service. We honour thy truth, obey thy law, and treasure the gifts of vision thou hast bestowed upon us. We give thee thanks to be born among the people thou hast chosen. So be it.'

'So be it,' they all responded.

Daphne again raised her hand, and they gathered around her. 'Let's make it brief this morning,' she said. 'Lieutenant Dex, your squadron was on duty last night, anything to report?'

'All quiet, Captain,' the young officer said.

'And I assume no messenger?'

'Correct, Captain.'

There was a pause as everyone in the room took a moment to let his words sink in. Sixteen days.

'Thank you, Lieutenant,' Daphne continued. 'Quartermaster, the supply situation, please.'

'Same as yesterday, Captain,' Quartermaster Billock said, 'except, you know, one day fewer until we run out. The switch to half rations will occur in nine days, based on the order to retreat being given today.'

Daphne calculated. If they left tomorrow, they would have eight days' full rations, followed by at least another twelve on half until they reached the assembly point. The journey took twenty days, which meant that in only another four days they would be on half rations for the entire trip back. After that, she imagined the quartermaster would start to speak obscurely of third rations, and so on down through their dwindling supplies. She hoped they would be able to spear a few of those boars once they moved out.

With surprise and relief she realised that she had at last made her decision. In four days they would leave, whether the orders came or not. She imagined herself facing the dark-robed military tribunal on her return, 'So tell me, Captain, exactly how did it come about that you abandoned your post?' If she was lucky they would just kick her out of the army, though she knew it was far more likely she would be shackled to one of the city's punishment pillars for a while first, enduring the humiliation, mockery, gobspit and worse from the busy crowds passing through the central market where the pillars were located.

She would keep this decision to herself until the evening before they began the retreat, when she would speak each officer individually, and have them pass her words down through the ranks.

'Very good, Quartermaster,' she said, scanning her officers and staff. 'In lieu of any contrary order, my decision is that we remain at our posts and stand fast. Lieutenant Chane, your squadron has the day, Mink, yours the night. Now, Engineer, today's work detail, please.' Her eyes moved to the handsome young Dreff, standing at ease in his dark brown uniform.

'Captain. Today I'll have Wilkom's squadron continue clearing the ditch in the north-west corner, then some of the palisade timbers need looking at further up the...'

As he was speaking Daphne noticed Chane and Mink share one of their looks. By their angry and knowing expressions, she imagined they were confirming to each other that the meeting had panned out as they had envisaged, with another day passing with no order to leave. She wondered if either would ever have the courage to speak up. She was tempted to reveal her decision at that moment just to see the looks on their faces, but knew she had to keep it to herself for a few more days. I'll make sure those two get rearguard duty the whole way back, she thought.

'Thank you, Engineer,' she said, as Dreff finished. 'Finally, doctor, an update on the sick list, please.'

Daphne found her attention drifting again as Manahan began, but unless a pox had descended in the night, she was confident she was aware of their situation. 'So as of this fine morning, there are twenty-seven troopers abed in the infirmary,' she heard Manahan conclude.

'Thank you, everyone,' Daphne said. 'You all know your orders, dismissed. Engineer Dreff, please remain.'

There were a few salutes amid the noise of tea cups against the tabletop, and the fug of several cigarettes being extinguished at the same time. As the others filed out, Engineer Dreff stepped a pace forward, sipping his tea.

'Captain?' he said, a faint smile touching the edge of his mouth.

She crossed over to the table and re-filled her cup. The tea was still hot, though a little stewed. Several sugars would cure that, she thought, spooning it in.

'I was wondering, Engineer...' she began.

'About our preparations to leave?' he interrupted, which he had the most annoying habit of doing. Bloody engineers, she thought, a half smile not reaching her eyes. 'I can assure you there, Captain,' he went on, 'everything is in hand. Just give the word, and we'll have this place dismantled quicker than an old mare takes to piss.'

'Well, that's nice to know,' she replied, 'but that wasn't what I was going to ask.'

She sipped her tea, waiting.

'My apologies for butting in, Captain,' he grimaced.

'Unnecessary, of course. No, what I wanted to know was...' She searched for the words. 'You served last year, didn't you, as engineer to the Fifteenth Loyal Foot?'

Dreff's expression changed from apologetic to troubled. 'Yes, Captain, I did.'

'And you fought at the crossing of the River Twinth?'

'Fought, no,' he said. 'But I was there, yes.'

'You saw the Sanang fight.'

'I suppose.' Damp patches were forming under his arms, and a bead of sweat was wending its way down the dark skin of his forehead.

'Then my question, Engineer, is this. How would our little fort fare if the Sanang attacked?'

Dreff hesitated, and the room was still.

'Engineer?'

'Well, Captain,' he said, looking at his feet, 'two things really. First, the whole River Twinth... battle, well, you can't compare it to us here at the fort. We were attacking them, see, trying to take the crossing and push them back. And second, there's no account of the Sanang ever assaulting one of the forward forts, not last year, and not this year neither, so far as I know.'

'I'm not asking for certainty, Dreff,' she said, catching his eye as he glanced up. 'We've been out here for much longer than last year.'

The engineer looked away, unable to maintain her gaze. 'You know, Captain,' he said, 'it's not my place, but... there have been some rumours.'

'What rumours?'

'Well, it's open knowledge among the officers that your father...'

'My father what?' she said, her voice raised.

'It's known that he petitioned the Queen's Council to extend this year's invasion into an occupation. That he wished for the forts to be maintained and held all winter...'

'The queen did not agree, Dreff,' she cut in, her annoyance showing in her voice. 'And we are the Queen's Own Cavalry. Our orders come from her Majesty and no one else. Is that clear?'

'Yes, Captain.'

There was silence, just long enough to be uncomfortable. So that was what the grumbles were about. How had they found out? She knew they thought she had received her command due to her father's seat on the council, but to think that some believed she was following his orders rather than the army's made her almost dizzy with rage.

'If I may return to my question,' she said, bringing her voice back to its usual even tone with an effort. 'If the Sanang were to attack this fort, what are our chances?'

'I don't know, Captain, that's the fairest answer,' he replied. 'Our forts were designed for the plains back home to repel cavalry and such-like, except of course out here we build them with wood. Look Captain, if you're after information on how the Sanang fight close up, you'd be better asking Chane. She was thigh deep in it last summer.'

'Yes of course, I'll be sure to speak with her.'

'And, Captain, don't forget our scouts are out there, regularly sweeping the riverside and forest. If the Sanang are coming, we'll know.'

She nodded. The scouts would give her a day at best to decide whether the company should stand and fight, or flee for their lives.

'Thank you, Engineer. That will be all.'

Dreff saluted, and turned for the exit.

'One other thing,' she remembered. 'You and Wilkom. Keep it discreet.'

A look of surprise flitted over his face for half a second, before his usual smile returned. He nodded almost imperceptibly, and left.

'Come on, Jaimes,' she said, without glancing over her shoulder. 'Time for our morning stroll.'

CHAPTER 2

THE SIGHTING

River Tritos, Sanang – 15th Day, First Third Summer 503

Where were the Sanang?

Daphne's mind buzzed around this question like a blood fly hovering over a carcass, as she and Jaimes undertook their daily inspection of the fort.

The scouts she had sent out to check in with their closest neighbouring outpost, some forty miles to the south-east, were due back that morning. Maybe they would have news about the reasons for their delay, or whether any Sanang had been seen. Were they licking their wounds and waiting for the Holdings to withdraw, or were they rallying and preparing to counter attack? Perhaps they were already on their way.

She knew what she needed to do to ease her nerves. She and Jaimes passed a row of workshops, and reached the entrance to the north tower. It had been constructed on the edge of the cliff, a hundred feet above the swift river waters, and was the highest point for several miles around. They climbed the three storeys to the top, where a guard from Chane's squadron had been posted on duty.

'Take fifteen minutes, trooper,' Daphne said. The soldier saluted and descended to the lower floors.

Daphne walked over to the wooden parapet. It was a beautiful sunny morning, and steam rose in winding sheets from the green carpet of forest spread out before her. The sun was a handswidth above the horizon, dazzling in the deep blue sky, and it was starting to get warm.

'I'm going to take a sighting, Jaimes.'

'Thought you might.' He had that look on his face that Daphne saw sometimes, which she hoped was concern, though it could just as easily be scorn.

'Get ready,' she said.

Nodding, he walked to the side of the parapet where a crate had been stowed, and started to unpack what she would need.

Daphne took a firm grip of the parapet with both hands, and looked out in the direction of the river.

There was a tree, taller than its neighbours, right on the edge of her vision, that she often chose as her target to scan the forest. Using her vision powers in such a way was exhausting, and she suspected it was contributing to her weightloss. Although in the past she had occasionally practised the line-vision skill she possessed on objects as far away as she could manage, she was more used to closer targets. Even a few seconds at long range was a mentally straining experience that left her sick and drained afterwards, as if she had been concentrating to the limit of her abilities for hours, while her head had been in a slowly tightening vice.

The pain she endured following each burst of line-vision was more than offset by the sheer joy and exhilaration she felt during the moments she was using her powers. Her spirit soared, and she felt borne up on a wave of energy, as her sight unchained itself from her eyes, and flew along a line between her body, and the target she had chosen. Along the length of that line she could look around unimpeded in all directions, just as she could from the target itself, once she reached it.

She was unusually blessed, in that she possessed more than one of the vision skills that, according to their scripture, the Creator had gifted the people of the Holdings. Her other power was battle-vision. Despite having never been in a real fight, in close combat training her battle-vision shone. It was as if she could see a slowed down version of everything going on around her, from all angles simultaneously, and she had learned she could easily put down those without a similar gift. Even if she hadn't been the youngest child of a Holdings lord, her abilities would have marked her out for a career as an officer. Almost everyone on the lower end of the vision scale entered the military. Those who had battle alone usually ended up in the ranks, while those with line or range often became officers or scouts.

The discovery, at age fourteen, that she held two of the seven vision powers had profoundly changed her life. Her father had been overjoyed when the priests had confirmed that she had passed both the battle and the line tests. Her elder sister Ariel had stormed off in a sulk, bitterly complaining about how Daphne was already the spoiled baby of the family, and now she would be insufferable. Her two brothers hadn't looked too pleased about it either. Like Ariel, Jonah had exhibited no vision powers, and was already the type of boy who railed against how unfair everything was. The eldest, Vince, had looked the least vexed. Daphne guessed that being the heir to the family's Holding, as well as possessing battle-vision, was some compensation to being trumped by his little sister. While her father had started loudly planning her future in front of them all, her mother had remained pensive. Though she had rarely voiced it, Daphne knew that her mother had wished to save her youngest from the army. With Vince already destined for the cavalry, losing another to the uniform had been a bitter blow. As far as her father was concerned, having sat through the disappointments of first Jonah's, and then Ariel's unsuccessful tests, here at last was a child who shared the same powers he possessed. In an instant she had moved from being mother's favourite to father's favourite, and seven years later, her family were still feeling the effects of that fateful day.

She focussed on the tree.

While her body remained motionless, her consciousness started to peel itself out from her eyes in the direction of the target. She felt an immense rush, and dizziness rose up as she felt her thoughts leave her head. At ten paces from her body, she paused to orientate herself. She looked around at the forest, down at the steep cliff bank to the dark river, then back at the palisade walls. She saw her own body standing at the parapet, blurry and indistinct, though everything else was picked out in precise detail. She could see the individual leaves on trees a hundred paces away, and could sense the motion from dozens of birds and small forest animals. A brown and red striped monkey clambered through the broad branches of a low and sturdy tree, up on the far bank of the river.

Controlling the surge of energy coursing through her, she began to systematically search the forest to the west. The tree she had chosen as her target lay along a line roughly parallel to the river, which flowed east to west, running swiftly by the north-western wall of the fort. She flew her line-vision out a hundred paces to a point between the river and the east tower, then wheeled around, to check the fort as it would look to anyone attacking, searching for weaknesses. The north-western wall was secure, with sheer cliffs along its entire length that fell down to the river. The south-western wall was more vulnerable. It was the longest wall of the fort, and the land in front of it sloped down a gentle incline for two hundred paces through the cleared zone, until it reached the line of forest. The wall was book-ended by towers, and protected by two deep, parallel ditches. She could see three helmeted heads above the parapet, keeping watch, and others atop the towers. Satisfied, she turned her vision back toward the tree and the river and soared ahead another hundred paces. Turn, search, soar, she repeated the pattern, heading further and further out to her target, which jumped up in size each time she got a step closer. Within a few minutes, she had reached the tree. She gazed out from its topmost branch, feeling a sense of contentment and a vitality of life she never experienced in her body. Focussing her mind back onto the task, she peered out to the west, following the line of the river and straining her vision to its furthest limit.

Then she saw it.

Movement in the trees. It was at the very periphery of her abilities, and hazy, but under a large, covering canopy, it seemed the forest floor was alive with movement. She could feel her physical body weakening, but held on, determined not to return without a clear message.

Just as she felt her body start to collapse, dozens of figures surged forwards, where there was a slight gap in the tree cover, and she was able to steal a good look. Warriors. Lightly dressed, the only metal any of them wore appeared to be pieces of stolen Holdings kit: the odd breastplate, helm or greaves. A few men held steel swords, also Holdings-made, while others had wooden and stone weapons: spears, axes and clubs. They seemed to be about the same range of heights as the Holdings soldiers, though broader, and their arms were longer and thicker. They were also paler than the dark-skinned Holdings. Judging by the area where she could see movement, there were hundreds of them, hurtling through the forest towards the fort. A last thought occurred to her as her body fell, and her consciousness snapped back to her head. None of the warriors were women.

A gentle whistling pierced her senses and she came to with a cough and a start. Blinking her eyes open, she saw she was sitting propped up against the parapet. Jaimes had put a blanket over her legs, and was attending to the boiling kettle at his side. He poured tea, spooned in a few sugars, and passed her the cup. She sipped, as a headache pounded behind her temples. She coughed again, sending a spasm of pain up her spine. Her toothache and earache felt even worse than they usually did after using her mage powers.

Jaimes lit two cigarettes, placed the end of one in his own mouth, then held out the other for Daphne.

'That was the longest I've ever seen you manage, Captain,' he said, balancing the cigarette on his lips. 'You see anything?'

She gazed back, her thoughts dislocated and numb, her head pounding.

Her eyes narrowed for a split second, then grew wide.

She tried to stand, and failed. Jaimes held her shoulder, easing her back down to a sitting position. 'Take it slow,' he said, knowing not to rush her when she came out of a vision trance.

'Sergeant,' she croaked, cursing the weakness the use of her powers entailed.

'Is something wrong?'

She waited a few more moments, drinking the hot tea, urging her voice to return.

She tried again.

'Assemble the officers,' she gasped. 'Bring them here, be quick.'

He got up at once and she watched as he sprinted down the stairs. Right, get a hold of yourself. Her lieutenants would be arriving soon, and would expect her to know what to do. It was fine to be weak for a moment in front of loyal Sergeant Jaimes, but she needed to think through what she had seen and come up with a plan.

Damn, she thought. No plan was going to get them out of this.

A tear formed in the corner of her left eye, and she sobbed for a quiet moment, regret filling her. She wished she were back home, wished she had never revealed the vision powers that had got her enrolled in the army and, above all, wished she had given the command to leave days before.

She heard feet on the steps in the tower below and, with an effort, donned her mask again. She wiped her face, now calm, serious and stern, and forced herself upright. She gripped the side of the parapet as she gained her footing. Just as the first head appeared in the roof opening, she moved her hand to the hilt of her sword and, after a brief wobble, stood unaided.

It was Jaimes.

He half cocked an eyebrow in surprise at the sight of her on her feet, and gave a low chuckle.

The four lieutenants were next, Chane and Mink, followed by Dex and Wilkom. The latter pair were chatting as they came up the steps, but fell silent when they saw the look on Daphne's face.

She waited until she had their full attention.

'Eight and a half miles west of here,' she began, each word emerging heavy as lead from her mouth, 'approximately six hundred Sanang warriors are fast approaching along the south bank of the river.' She pointed downstream, and the eyes of her officers were pulled in the same direction, as if they half expected to see the enemy appear on the treeline at that moment.

'The scouts, Captain!' cried Dex. 'We would have had word from the scouts!'

'I know what I saw, Lieutenant,' she said. 'At the rate they were travelling, they will be here in little over two hours, three at the most. We must be ready to defend this fort and hold it against them.'

'But, Captain,' said Mink, 'shouldn't we evacuate?'

'A little late for that,' muttered Chane.

'Quite,' said Daphne. 'Retreat now, and we'd have to drop everything and flee as fast as we could, with nothing but the clothes on our backs and the swords in our hands. It would be a slaughter.'

Mink said nothing, his hands screwed tightly into fists.

'Should I order battle stations, Captain?' asked Wilkom.

'No,' replied Daphne. 'We'll get battle ready, but quietly. The only advantage we have is that they don't know we've seen them coming. We'll bring in everything from outside and get the fort locked up nice and tight. Move the crossbow bolts and slingstones to the walls, and break out whatever armour we've got that hasn't yet rusted. Get the forge working flat out; sharpen every damn thing in sight. Each of you, talk to your squads, steel them for the struggle to come. We will not be surrendering this fortress to the Sanang. We are Holdings cavalry, the Queen's Own Fifth, we do not run, and we do not surrender. Is that understood?'

'Yes, Captain.'

'Good,' she said. 'We're going to take up the standard defence, nothing fancy. All of you, send your battlers to the armoury to get kitted up. Chane, you're on south tower; Dex, the gates. Mink, you take north and west. Wilkom, you're on east. And Wilkom, find your two fastest runners, and send them back to the assembly point. Get them armed and supplied, but make sure they leave within the next twenty minutes. You all know your orders, dismissed.'

As soon as they had departed down the stairs, she slumped against the parapet, grimacing.

Jaimes lit another pair of cigarettes.

'Thanks, sergeant,' she said, taking one. They leaned side by side against the parapet while they smoked, gazing out over the peaceful forest.

'Did you always want to be a soldier, sergeant?' she asked, starting to feel a little better.

Jaimes thought for a moment. 'Always wanted to be near horses.' He looked around at the fort's distinct lack of any equine beast, and shrugged. 'Seemed a good idea at the time. Would have been better off getting a job on your father's estate, Captain.'

'It's not too late,' she smiled. 'I could put in a word for you when we get back.'

Jaimes frowned.

She thought of home. Her family's Holding had by far the largest herds in the country, and she had been around horses every day of her youth. She probably missed them more than she did her family.

'What about you, Captain?' Jaimes said after a while. 'Why did you volunteer?'

She turned to him. 'For the honour of serving the queen, of course.'

Jaimes frowned again.

'It was the only job I ever wanted,' she said. 'To be an officer in the cavalry.'

She wondered if that was true. Her father had always insisted it was.

Daphne walked to the opposite wall of the parapet and looked down over the fort. There had been an increase in the bustle of the soldiers, gradual at first, but now unmistakeable, as they rushed to get the fort prepared. Several squads were beyond the walls, carrying out a series of quick repairs to ditches and palisades, while others were gathering in anything that had been stored outside. By the riverbank a squad was filling buckets with smooth riverbed slingstones, while others reinforced the picket fence that snaked down the cliffside, protecting their access to fresh water.

Inside the fort, the forge was reeking smoke and sparks, and a great clanging of metal came from within. A large basket filled with notched and bent swords sat by the entrance for repair. Over by the armoury on the main road, which stretched from the gates to the front door of her command tent, soldiers were breaking open crates of armour that had been wrapped against the damp and humidity, and in the front row to receive it, Daphne saw the soldiers under her command who possessed battle-vision. There were fifteen battlers in all, excluding her, which matched the proportion in the rest of the army: about one in ten soldiers had the ability. She knew they would be getting the best of the armour, and their pick of weapons. Daphne's battlers were normally distributed among the four squadrons, but for this engagement she was going to hold them together centrally, ready to respond to any threatened breach in their perimeter. It was in close combat where they would be most useful, rather than shooting down from the walls.

Further along the main road, stood those who would be doing the shooting. The company had a supply of crossbows, but not nearly enough to repel any serious attack. The dearth of trees in their country had naturally led to a lack of wooden weapons. This deficiency had cost them dearly in their long wars with the Rahain Republic, which had finally ended over twenty years before. The Rahain had used crossbows, catapults, mangonels, and a whole range of projectile weaponry that was completely alien to the Holdings military, who instead held to heavy cavalry charges. And since those days, the Holdings had been slow to learn and adapt. The aristocratic traditionalists in charge of the army claimed that using a bow was cowardly, and that shooting people from a distance would sap the martial vigour of the Holdings. Despite this, since the start of the war with the Sanang, a few shipments of crossbows had been purchased from the Rahain, with whom they were now ostensibly allied. Daphne had been present at the frontier wall when such a shipment had been delivered, not long after she had been posted there the previous year. The merchants who had accompanied the crossbows were not the first Rahain that she had seen, there being several exorbitantly paid carpenters camped near the fort, there to pass on their skills in woodcraft to the ignorant Holdings.

Behind their backs, the soldiers called them snakes, and, though it made her feel a little ashamed to admit it, she could see why the appellation had stuck. While their eyes were the same size as Holdings folk, those belonging to the Rahain were generally yellow or green, with vertical black slits for pupils, while on their silvery grey skin a faint and delicate tracing of scales could be discerned in a certain light. What struck Daphne the most, however, was that their pink tongues still held the vestiges of a cleft. Forked, like the snakes from the great plains of her homeland. After she had dealt with the crossbow delivery, it had become one of her jobs to liaise with the Rahain carpenters, and any other merchants who arrived. They had taken the trouble to learn the Holdings language, and so Daphne had thought it only fair that she make an effort to learn their tongue, and she had found a friendly and willing Rahain woman who had tutored her over the season she was posted there.

This year, now that timber was being taken in great quantities from the Sanang forest, there had been some tentative attempts by the Holdings army to replicate the simplest Rahain designs, and it was thirty of these new Holdings-made crossbows that the company had to fend off the imminent Sanang attack. Down by the fort's main road, she could see them being handed out to the troopers who had received training in how to use them. The crossbowmen and women took their weapons and sleeves of bolts from the quartermaster's armourers and returned to their squadrons.

All across the fort, she could see squads assemble under the shadows of the towers, staying out of sight. Once all of her soldiers were back inside, she would put just a few on the walls, to make it look like they were unprepared, while the others would each be given a sling and a bag of stones, to go with their cavalry-issue sword and shield, and would join the others waiting by the tower stairs.

She rolled her shoulders and straightened. Almost ready.

There was a noise behind her, and she turned to see three of Mink's troopers come up onto the roof, carrying signal flags. They paused when they saw her.

'Carry on, troopers,' she said, giving them a small nod. 'Sergeant, time to go.'

***

Back on the ground, Daphne and Jaimes made their way between the command tent and a long, low timber building containing the fort's workshops and stores. They came to the dusty crossroads at the heart of the fort. Ahead was engineering and the forge, the command tent was to their right, and to their left stretched the long road that led to the main gate in the south-eastern wall.

'South tower, via the gate first, I think, Jaimes,' she said, taking in the scene of bustle surrounding her. She saw the group of armoured battlers stand hulking by the forge, getting their weapons straightened out and sharpened.

They walked at pace towards the gate, passing the armoury on their left, and then the troopers' barracks on both left and right.

The gates were wide open as they approached. Lieutenant Dex was directing the traffic coming in, as soldiers returned from their errands.

He saw her, and turned.

'Good morning Captain,' he said. Daphne could see anxiety shot through his eyes, but he was doing his best to master it. 'The troops are almost all back, we'll have the bridge in and these gates locked up shortly.'

'No, Lieutenant,' she said, an idea forming in her mind. 'I think we'll be leaving them as they are for now.'

He glanced at her, eyebrows raised.

'We want them to think we've been caught like an old nag in a knacker's yard,' Daphne said. 'Keep one of the gates open, and leave the bridge in place, but lay its pull ropes out so the handles are inside. The Sanang will see the open gate and run straight for it. I want you to have five troopers here behind the door, ready to haul in the bridge and lock up the gate as soon as the enemy get within ten paces of the inner ditch. Find a sergeant to lead them.'

'Yes, Captain.'

'Are all of your crossbows in the gatehouse?'

'No, I have some up on the wall.'

'Move them all into the gatehouse, upper storeys,' she said. 'I'll have Chane and Wilkom's crossbows cover the wall.'

Dex nodded.

She looked through the open gate towards the east. The south-eastern wall was the narrowest, and the ground before it was more level than on any other side. The forest had been cleared back, and there was a double ditch, just as on the south-western flank. The narrow, three-storey gatehouse stood in the middle of the wall, and the palisades connecting it to the east and south towers had been built with a para-peted walkway along the full length.

'One last thing. Send a runner to my aides in the command tent, have them prepare my armour and bring it to the south tower in ten minutes. And summon Wilkom.'

'Yes, Captain.'

'Very good, Lieutenant, carry on.'

Daphne turned to her right, and walked towards the south tower, passing the barracks of Chane's squadron.

They found Chane at the base of the tower, talking to a runner. Standing tall in her polished armour, giving orders while her troopers got ready, she looked to be in her element. 'Captain,' she said, as she saw Daphne approach.

What a change in her, Daphne thought. Her attitude had been consistently dour and borderline sullen for the entire campaign, and now she was smiling? Was it the proximity of violence? Whatever it was, it made a pleasant surprise.

'I was about to send this runner to you, Captain,' Chane continued, gesturing towards a young trooper. 'The enemy has just been sighted.'

'Show me.'

'Yes, Captain.'

Daphne and Jaimes went into the tower after Chane, and followed her up the wooden stairs.

They reached the open trapdoor and crawled out onto the roof. Daphne cursed as she snagged and ripped her left trouser leg on a large splinter jutting out from the dirty planks.

'Over here,' Chane beckoned. She was squatting by the wall, keeping her head under the height of the parapet. At her knee was a crossbow slot, two inches high, by six wide.

Daphne crouched by it and looked out.

'Just at the turn of the treeline, where it curves from south-west to south-east.' Chane paused to allow Daphne time for her eyes to adjust. At this proximity to her, Daphne sensed a possible reason for the lieutenant's mood, detecting a faint smell of alcohol on her breath.

'Do you see that stand of tall silvery trees?' Chane asked. 'To the right, close to the ground there are some thick, dark brambles. One of my best spotters saw something move just there, about five minutes ago. Said it glinted like metal.'

Daphne located the spot. It seemed still and deserted. She considered using her vision again, but decided against it. There was nothing to learn, and she was better off saving her strength.

'Alright,' she nodded. 'Let's go.'

Daphne, Jaimes and Chane crawled back the way they had come and descended the stairs to ground level. Outside, Daphne's aides were waiting for her. One was holding up her shining breastplate. Wilkom and one of her sergeants stood a pace to the side.

'Chane, Wilkom, with me,' she said, taking off her dress uniform jacket as she walked over to them. One of her aides took the jacket, while the other two started strapping her into her armour. She looked at her two lieutenants. 'I want all of your crossbows stationed up on the wall between the corner towers and the gatehouse when the signal is given. Once up there, keep them out of sight until the second signal, then open up with everything you've got.'

'Yes, Captain,' they replied.

Her aides stepped back. She now stood in polished and shining breastplate, greaves and arm vambraces. Jaimes held out her red-plumed helmet. She took it, and stowed it under her arm.

'Lieutenant Dex will draw them in, and you two will support his position. If anything threatens the long walls, have runners sent to the battlers, who'll be on the parade ground in front of Mink's barracks. Understood?'

They nodded.

'Let's give them such a bloody nose they'll think twice before trying again.'

Wilkom nodded, while Chane smirked, looking more than a little drunk. Perhaps she had the right idea, thought Daphne. She could do with a drink herself.

CHAPTER 3
INTO BATTLE

R iver Tritos, Sanang – 15th Day, First Third Summer 503

Noon came and went. Holdings soldiers lounged in the shade beneath the walls in silence. Many slept, their helmets pushed over their eyes as they stretched out in any dark corner they could find. The quartermaster and her staff regularly made the rounds, handing out food and water while they waited.

The hours crawled by.

Daphne kept busy. She toured every inch of the fort, trying to have a word with each of the near two hundred people that were inside. She had talked with the battlers, and visited her lieutenants up in their towers. The hospital held fewer than before, as everyone capable of fighting had been put back onto their feet and sent to their units. Their beds would be needed soon enough, Daphne guessed.

She returned to the south tower as twilight was descending, and the soldiers were lining up by the walls to receive their dinner. She wondered if the Sanang would wait until morning before attacking.

'Sergeant Goldie,' she ventured, catching sight of a veteran she had not yet spoken to.

Before the woman could answer, there was a low blast on a whistle from the upper storey of the gatehouse, and everyone froze. Seemingly in reply, an angry noise erupted from the direction of the forest, building into a roar of voices.

Daphne nodded at Goldie. The sergeant turned and gestured to her crossbow squad, who put down their bowls and trooped to the parapet.

Daphne raced up the stairs of the south tower and onto the roof, where she crawled to the edge. Looking down in the dim light of dusk, she could see scores of Sanang warriors running out from the forest, and across the area cleared of trees. They were sprinting for the gate, two hundred at least in this first charge. Behind the walls of the fort the Holdings troopers waited in silence. It was growing darker by the second.

The Sanang charge funnelled towards the gap in the outer ditch, opposite the open gate. They pulled up as the wooden bridge was hauled back inside the fort and the gate doors were slammed shut. Several Sanang toppled into the deep inner ditch, unable to stop their headlong charge. As the others hesitated, their bodies cramming into the space between the two ditches, Daphne stood and blew her whistle as loudly as she could.

Torches that had been kept hidden were thrown out from the wall, providing illumination for the teams of crossbows and slingers, who sprung up from behind the parapet and began shooting at the Sanang. Twenty four crossbow bolts were released, and Daphne guessed at least a dozen hit the enemy. She saw them strike thighs, shoulders, chests, but with the exception of one Sanang who received a bolt to his right eye, none fell. Slung stones the size of hens' eggs whipped into the crowd of Sanang, raining down on the front row, and more warriors were hit. The majority of the attacking Sanang appeared to be merely angered by the wave of projectiles striking them, and they started to jostle each other to get closer to the fort. This was the opposite direction that Daphne had been expecting, but the effect was much the same, as the pushing and shoving caused several more to tumble into the ditch, where they were impaled on the stakes at the bottom. Several Sanang were now screaming abuse and threats at the fort, a few were beating their chests, oblivious to the bolts and stones flying around them. She saw some wrench bolts from their bodies, while remaining on their feet, hurling insults at the Holding soldiers. As waves of stones and bolts peppered them, more started to fall, some with several bolts embedded in their bodies, and some due to the incessant pushing, yet they showed no sign of wanting to retreat.

What were they doing? she wondered. They were behaving like blood-crazed animals. Daphne almost allowed herself to smile. They might not have many crossbows, but they had plenty of damn bolts.

Suddenly a harsh, blaring horn was heard from within the forest, and her hopes fell, as hundreds more Sanang emerged from the tree-line. This force was moving in ranks at a steady, disciplined pace, each warrior bearing a light shield on his left arm. Their ranks stretched out over a hundred yards, with torches held aloft every twenty paces or so. Behind four lines of soldiers, teams carried several large tree trunks they had cut down. The smaller branches had been hacked off, but the Sanang had left the larger limbs intact. Damn, she thought, this lot knew what they were doing.

'Captain!' shouted Dex from the upper storey of the gatehouse. He was waving at the new force.

'I see them, Lieutenant,' Daphne called back. 'Keep shooting!'

It soon became obvious that the Sanang between the ditches had also seen the approaching ranks of their compatriots, for the jostling and shouting increased. She watched one of them, a short, bald warrior, whose entire head was covered in tattoos. He was holding a longsword aloft, and was gesticulating wildly towards the inner ditch. In response, several dozen Sanang lowered themselves off the edge of the outer bank, and started scrambling down the slope. With the tattooed man urging them on, more joined in, and soon the inner ditch was filled with Sanang warriors wending their way through the stakes and corpses, while a continual shower of stones and bolts pelted them from above.

They moved out of sight, shielded by the steep angle of the inner ditch. Daphne looked up, squinting into the darkness, and saw that the second force had reached the edge of the outer ditch. The tree trunks were hauled forwards through the ranks, and warriors manhandled them into position over the ditch, their length comfortably reaching the other side. The Sanang then began to file over these improvised bridges, using their large arms as much as their legs, like scampering apes.

'Runner,' she said to the wide-eyed young soldier to her left.

'Yes, Captain?'

'Send this message to Sergeant Harrian,' Daphne said. 'She is to bring the battlers to the gatehouse immediately. Tell her the Sanang are preparing a full assault on this side of the fort.'

The runner nodded, and sped off down the hatch to the tower's lower levels.

'Do you think that's all of them?' Jaimes asked her.

'I saw six hundred in the forest,' she said. 'There are six hundred here, coming straight for us. If there are more out there...' she almost shrugged as she let the sentence die in the air.

Jaimes nodded, his expression unreadable in the gloom.

Damn the dark, she thought, why couldn't they have attacked in daylight like civilised people, when she would have been able to use her line-vision to full effect?

'Chane,' she called down to her lieutenant, who stood directing her crossbow team on the wall beneath her. She looked up at Daphne, her face grimy, and her eyes wild.

'Captain?' she cried.

'I'm going to the gatehouse, that's where the first assault will land. Keep your eyes on the second force; don't let them get near the wall.'

As she said that, the heads of the first wave of Sanang starting appearing over the rim of the inner ditch. Daphne cursed under her breath, and ran to the hatch. She jumped down the stairs of the tower, each flight lit by flickering oil lamps, then out into the fort. Sprinting between the barracks and the wall, she reached the gatehouse, where five troopers were standing, armed with long pikes and short axes. The gate consisted of a double door, each constructed from sturdy upright timbers braced crossways with thick beams. It was positioned halfway along a passageway running through the gatehouse. Slots in the wooden ceiling ensured that anyone entering could also be attacked from above.

The noise was intense, the screaming from the injured and enraged Sanang beyond the gate drowning out everything else. Her soldiers looked grim and sullen in the torch light, as they saluted her.

'I've sent for the battlers,' she said.

A wave of relief passed over the troopers' faces. Any response was cut short as a roar of voices came from the entrance passageway. By the time it had taken for Daphne to draw her sword, there was a great thud as a weight of flesh slammed into the gate, which shook and bulged inwards. There was a small gap between the top of the gate and the ceiling, about a foot in height, and hands began to appear there, grasping the timbers, then heads rose up, and for the first time Daphne locked gazes with a Sanang warrior, and she saw the deep hate in his eyes.

'Cut them down!' she shouted.

The half-squad moved into position, slashing and jabbing the barbed steel at the end of their long pikes into the heads, arms and shoulders of the Sanang climbing the gate. As they fell, clasping at their ripped faces, Daphne could see movement behind them, where Sanang had scaled the passageway wall, and were now hacking with axes at the beams and planks above, which led to the first floor. Why was no one up there fighting back? She couldn't see any activity on the first floor from where she stood, and at this rate the Sanang would be inside in minutes.

She would risk it. She glanced at Jaimes, who, from the look in his eyes, seemed to understand immediately what she meant.

Together, they backed up from the gate, to where Daphne could get a good view of the top of the east tower. It had a turret with an overhang that she had used before, and she knew it afforded a good, though tightly angled, view of the front of the gatehouse.

She looped her left arm around a post holding up the canopy of a barracks block belonging to Dex's squadron, and leaned into her line-vision. As her sight shot up to the corner turret, a wave of bright white energy exploded within her, and she staggered, dizzy and disoriented.

Control, control, she breathed.

Years of practice had taught her how to bring her ability under her control, especially in times of stress, but never had her training come close to replicating the feelings that ripped through her now, with the roar of the enemy battering at her senses.

She was terrified. She froze, fighting her instinctive panic. Regret and guilt, all the lives of her troopers, her heart shuddered from the responsibility. So many people depended on her. What had her father been thinking?

Somehow she mastered her breathing, her vision cleared, and she found herself looking down from the vantage point of the turret, the front of the south-east wall on her right, extending down to the gate-house, which jutted out from the line of the palisade.

Despair filled her. In a dozen places, the Sanang from the second force were laying their tree trunks against the wall, propping them up at an angle. Even as she watched, they were beginning to climb towards the top of the stockade. Crossbow bolts and slingstones rained down upon them, but they were holding their shields high to cover themselves, and were moving steadily upwards.

Over at the gatehouse, the situation was worse. Sanang warriors had scaled the front of the building, and were engaging the Holdings troopers within through any available opening. Daphne saw a trooper being flung from the upper storey, his body tumbling through the air to the ground below.

She absorbed this in an instant, then pulled her vision back to her body. She fought the urge to fall to her knees and vomit, instead settling for scrunching her eyes closed as her world span. She felt Jaimes at her right, supporting her arm.

'The battlers approach, Captain,' he whispered.

She needed to steady herself, and knew only one certain way to do so. Her body would pay the inevitable toll of exhaustion and crippling aches afterwards, assuming there was an afterwards, but she could see no other way. It would be so easy to lie down, let sleep overwhelm her as soon as she released her will, and let her vision slip away. She longed for oblivion.

Instead, she switched to battle-vision, and calmed, energy and clarity rippling through her. She raised herself upright from where she had been hugging the barracks post, and watched as her fifteen battlers jogged down the road towards her. Battle-vision would enable her to carry on for much longer than normal, but there was nothing supernatural about it, she was depleting her body's reserves, and when they were gone, they were gone. Instructors at the military academy had always been insistent on this point: never switch between visions without a break in between. She had only done it once before, and it had laid her out for days.

'Sergeant Harrian,' she said, as if she were out for a stroll.

The veteran battler came to a halt before her. She looked to be in her mid-forties and carried a large double-headed battle-axe. Judging by her scars, she had survived plenty of earlier engagements, and Daphne wondered if they had still been at war with the Rahain when the sergeant had enlisted.

'Captain,' she said, her gaze flickering upwards and around to take in the scene. Sanang could be seen over the tops of the walls, attacking the troopers on the palisade.

'Split your battlers into three half-squads, one to Wilkom, one to Chane, and one with me.'

Harrian nodded and turned to her armoured battlers. With a few quick gestures, the group divided. Five ran for Chane's squadron by the south tower, while five headed the other way, to assist Wilkom. Harrian, Daphne noticed, had chosen to remain with her.

'Sergeant,' she said, speaking loudly enough for the troopers to hear, 'the Sanang first wave are scaling the front of the gatehouse, and are getting in over the top.' She pointed at the door to the building's ground level, a few paces behind her. 'We're going in.'

Harrian looked up at her and nodded. Daphne watched for a moment as each of the battlers drew upon their vision. The intensity in their eyes changed somehow, in a manner only those who had experienced it themselves could discern. They would have known that Daphne was using battle-vision as soon as they had seen her.

She set off towards the entrance. As she ran, she looked up to review the situation at the gate. The great doors were holding firm, though the bulge at their centre remained. The five guards posted there were still busy keeping back those attempting to climb the gate. She could see the sweat running down the troopers' faces, and the grim determination that was sustaining them. Every detail of the scene she comprehended in a fraction of a second, her minding sorting out and understanding what she had seen at a far faster rate than she was capable of in normal life.

She entered the empty lower floor to the left of the gate. There were wooden steps against the back wall, and she reached them in seconds. At the base of the stairs she paused, conscious of the racket her steel-clad soldiers had made behind her. She motioned for them to stop, and tilted her head to listen. Aside from the constant background roar, she could distinguish nothing coming from above.

She jogged up the steps, her sword out low, before Jaimes could insist on going first. At the top she came into another room, with a door leading to the large hall containing the murder holes over the gates, where she seen the Sanang trying to enter. As the others joined her on the first floor, she signalled towards it.

This time both Harrian and Jaimes gently pushed Daphne behind them as they approached the door. A battler took the handle, yanked it open, and Harrian sprinted through, closely followed by Jaimes and the others. Daphne went in last, to the sound of yells and screams from fights across the room, which extended all the way to the front of the gatehouse. A Sanang warrior, armed with a Holdings blade, rushed towards her.

Daphne fought back her fear. She relaxed her muscles, and used her battle-vision to evaluate the entire scene within the room in an instant. Over by the front wall, troopers were holding back Sanang warriors, who were hacking their way through any weakness in the timbers. Already several holes had been opened up, and bodies littered the floor. Sanang were coming in through the gaps, and it looked as though the Holdings force would soon be overwhelmed. Of more immediate concern were the Sanang warriors standing around the large, ragged hole in the floor above the outside of the gate. Her battlers were engaging this group, and seemed to have caught them as they were preparing to secure a rope ladder to help the warriors below ascend.

She breathed, and turned her attention to the man rushing her, his sword raised. She sidestepped the slashing blade at the last instant, and brought her sword up to slice across the warrior's chest, a trick that had always worked at the academy. Except somehow the Sanang parried her attack, his blade grinding and sparking its edge upwards against hers, his superior strength pushing her over, as he strained his enormous shoulders and shoved.

Fast and strong, she thought, as she fell backwards into a roll, coming to her feet and spinning to her right in a single movement, the tip of her sword arcing out and cutting deep into the throat of the warrior before her.

He staggered to a halt, putting a hand to his neck. Crimson blood pumped out between his bruised knuckles, and he glared at her in angry disbelief.

And that was it, the first person she had ever killed, except he wasn't dead yet. She couldn't tear her eyes away, staring at him gurgling up bloody saliva as he mouthed what she presumed to be deadly curses and insults. His sword was still pointed at her, and his eyes screamed violence. He spat at her but missed, sending red flecks across the timber floor, before finally slumping to his knees, making a guttural snorting sound that sounded like harsh laughter, his weapon clattering to the floorboards.

'Captain!' she heard Jaimes shout.

She pulled her gaze away from the dying Sanang, and saw her aide limping towards her, a wound above his left knee. As he approached he swung his sword and beheaded the kneeling Sanang warrior from behind, grunting with the effort.

'You're hurt,' she said, realising that she had lingered.

He shrugged. 'Your first Sanang?'

'My first anyone.'

He nodded.

'You clear the rest of them?' she asked.

'Yes. We got them all.' He pointed at the sprawled Sanang bodies by the holes in the floor. 'But we lost Bodin and Laury, and Harrian took a wound to the gut she won't be coming back from.'

'What?' she gasped.

She ran over to Harrian, who lay leaning against a pile of crates. She held her hands against her opened stomach, keeping her insides from dropping out. Her dark face had greyed, and her eyes were half closed.

Daphne knelt, and gently placed a palm over one of Harrian's hands.

'They were too quick, Captain,' the sergeant gasped, risen blood edging from her lips. 'Sorry.'

'You fought well,' Daphne said, but it was too late. The sergeant's head slumped to the side.

She turned to her two remaining battlers. They looked as stunned as she felt. She gestured to the front wall, where the Holdings soldiers were being pushed back from the gaps the Sanang had hacked from the timbers.

'Get over there,' she ordered. 'Help them.'

They saluted, and trotted over to the far wall, defeat heavy in their eyes.

Daphne made her way to the edge of the large hole in the floor and looked down. It was dark below, but she could discern the roiling mass of Sanang as they continued to press at the gate, shoving it, hacking at it with axes, and scaling its height, only to be pushed back into the mob.

She caught Jaimes' eye, and glanced over at the crates, several of which were stamped as containing lamp oil. He nodded, and they set to work.

Within minutes they had a dozen large, sealed clay jars of the clear, viscous liquid ready at the lip of the hole. Daphne held a lamp in her hand.

'This could bring the whole gatehouse down, you know,' Jaimes frowned, sitting on one of the empty crates, resting his injured leg, and tying off the wound with a piece of ripped shirt.

'If we're lucky,' she muttered, heaving the jars over the edge, through the hole and smashing onto the scrum beneath them. There were yells of outraged surprise from below, and the Sanang's attention was directed upwards. As she hurled the lamp towards them she caught a brief sight of dozens of upturned faces staring at her, before throwing herself backwards away from the edge.

There was a great whomping sound, and light and a blistering heat blasted upwards from the gate passage as the lamp oil ignited. Screams rose with the stench of burning leather, hair and flesh. The flames died down quickly, and Daphne crawled back and peered over the hole's edge. In the grimy light of a dozen small pockets of burning oil, she saw bodies piled up before the gate, blackened corpses, scorched and smoking. Her gorge rose and before she could stop herself she had vomited her dinner through the hole, splashing the sour contents of her stomach onto the bodies and burnt earth beneath her.

Dizziness threatened to overwhelm her. She closed her eyes, but the scene below was etched into her mind. What had she done? She had gone from killing one Sanang to a score of them in a few minutes. Guilt and disgust sapped her concentration, and she felt her battle-vision start to slip away from her.

Strong hands pulled her up by the shoulders.

'Not yet, Captain,' Jaimes said. 'More to do.' He held her by the arms as she steadied herself. Focus, breathe, come on.

She took an offered drink from his water canteen, then dowsed her face and slapped herself on both cheeks, shaking her head like a wet dog. After a moment she opened her eyes again.

Another burst, she could do another burst.

'Thank you, Jaimes.'

She turned to the front of the large hall, where the addition of the two battlers seemed to have succeeded in halting the Sanang's advance. As she was about to assist the troopers there, she heard a piercing whistle blast three times, from the direction of the interior of the fort.

Jaimes glanced out through a slot in the rear wall, which overlooked the main road leading up to the command tent.

'Runner coming,' he said.

'I'd best go meet them,' she said. 'Come after, but go easy on the leg.'

He nodded, and she sprinted for the door. She leapt down the stairs to the ground floor, and rushed back outside, to the open area behind the gate. The five troopers stationed there were taking a break, the fire having dissuaded any more attacks for the moment. She stopped as the runner skidded to a halt in front of her, panting, terror in her eyes.

'Take a breath, trooper,' Daphne said.

'Sanang,' she gasped, 'attacking the west tower, Captain, at least two hundred. Lieutenant Mink's position is being overwhelmed, and he urgently requests reinforcements.'

'Tell him to hold on, trooper,' Daphne said. 'I'll send him whatever I can spare.'

The runner stared up at the conflict raging along the entire length of the wall in front of them. Sanang warriors had gained a few sections of parapet, and were slowly pushing the Holdings forces back, despite the presence of the remaining battlers. The runner's face fell, and she hesitated for a second before turning, and sprinting back the way she had come.

As soon as she had gone, Daphne's mask slipped, and a surge of despair and helplessness washed over her.

They were all going to die, and it was her fault.

CHAPTER 4
BLOODY-MINDED

River Tritos, Sanang – 15th Day, First Third Summer 503

By the time Sergeant Jaimes had struggled down to the ground floor Daphne had regained some of her composure.

'Bad news?' he asked when he saw the look on her face.

'West tower's under attack. Another two hundred.'

'Shit,' he said. 'Sorry for the language, Captain.'

'I think we're a little beyond that, sergeant,' she said. 'Tell me honestly, is there any hope for us?'

'Mink's got a whole squadron up there, three dozen troopers,' Jaimes said, shrugging. 'He might push them back.'

She snorted, put her hands on her hips, and bowed her head.

'You can't stop now,' he said. 'You drop that battle-vision, you'll be out cold for days. We need you.'

She laughed.

He took a step closer, catching her gaze and holding it.

'Don't give up, Captain.'

'I feel so helpless, Jaimes.'

'Then do something. We might all be dead by morning, but right now we're alive. Let's make sure that when we meet the Creator we can at least look him in the eye. If it's truly our time, then we'll die fighting as Holdings cavalry, the Queen's Own, under the gaze of the one who made us.'

She nodded.

'You're right,' she said, focusing her strength, channelling the vision's energies through her exhausted body. 'Let's find some Sanang to kill.'

There was a tremendous pounding upon the gate, and it bulged inwards, shaking and creaking. The five guards leapt to their feet, hoisting their pikes aloft. The noise ceased, and the air grew still again.

'I think they might be coming to us, Captain,' Jaimes said. 'Wait.' He pointed over in the direction of the south tower. 'Chane.'

She turned her head, and saw the lieutenant, trailed by a dozen troopers.

'Captain!' she cried. 'The south tower has fallen. The enemy breached the upper floors. We need Mink's squadron and the battlers.'

Daphne shook her head. 'That's not going to be possible, I'm afraid.'

Chane came to a halt, as if all energy had been sapped from her. 'Fuck.'

Before Daphne could reply, there was another almighty crash against the gates, the upper timbers of which splintered and cracked. The five guards stood staring at the doors, motionless.

Daphne ran towards them. 'Troopers,' she cried. 'Brace the gates! Find anything, beams, barrels. Quickly!' She turned to Chane as they scattered. 'Lieutenant, your assistance, please.'

Chane jogged over, hanging her head, while her dozen troopers followed.

'You six with the crossbows,' Daphne said to a group of them. 'Over there, climb up onto the barracks wall behind us. As soon as you get a glimpse of the enemy, start shooting and don't stop.'

They nodded and ran off.

'And you six,' she pointed to the rest. 'Get yourselves a pike each and form a line here.' She gestured with her arm to a position four yards in front of the gate.

As they shuffled off to the armoury racks by the wall, Daphne turned to Chane.

'Lieutenant?'

Chane spat on the ground, her eyes red. 'I lost the tower, Captain.'

'The Sanang are going to be bursting through those doors any moment,' Daphne said. 'I need you by my side.'

Chane looked up, her expression clouded.

Another great thud battered against the gates. More cracks appeared, and the cross timbers buckled, but held.

The five troopers reappeared. It looked like they had ransacked the nearby barracks as they were carrying several of the long beams that were used to support the rows of bunk beds. They propped the beams into position against the damaged doors, digging shallow pits in the earth to brace them. Two of the troopers were hammering in nails to secure the tops of the beams when the largest impact yet struck the very centre of the doors. The two troopers were hurled back from the force of the blow and the middle pair of timbers exploded towards them in splintered fragments. The tip of a fire-hardened ram appeared in the gap, easily over a foot in diameter. It withdrew, leaving a dark space behind, through which no Sanang were visible.

'Get ready!' Daphne commanded. 'Two lines! Shields out, pikes up!'

Her troopers obeyed. The two who had fallen hauled themselves to their feet and picked up their pikes to join the front line. Daphne placed herself in the middle of the back row, Jaimes to her left, Chane to her right. There were seven of them in each line, enough to fill the passageway from one side to the other, their shields overlapping. She unsheathed her longsword, and held it high. Its weight felt good in her hand.

'For the Holdings!' she shouted. 'For the queen!'

There was another crash, and the right hand door of the gate was battered inwards, swinging on its iron hinges and crashing into the wall of the passage. The braces on the left side had done their job, and that door remained in place. The ram withdrew, and there was a great shout from outside. The first Sanang were seen coming at a run through the open doorway, swords, clubs and spears brandished.

'Crossbows, now!' Daphne shouted.

From their elevated position on the barracks wall, the six loosed their bolts into the advancing Sanang, felling one, and slowing another two.

'Pikes out!' she yelled.

Her two rows of troopers lowered their lances and braced themselves. The first Sanang were sprinting toward them, trying to avoid the flying crossbow bolts, and three impaled themselves on the barbed steel blades of the wall of pikes held against them, unable to stop in time.

The Sanang behind had not paused, and more were rushing through with every second. One of them slipped between the long pikes, but Daphne anticipated him, and thrust her sword into his chest, her strength and his momentum forcing the blade out through his back.

She pulled the sword out, letting him fall to the earth. Her soldiers' pikes were jabbing and cutting ferociously, and bolts were striking Sanang flesh with regularity as they bunched together in the narrow entranceway. She saw Chane hack down a warrior to her right, her blade blurring through the air. Still the Sanang pushed and pushed, the press of those in the tunnel behind shoving the others forwards onto the pikes and swords of the Holdings cavalry. Soon the passageway was thick with the piled corpses of Sanang, and the sheer bulk of them became a hindrance to the attackers, blocking them on the other side of the gate. The assault slowed, then ceased.

Two of her troopers were down injured, but none had been slain.

Daphne glanced over to Chane.

The lieutenant pulled a hipflask from her jacket. She unstoppered it and drank. She wiped her lips and held it out to Daphne.

'I haven't had a drink since the academy,' she said, taking the hipflask.

'Captain,' Chane replied, 'I wouldn't be surprised if you'd never drunk in your life before. You are, after all, someone who follows the rules.'

Daphne remembered her student days, when the official Holdings proscription on the consumption of alcohol was flouted on campus with regular and enthusiastic abandon.

She took a generous swig. It was dark rum, cheap by the taste, and it burned her throat.

'Hey, Captain,' Jaimes butted in as he limped over, the wound on his leg bleeding heavily again. 'Save a drop for me, if that's alright with you, Lieutenant?'

'You look like you need it, sergeant,' Chane said.

Daphne handed him the hipflask.

Jaimes nodded his gratitude and drank deep, using a pike as a crutch.

'Back to work,' Daphne called out. She pointed to the Sanang corpses lying closest to them. 'Front line, throw these bodies onto the pile by the door, block it up with their dead.'

The troopers sighed and grumbled, but started lugging the bodies over to the broken doorway.

'You lot, make sure the left door is firmly braced,' she ordered the second line.

Daphne started to hear the sounds of a commotion coming from the road to the east tower, and Holdings soldiers ran into the square from that direction, in groups of twos and threes.

As they passed the gatehouse, Daphne shouted. 'Troopers, form up!'

A few turned to look, and some paused, while others kept running. Several seemed to have lost their weapons, and panic danced on their faces.

'They're coming, Captain!' cried one.

'Chane,' she said, 'with me. Jaimes, you command the gate.'

The two walked into the mass of Holdings troopers. The soldiers had stopped running, and about two dozen had now assembled in the square in front of the gatehouse.

'What are you seeing, trooper?' she called up to a crossbowman on the barracks wall, wishing she had the strength to draw on her line-vision.

'Nothing yet, Captain,' he yelled back.

'You,' she said, grabbing hold of a sergeant's blood-smeared leathers. 'Tell me what's happening.'

'Captain,' he stammered, trying to get to attention. His face was grimy and sweat stained, and his nose bloody. 'We lost the east tower, and the north-east wall. There was just too many of them.'

'Where are the battlers I assigned you, and where is Lieutenant Wilkom?' Behind her, she could hear Chane firing angry commands at the others, ordering them to re-arm themselves and get into lines.

'I last saw two of the battlers on that end of the wall,' the sergeant said, pointing over to the section of parapet to the left of the gatehouse, but it was shrouded in darkness. Sounds of fighting could still be heard, but from where it was impossible to tell. At night in the forest, without torches or lamps, the darkness was utter and complete.

'And Wilkom?' Daphne said.

'Dead, Captain.'

Chane approached. 'Did I hear right?'

'Yes,' Daphne replied. She turned to the sergeant. 'Your remaining squads are now under Lieutenant Chane's command.'

'Yes, Captain.'

'Lieutenant,' Daphne said, 'presumably the Sanang now hold at least three of our towers.'

Chane nodded.

'Then what in the name of the Creator are they waiting for?'

'I don't know, captain,' Chane said. 'The first wave that attacked us tonight, that's what I'm used to, that's how I've seen the Sanang fight before. All guts, no brains. The other lot, though, they were different.' She shook her head.

'How different?'

'Like they'd been trained, Captain. They were disciplined, and were working together. Not like last year, where they would shove, fight, and sometimes even kill each other to be the first to attack us.'

'As the mob at the gate behaved?'

'Exactly,' Chane said, 'but the second wave acted like they actually knew what they were doing. Behaving like fucking soldiers. Ma'am.'

'Then why are they waiting?'

'My guess, Captain, is that they're securing the perimeter of the fort to ensure they've got us surrounded, and when they're ready, they'll come at us from all sides at once.'

'That sounds like they might be wanting to capture us alive,' Daphne said.

She met her captain's eye. 'The Sanang don't take prisoners.'

'But like you said, maybe this lot are different.'

Chane snorted. 'I wouldn't count on it.'

There was a long low blast on a horn, followed by another, then a third.

'Movement from the main road,' shouted one of the crossbow team from the barracks wall.

Daphne and Chane squinted through the gloom in the direction of the command tent, as a line of flickering torches appeared. At the same time, lights could be seen coming along the roads in the direction of both the east and south towers.

Daphne moved into the centre of the square. 'Everyone, to me!' she cried. 'Four lines, shields on the outside.'

The Holdings troopers, about fifty in total, quickly drilled themselves into a rough square, two deep. Most looked terrified, but Chane had ensured they were all armed.

They watched as the torches approached from three sides. Despite her battle-vision, Daphne was starting to feel a deep exhaustion take hold within her, a dull throbbing ache in her bones that screamed at her to lie down and sleep, and it took all of her will to remain alert and on her feet.

Just as the first Sanang were becoming visible under the light of their torches, there were shouts at her back, and she turned towards the gatehouse.

There stood the Sanang warrior with the tattooed head, who had led the chaotic first wave. He was in front of the gatehouse door, grinning at them as dozens of his warriors rushed out of the building behind him.

He was gripping something in his left hand, which he lifted and hurled into the mass of Holdings soldiers. It thudded and rolled over by

Chane's feet, but Daphne's view was obscured.

'What is it?' she called over.

Chane looked up, grimacing in disgust, 'What's left of Lieutenant Dex, Captain.'

The tattooed Sanang started shouting and gesturing at his warriors, and they roared in reply, raising their weapons, and beating their chests. At his command, they charged at the troopers.

The Sanang crashed into the locked shields of the Holdings square with heavy ferocity, pushing the exhausted troopers back several paces. Gaps opened up, and their lines collapsed into a chaotic melee.

'Time for a prayer to the Creator,' Jaimes muttered.

'For victory?'

'For a quick death, Captain,' he replied, raising his sword as the first Sanang broke through to the centre. The sergeant's sword hacked downwards, taking off an enemy's right arm at the elbow. Daphne parried one blade, twisting to dodge another that glanced off her breastplate. She lunged out at the first attacker, aiming for his throat, but she was tired, and the tip of her blade grazed off his shoulder. She was over-extended, and as the Sanang raised his sword to finish her, she saw Jaimes' arm sweep past, hitting her attacker across his chest. He went down, but another Sanang rushed forwards and struck the sergeant a cleaving sword blow to his neck and shoulder. Jaimes spun on his feet and crashed to the ground, his throat opened.

Daphne roared in anguish and fury, and starting swinging her sword wildly at the Sanang, surging her fading powers to batter him backwards. Surprised, he tripped and fell to the earth. Daphne leaped forward and with a great stroke cut his head off.

She screamed. Not Jaimes, her Jaimes. Her head swam, and her sight blurred with tears. All around, she could hear the sounds of her troopers fighting and dying. She dropped her sword and fell to her knees, looking down at the bloody earth, red and brown. This was where she was going to die. As she started to fade, she heard more horns blowing, and she slowly drifted...

She came to as Chane slapped her hard across the face, her other hand gripping the edge of Daphne's breastplate.

'Wake up, ma'am!' she shouted, shaking her. 'The fighting's stopped.'

Daphne felt a lit cigarette placed between her lips.

'I hope you've got more to drink,' she croaked, her cheek starting to swell.

Chane reached into her tunic and produced another flask. She passed it to Daphne, who took a drink. Rahain brandy this time. She moved from her haunches into a sitting position, grimacing at her aching limbs. 'Better than the last stuff,' she said, handing the flask back to the lieutenant.

Chane sat down on the earth next to her, and took a swig. 'Was saving this one.'

Daphne looked around. There was a wedge of piled-up corpses in front of her, mostly Holdings. Somewhere in that pile was Jaimes, but she couldn't see where. The surviving soldiers of her company now sat around her. Many had injuries. A few still clutched their weapons, but she saw that several were unarmed. There was not a single battler present among them. A few paces beyond, a solid wall of Sanang spears and shields ringed them. These warriors eyed them with cold professionalism.

'What did I miss?' she asked Chane.

The lieutenant studied her for a second. 'The first group from the gatehouse were cutting their way through us, when this lot arrived.' She gestured at the lines surrounding them. 'They ordered the first group to withdraw, and when they weren't obeyed, they waded in and pulled them off us. Since then they've just been standing here staring. Looks like you were right, Captain. Maybe some of them want us alive.'

The wall of Sanang suddenly opened to the east, allowing a group to approach. It was more Holdings survivors, rounded up from the other end of the fort. Sanang soldiers shepherded them into the square. Around half of the group were civilians, including doctors and engineers. In among the dozen or so troopers, she recognised Lieutenant

Mink, one eye blackened, and his head bowed. The ring of Sanang expanded to allow the new group to settle down with the others.

'Good to see you, Chief Engineer,' Daphne said, as Dreff limped over and sat next to them. Manahan and his three junior doctors also joined them, looking shocked but unhurt.

Dreff glanced around.

'She didn't make it,' Daphne said. 'Sorry.'

Dreff's face crumpled, and he closed his eyes. Chane glanced at her in surprise.

There was a noise to their left and both Daphne and Chane looked up to see Mink approach.

'Lieutenant,' Daphne said. 'Please report.'

Mink looked away, saying nothing as he sat down.

'Maybe the black eye from the Sanang has left him concussed,' Manahan said.

A sergeant strode up. 'Was me that gave him that, sirs,' he said. 'The lieutenant was experiencing an attack of the nerves when the Sanang assaulted our tower. He wasn't making any sense, so I helped calm him down a bit.'

All eyes turned to Mink in silence. His head was bowed, and he looked humiliated. So the rumours about her lieutenant's courage in combat were true she thought, feeling sorry for the man.

'Very well, Sergeant Weir,' Daphne said. 'Let's hear the report from you then, if you would.'

'They snuck up on us in the dark, Captain,' Weir said, crouching by the surviving officers. 'Scaled the wall like monkeys. The guards on the parapet never heard a thing, not until they were right on top of us. A whole two hundred, we think, including their chief, who was armoured like one of our battlers. He cut his way through half of us on his own. Lieutenant Mink surrendered, and their chief accepted. He's got a Holdings man with him...'

'What?' Chane asked. 'Who has?'

'The armoured Sanang chief. He has a Holdings man as a slave...'

This was too much. 'A slave?' several of them of called out at once, in tones ranging from outrage to disgust.

'That's what the man told me,' the sergeant replied.

'You spoke to him?' Daphne asked.

'Yes. The Sanang chief's using him as a translator. That's how we knew he'd accepted our surrender.'

'I had to surrender,' Mink muttered. 'I had no choice.'

'No one blames you for that, Lieutenant,' Daphne said.

Mink glared in anger and hurt pride, but said nothing.

Manahan leaned over, and peered at Daphne.

'Are you alright, Captain?' the doctor asked. 'Are you injured?'

'The captain's been running battle-vision for hours,' said Chane. 'She's now so exhausted, she's liable to lapse into unconsciousness at any moment. And when she does, she could be out for days. I've seen what happens when battlers burn out.'

'I'll be fine,' Daphne said, lighting a fresh cigarette from the smouldering end of the one she had just finished.

'Has anyone seen the priest?' she asked after a while.

There were headshakes and shrugs.

'I haven't seen him since the briefing this morning,' said Chane. 'Yesterday morning, now.'

'Did you doctors not see him in his quarters?' Daphne asked.

'There was no sign of him all day,' Manahan replied. 'I assumed he was out ministering to the troopers.'

'And I assumed he was praying in his rooms,' Daphne said.

Chane sneered. 'Are we to believe that the company priest, our spiritual leader, has absconded?'

'I happened to see Father Rijon this morning,' Sergeant Weir said. Daphne had forgotten he was still crouching by them. 'He was outside the walls, said he was off to collect some things he needed for a prayer ritual or something.'

There was a collective groan.

'He'll never make it,' Dreff said, speaking his first words in some time. 'It's twenty days to the assembly point.'

No one disagreed.

There was a noise growing from beyond the ring of Sanang. The shield wall parted, and a group walked through towards them. There were eight in all. Four guards each had breastplates and spears, and one held a torch. The other three Sanang were also armoured, and carried swords. One of them was decked head to toe in an almost complete panoply, except for a helmet under his left arm. He was broad and powerful, and his eyes shone with a grim intelligence. The eighth member of the group was a dark-skinned Holdings man, poorly dressed, slim with long hair, who looked to be in his early thirties. He was wearing a wooden and leather collar around his neck, with a rope attached, the other end of which was held by one of the guards.

They stopped at the edge of the gathered troopers, and the chief said something to the slave. To Daphne's ears, his language sounded like a combination of chewing leather and spitting.

The Holdings slave nodded and stepped forward a pace to scan the prisoners. He looked from left to right, stopping when he saw Daphne's party. He pointed and spoke in the Sanang tongue.

The chief nodded and started walking towards them. His guards went ahead, gesturing with their spears to the folk in the way to move aside, and a path was cleared. The chief halted a few paces away. His slave scanned them again, staring at each. He started pointing, at her, at Chane, and Mink and Manahan, each time saying something to the Sanang chief.

Daphne summoned her strength.

'Who are you?' she called out to them.

The slave and the chief exchanged a glance and a few whispered words. The slave nodded and stepped closer.

'You are blessed by the presence,' he said, gesturing at the armoured Sanang, 'of the great Chief Agang Garo, the mighty and the merciful lord of the Beechwoods, commander of a thousand spears and two hundred swords.' He paused. 'Probably more like three hundred now.'

He pointed at the small group sitting before him.

'The great Agang claims you as his prisoners.'

He turned and spoke to the Sanang guards who, to Daphne's surprise, obeyed him. The slave began to point. He started with Daphne, then Chane, Mink, Dreff and the four doctors. The guards started to urge them to their feet. Daphne looked at the slave and nodded at Sergeant Weir. The slave shrugged and motioned at a guard to include him.

Chane and Weir helped Daphne to her feet, each taking an arm over their shoulders, and together the small group were shepherded apart from the others to a separate section of the square. They reached a clear space where they were ordered to sit, while a new ring of shields moved efficiently into position around them. On its edge, Daphne saw the slave talk to Chief Agang. After a brief exchange, Agang nodded and strode off, his officers and guards following. The slave remained. He turned towards where Daphne's group huddled, and edged his way through the shieldwall.

'You're safe now,' he said to her. 'The chief has claimed you, which means that no one who values his life will come anywhere near.'

'Who are you?' she asked. Chane and Weir sat beside her, one at each shoulder.

'My name is Ethan, once of Long Holding.' He looked up into the dark sky, the first signs of the dawn's light a mere smudge in the east. Daphne saw that he would be a handsome man, if cleaned up. 'Listen carefully,' he said. 'At sunrise, Chief Agang Garo will be leaving, to inform the other chiefs of his victory.'

'And us?' she asked.

'We'll be staying here,' he replied, a frown passing over his face. 'Agang will be leaving a detachment, and he has also ordered one of his... allies to garrison the fort. He will be back in seven days.'

Daphne's heart sank. 'Which ally?'

'You might have seen him,' Ethan said. 'Has tattoos all over his head.' He looked into her eyes. 'He is B'Dang D'Bang. He is not someone to anger or provoke, regardless of the chief's claim on you.'

'Why him?'

'A punishment,' he replied. 'He disobeyed orders, attacked without permission. Did you think the chief had planned to attack at night? No. Agang had ordered them to bunk down and wait for dawn. B'Dang ignored him and charged. So Agang is making him stay here, to guard the fort. He wanted to go along to see the chiefs, to boast and brag, so Agang told him no. I'll be staying too, to keep an eye on things.'

'Have you truly turned to the Sanang?' Daphne asked.

'Agang is different,' he said, 'as are his men. Nothing like the mob led by B'Dang D'Bang. Agang may look like a fierce warrior to you, and he is when he has to be, as do any who wish to lead the Sanang. But he's a reluctant warrior, more fond of books than he is of fighting. Look,' he said, 'just keep your heads down, stick close to me and these soldiers here, and you'll get through this just fine.'

He got to his feet.

'Wait,' Daphne called.

He looked down at her.

'What will happen to the rest of my troopers?' she asked.

He stared at her for a long moment, then turned and made his way back through the shield wall.

Dawn was soon in coming, though not as swift as on the endless plains of home. The Holdings officers watched as Agang's men picked up their weapons, shields and packs, and marched out of the fort. Agang himself was still by the broken gates, hectoring B'Dang D'Bang, pointing back at his prisoners, and making slitting gestures across his throat. B'Dang gazed past him, bored and unimpressed.

Once the chief had left, his slave Ethan strode across to the squad of Agang's warriors left behind to look after his personal captives. He motioned to them, and the warriors ordered Daphne's group to their feet.

Again, Chane and Weir assisted Daphne to rise. She clenched her jaw in grim determination as she forced herself upright. After hours of sitting, every muscle screamed.

They were herded towards the nearest of Chane's barracks blocks, which necessitated passing the rest of the Holdings prisoners. Three dozen or so exhausted troopers huddled together in the morning light. B'Dang's men had replaced Agang's force, and were surrounding the sitting prisoners in lazy groups, drinking and smoking narcotics.

B'Dang appeared, hands on hips. He looked over at Daphne and her small group with contempt as they went past, and she saw the ring of B'Dang's men tighten around the remaining troopers. B'Dang D'Bang raised his sword, his eyes still on her, a smile on the edge of his lips. He roared out to his men, and they fell like wolves upon the exhausted prisoners. A few fought back, but were cut down in the onslaught. Rage gripped Daphne as she watched her soldiers massacred.

As they approached the barracks, Daphne wriggled free from the grasp of Chane and Weir. She rolled to the ground in a tight bundle, avoiding the onrushing limbs of their Sanang escorts. Once out of their reach, she staggered forwards, unsheathing her sword, which throughout the night they had never taken from her, the Sanang too arrogant to bother disarming such a worthless foe. She ignored the angry and fearful shouting coming from behind her.

Ahead, B'Dang and a few of his cronies were standing, watching her unsteady approach with amusement.

Well I hope you find this funny, she thought as she ceased staggering, and leapt at B'Dang, swinging her sword, expending everything she had for one final burst. Her blade flashed through the air, but B'Dang was faster. He grabbed one of the smaller warriors standing next to him, pulling him between Daphne's sword and himself, the blow slicing the hapless warrior through the neck. His body slumped to the ground as Daphne landed, falling to one knee onto the hard earth.

She looked up to see B'Dang laughing. He bowed his head to her in approval. He sheathed his sword, smiled, and picked up a large studded bat.

'Please forgive me,' she said to the ground, not knowing who she was talking to, but feeling sick and overwhelmed with loss and guilt, and wanting it to end. 'I'm so tired.'

She felt a crippling blow to her left arm and side, and fell to the ground, crying out in pain. She clasped her shattered limb with her other hand as excruciating agony tore through her, enveloping her every thought.

She closed her eyes.

CHAPTER 5
FRACTURED

R iver Tritos, Sanang – 22nd Day, First Third Summer 503

The sun is shining overhead, and a warm wind blows across the plain, rustling the long summer grasses. Daphne runs, holding out her hands to either side, brushing them through the few remaining stems of blue and yellow wild flowers. She is wearing a dress, and her legs and feet are bare. As she approaches the top of a small incline, she can hear the noise, thundering and pounding. The powerful roar frightens her, but she finds it comforting at the same time. She reaches the prow of the gentle hill and stands there, gazing out over the endless savannah. Covering the plains below are thousands upon thousands of horses, their hoofs beating against the ground as the great herds gallop in synchronised swirls through the grass, sending a thick cloud of dust up into the deep blue vastness of the open sky above. Home.

She cried out in pain as her left arm was held and lifted, bolts of flagellating agony scourging through her. She struggled, and more hands gripped and restrained her. She was flat on her back, but couldn't tell if her eyes were open or not, the pain from her arm all-consuming. Firm palms pressed against her head, and something like a cigarette was held to her lips. In her panic she inhaled. The pain faded, and she fell back into oblivion.

'Is it true the Sanang have skin as pale as milk? Do they really look like apes?' Jorge asked her, as he lay naked on her bed, smoking a cigarette. 'You hear such dreadful nonsense about them from the more excitable students, first years mostly. About how they all live up in the trees, swinging from the branches like monkeys, beating their chests. Come on, Lieutenant, is it true?'

Daphne laughed. 'I've already told you. There were no Sanang at the frontier wall. But yes, I suppose that's roughly the sort of thing the soldiers returning from the front would say.'

'Could you not just pretend you'd seen them, make something up?' he grinned. 'Something ferociously savage and gruesome, which will turn stomachs at tonight's dinner party. There's a certain priest coming whom I'd particularly enjoy upsetting.'

She gazed around her university room. She was using it again over the winter, to catch up on the studies she had missed while being stationed at the wall all summer. Someone else had been living in the room during the previous term, but Daphne had made it her own again. Jorge flicked ash into a tea cup, and passed her the cigarette. She looked at the dark skin of his chest, and his stomach, grown a little flabbier since the last time she had seen him.

'On the subject of making things up,' he said, a gleam in his eye. Daphne groaned.

'The bloody so-called prophet, letting it be known that the voice of the Creator commands us to end the war? Did you hear? I mean, does he really think anyone believes that codswallop anymore? To imagine he's actually got a little voice in his head, telling him what to do, it's utterly barking. The queen should damn well order the prophets and priests to bugger off, stay out of politics and get back to reading their dusty old books. No one's buying it any more.'

'You finished?'

He put on a hurt face, and pouted. She stifled a laugh. Such an angry boy.

'Remember,' she said, 'you can get away with saying that sort of thing to me when we're alone, but...'

'Yes, yes, I know,' he said. 'Don't worry, I won't go embarrassing you with my unbelief in public.'

'...all a favour and stop complaining. By the Creator's balls, you're starting to be a pain in the arse.'

'Fuck you.'

Where was she? She couldn't move, not a toe, not a finger, nor would her eyes open.

She heard movement.

'No, Lieutenant.' It was Sergeant Weir. 'Put Lieutenant Mink down, sir. Please.'

'Do as the sergeant says, there's a good chap.' Manahan, sounding tired but calm.

More movement. A sigh as Chane sat back down.

So they weren't in immediate danger, Daphne thought, before starting to feel an ache build up from her left arm, centred on her elbow. It was manageable, but growing.

'Whatever are you doing over there, Delia?' Manahan said. 'The captain needs her rest, don't you be disturbing her.'

'I thought for a moment I saw her move, sir,' the junior doctor said, surprising Daphne with her proximity. Her voice sounded like it came from a foot away, to her left side. 'Her poor arm.'

'Don't touch it, Delia,' Manahan said. 'We all saw what happened last time. We were fortunate that the slave was here with one of those narcotic cigarettes of his. Besides, without equipment, surgical instruments, and everything else we would require, there's nothing more we can do. We saved her arm, but it will be crippled and useless the rest of her days. Her hand will be like a withered claw.'

'That's enough,' said Chane. 'No need to be cruel.'

'My dear Lieutenant,' the doctor said, 'I am merely being factual regarding her injury. If the gory truth of battle upsets you, then perhaps the army wasn't the best choice of career.'

As they bickered, Daphne screamed inside. The pain was inexorably building, shooting fire from her fingers, wrist and forearm all the way up to her shoulder, but centred on her shattered elbow, a tight knot of agony. And now to discover that she would never use her arm again, her future dimmed and narrowed. A crippled prisoner in the Sanang forest. Would she ever be able to ride a horse again? The pain filled her, and she bathed in its tears for a moment that felt as long as an eternity.

'Jaimes,' she groaned, turning her head. 'Jaimes, help me.'

She heard whispering.

'Jaimes, is that you?' She felt sick, opened her eyes, and saw Chane leaning over her, shrouded in darkness, a guarded half-smile forming on her lips.

'Captain,' she said, 'can you hear me?'

'Here,' said a voice to her left. She looked over, her head swimming, to see a young woman holding a water canteen. She held it to her lips. 'Slowly,' the young woman said, as Daphne gulped it down.

Where was Jaimes? If she were ill, shouldn't he be here to help her?

She tried to lift her neck to see if he was there, but her muscles were too weak and she only succeeded in flopping her head from side to side, gasping.

'Be still,' Chane urged.

Her nausea rose, and she felt the liquid she had just drunk start to come back up. She vomited, but couldn't turn her head, and started to gag.

'Turn her over, quickly,' Delia whispered. 'Try not to touch her arm.'

She was choking now, and panicking. Hands took hold of her shoulders, and began shifting her onto her right side. Her head was tipped sideways, a hand pushing down on her cheek. She stopped choking, and water and bile gushed out of her mouth onto the sweat-stained sheets of the bed. She shuddered all over, her body shaking violently from exhaustion and pain.

The hands were trying to push her over onto her back, but her spasms shook her from their grasp, and she fell onto the bed, cracking her left elbow against the frame as she landed.

A skull-splitting scream tore through her ears, and it was only in the moment before she passed out that she realised it had come from her.

A damp cloth was pressed to her forehead, and the sudden coolness of it was enough to wake her. She kept her eyes closed as the cloth tenderly wiped away her sweat and tears. She remembered being ill, back when she had been ten summers old. It had been the horse-fever, a rite of passage for most Holdings youth. Her mother had tended to her every day, applying soothing balms and creams to her blistered skin, so that she wouldn't suffer any scarring that might endure into adulthood. She felt a pang of guilt at the thought of her mother. Had Daphne ever really expressed her gratitude for all that she had done?

She opened her eyes to thank her, and instead saw a tall, strange man leaning over her bed.

'Who...?' she gasped, trying to shout.

'Lieutenant!' the man said. 'Come quickly.'

She realised there were more people in the room. They were rising and moving towards her. Panic rose to overwhelm her, and her arm started to ache.

'Give it to me, hurry!' a female voice said. She thought she detected a faint scent of smoke. A woman appeared on her left, holding what looked like a cigarette. Daphne thought she recognised her from somewhere.

'Here,' the woman said. 'Don't be afraid. Smoke this. It'll make you feel better.'

She did know her, Daphne thought, as the pain from her left elbow grew. She would have to trust her.

The woman held the lit brand to Daphne's mouth, and she inhaled. She blew out a long low exhalation of grey smoke, and the panic and pain started to recede. She closed her eyes and relaxed back onto the mattress.

'Get her some water,' the woman said. 'And let's prop her head up this time.'

She felt strong arms lift her by the shoulders, and pillows were pushed behind her head to raise it. She felt safe, and didn't resist.

'Here, Captain,' the female voice said. 'Drink.'

A cup touched her parched lips, and she took a sip. 'And have another smoke.'

She inhaled again, and the last of the pain vanished.

She opened her eyes.

'Chane?' she asked in surprise, her voice a weak whisper.

'Yes, it's me,' the woman said. 'How do you feel?'

Daphne thought for a moment. 'Numb. Where's Jaimes?'

There were a few nervous glances among the people gathered around her bed. Mink, she knew, Dreff, and Manahan... Memories began to seep back. Were they in the Sanang Forest?

'Sergeant Jaimes is dead, Captain,' Chane replied, looking right at her. 'I'm sorry. Do you remember anything?'

'Some... things. Were we attacked?' A vision jumped into her mind of a tattooed man standing by a ditch, brandishing a sword, eyes afire, grinning at her.

'Yes, Captain,' Chane said.

'We're all that's left,' Mink muttered. Chane shot him a dark glance.

Whatever she had smoked was making her thoughts slow and fuggy, and she took a moment to register what Lieutenant Mink had said. As the memory of what had happened finally returned, she started to cry. It was an odd feeling, as if it were someone else's body that shuddered with sobs, her consciousness observing from a safe distance.

'Great work, Mink,' Chane said.

She felt an arm go round her shoulder. 'Everyone,' Chane called out, 'back to your bunks, give the captain some space. Delia, could you please dig out whatever food we have left?'

Chane sat on the side of the bed, and held her as she wept.

A voice in Daphne's head that sounded a little like her father's told her to pull herself together and act like an officer, and despite the temptation to burrow into Chane's reassuring embrace, she stopped weeping. She tried to raise her left hand to wipe away her tears, but her arm wouldn't respond. She glanced down at it. She knew what she would see, she could recall the words of Doctor Manahan when she had partially awoken some time before, but she had a tiny hope that she may have dreamt it.

Her left limb was bandaged, with splints along her upper arm and forearm. Her elbow was bent in a position halfway between a straight line and a right angle. The hand was also bound, but she could see that her fingers had curled inwards on themselves.

'I'm not going to lie to you, Captain,' Chane said, as she disengaged from the embrace. 'The doctors believe you have lost the use of your left arm.'

Daphne nodded.

'Thank you, Lieutenant,' she said, her voice steady. 'My thanks to you all, for looking after me. How long has it been?'

'This is our sixth morning, Captain,' Chane replied. 'We're in what was Sergeant Goldie's squad barracks. Mink spoke the truth before, we few are all that remains of the company.'

Daphne looked around. There were nine of them in the room. Four soldiers: herself, Chane, Mink and Sergeant Weir, who sat crouched on a table by the far wall, peering out of a small opening to the outside. There were also the four company doctors: Manahan, Delia, Garrick, and Jonnas, who had been the one wiping her brow when she had awoken. There was also Dreff, who was lying motionless in his bed, near to the barrack's doorway.

'They killed all of the troopers,' Daphne said.

'Yes, Captain, they did,' Chane replied.

'Took a few days over some of them,' Mink said, his eyes bloodshot and heavy.

'The captain doesn't need to hear the details,' Chane said.

'No, Lieutenant,' Daphne replied. 'It's alright. Tell me.'

Chane looked down, grief and rage on her face.

'B'Dang kept a few of them alive, for a while,' she said. 'For sport. And to torment us. He made sure we heard it all.'

There was silence in the room.

'Has B'Dang been in here?' Daphne asked after a while.

'No,' Chane replied. 'Agang's guards have kept him away. Although there's only twelve of them, they're more disciplined than B'Dang's crew. Those clowns spend whole days and nights getting drunk and smoking drugs. If it came to a fight, Agang's men could probably handle them without too much difficulty.'

Chane lit a cigarette.

'I've been remembering the battle,' she went on. 'I'm reasonably sure we killed at least as many of them as they did of us all told, only the vast majority of dead Sanang were from B'Dang's force. Looking back, I don't think we killed all that many of Agang's soldiers.' She paused. 'Here's the thing. If Agang's trying to organise the Sanang, train them up... Well, if he succeeds, then this war will take on an entirely new flavour.'

'Nonsense,' called over Doctor Manahan. 'They are savages, plain and simple. This Agang character may have gotten himself a dressed-up little troop of make believe soldiers, but the Sanang as a people? Organising themselves? Pah.'

'Where are the women?' Daphne asked.

'What?' replied Chane.

'Among the Sanang warriors. Why are there no women?'

Chane shrugged.

'Maybe the Sanang female is unsuited to combat?' suggested Manahan.

From his little window, Weir snorted. 'Not likely,' he said. 'I seen plenty of Sanang women in a village on the first year's invasion, some of them fought well enough when we were clearing them out. None of them were dressed as warriors, though.'

Daphne pondered. Why would an army exclude half of the population? Had the Sanang women refused to fight?

Delia approached from the left. 'I have the food you asked for,' she said, holding out a greasy plate. On it was a small selection of dried grey meat, a husk of stale bread, and a couple of small wrinkled oranges. 'It's not much,' she said, putting down the plate, 'but I do also have this.' She reached into her pocket and pulled out a small rectangular wrapping. 'Chocolate,' she whispered. 'Been saving it for you, Captain. It's not much, but if you clear the plate, I'll give it to you.' She held it out.

'You're bribing me like a child,' Daphne said.

Delia nodded. 'Is it working?'

Daphne picked up a piece of dried meat and started chewing. She grimaced at its rancid saltiness, and tried to keep her mind on the chocolate, the one thing, in her opinion, that might justify the entire invasion of Sanang.

Daphne awoke again as the last light of day was filtering through the slats in the wooden walls. She had fallen asleep with the taste of chocolate in her mouth, but now she felt the pain from her arm arise once more.

She rolled over, retching.

From the bed opposite, Delia sat up. 'Captain?'

Daphne grimaced. 'The arm.'

Delia walked over to a small table next to Daphne's bed. She rummaged around in a drawer for a few moments, then produced a flint and taper. She sat on the stool next to the bed and sparked up a small light. She lit a drugged cigarette, and passed it to Daphne.

She inhaled, and the pain abated.

'Thanks,' she said. 'Is it like alcohol, might I become addicted?'

'I don't know, Captain,' she said. 'We have no idea what herb it is you're smoking. Ethan, the slave, he had a packet of them, already rolled. It does work, though?'

'Yes,' Daphne said. 'Leaves me a little confused, but it takes away the pain.'

The young doctor smiled. 'The pain will fade in time.'

Daphne nodded.

She heard a low cry, and looked over at the bed on her right where Chane was sleeping. Her face was troubled, the sheets twisted round her body.

'Bad dreams,' Delia said.

One of the other young doctors, Garrick, joined them. 'Captain,' he said, 'do you think you're ready to try a little walking?'

She was always stiff and sore after coming out of a protracted vision coma, and this had been one of her longest. Nodding, she pulled back the sheets from the bed with her right hand. Below the hem of her under-armour longshirt, her legs had thinned, and there were a few cuts and bruises marring her dark skin.

She held out her right arm, and Garrick took it. She swung her legs and placed her bare feet onto the wooden floor. Leaning into him, she stood, and was surprised not to feel her joints screaming in pain. She straightened, and started to walk, keeping her left arm close to her body.

'Whatever it is I'm smoking,' she said, stretching out her legs in relief as she walked across the floor with ease. 'It damn well works!'

She practiced for a good while, exercising all the muscles she hadn't used in days. One particular stroll to the far end of the barracks, away from everyone's beds, taught her what that area was being used for. In a corner, a desk had been turned on its side to afford a little privacy, but the stench was unbearable, and she quickly retreated the way she had come. Back at her bedside, she realised the smell had been present the entire time, and she was just noticing it now.

'Someone's coming,' Weir called from the window. 'It's alright, it's Ethan.'

Daphne turned her head towards the door at the end of the room just as it opened. Outside, two black-clad guards were flanking the doorway, while three others entered the room, along with the Holdings slave.

'Good evening,' Ethan said. He noticed Daphne standing by her bed. 'You're up, excellent.' The guards shut the door behind him.

'I have some news.' He paused, wrinkling his nose. 'Creator's cock, it stinks like a dirty stables in here. Well, hopefully it won't be for too much longer.'

The guards had brought in a sack, and they started to unload its contents.

'Here are tonight's rations,' he gestured to the food and drink being stacked onto the table. 'Possibly your last night here.'

Chane sat up and pulled herself out of bed. 'We're leaving?'

'A scout arrived,' Ethan went on. 'He told B'Dang to expect the arrival of Agang Garo this time tomorrow. Knowing the chief, that probably means he'll be here in the morning.'

'And then what?' asked Daphne.

'That depends on how well his meeting with the other chiefs went. If all goes according to plan, the Sanang warbands will soon be striking at the Holdings invasion forces, leaving Agang free to return to Beechwoods.'

'He won't be leading the counter-attack?' Chane asked.

'No,' Ethan said. 'He has no desire to fight any more than he has to. And anyway, as soon as the other chiefs are involved he technically becomes out-ranked by half a dozen of them. He wants them all to fight back against the Holdings, he's been trying to organise them for thirds, but they won't allow him to lead. And if he can't lead, he'll be going home.'

'Why did he attack us if he doesn't want to fight?' Chane said.

'To show the chiefs it could be done,' the slave said. 'The Sanang warbands have been sitting cowering and skulking, bickering and fighting each other, all terrified of being the ones to make the first move against the Holdings. As soon as Agang heard that this fort was still occupied, while the others had been evacuated days before, he knew he had to lead the attack himself…'

'What?' cried Daphne. 'He knew? The other forts had evacuated?' She sat down on the bed, her mind spinning, trying to fit together events that had moved far from her control.

Mink got to his feet. 'You fucking bitch! I knew it!' He raised his finger at Daphne. 'You betrayed the Holdings and killed us all. You!'

As Daphne stared open-mouthed, Weir strode up the aisle of the room, until he stood between her and Mink.

'You need to watch your mouth, Lieutenant,' he said.

'What is this?' Mink said. 'You all know I'm telling the truth, we've just heard Ethan confirm it. The other forts had evacuated, while we alone remained. Why? Because she would rather obey her father than the queen.'

'No orders arrived,' Daphne said, her voice sounding desperate to her ears. 'Do you hear me, we did not receive any orders to evacuate!'

'I believe you, Captain,' said Chane, joining Weir by Daphne's bed.

'But, Chane,' Mink called across the room, everyone's attention on him. 'We talked about this, about how her father wanted her to stay on, occupy the fort all year. We agreed…'

'No Mink,' said Chane. 'You agreed. I confess to thinking that the captain was incompetent, and that she'd only got the commission because of her father. Sorry about that.' She glanced over at Daphne, who shrugged. 'But I didn't believe any of those bullshit rumours that she was deliberately ignoring orders. She's not a traitor.'

Daphne noticed Ethan nodding his head.

'Thank you for your support,' she said. 'But I'm not sure we should be discussing this while he's here.' She jerked her thumb in the slave's direction.

'It's been enlightening,' he smirked. He motioned to the guards to leave.

'I'll be off now,' he said. 'Try not to quarrel too much. It could be a busy morning.'

CHAPTER 6

TRAUMA

River Tritos, Sanang – 22nd Day, First Third Summer 503

Later that evening, Daphne made a point of going to speak to Dreff. He had not uttered a word since she had awoken, nor had he left his bed. As she approached, she could smell his odour, rank and sour, and she suspected he had soiled himself.

'Hello, Engineer.'

He cracked open an eyelid, grunted, and rolled over.

She looked around and caught Chane watching her. The lieutenant shrugged, mouthing 'I've tried'.

'Do you want to talk, Dreff?' Daphne persisted, speaking in a whisper. 'About Wilkom?'

She saw the veins on the back of his hand stand out as he gripped the bed sheets, but he said nothing.

'Maybe later,' she said. 'Listen, I don't know if you were awake when Ethan was here earlier, but we might be leaving tomorrow.' Continued silence from Dreff, motionless except for his shaking hand. She sensed waves of pain emanating from him, and remembered how she had felt earlier, held by Chane while she cried for Jaimes and the dead troopers. She felt that ache within her still, that loss, all the faces and names of the young soldiers who would never return to their families. And with

Jaimes' death came an absence, not only at her shoulder, but in her mind, where her thoughts seemed one-sided and small without him.

But she was an officer in the queen's cavalry, and she would not allow herself to weaken.

There was a knock at the door. It swung open, and Ethan walked in, a bag slung over his shoulder. He nodded to a black-clad guard, who closed the door behind him.

'Good evening,' he said in the candle-light.

'A little late for a visit,' Daphne said, getting up from Dreff's bedside.

'I hope you don't mind. I was at a loose end.'

He put his bag down on the small table by the door.

'Take a seat,' she said, right hand gesturing.

He sat and stretched his legs. She saw Chane approach from the corner of her eye. The rest of the room lay still. The doctors seemed to be sleeping, excepting Jonnas, who was sitting meditating, or possibly praying. Mink was sitting on his mattress with his knees up at his chest, but she could see his eyes watching her from the other side of the room. Weir lay on his bed, arms folded behind his head, eyes closed.

'How's the arm?' Ethan said, keeping his voice low.

'Painful,' she replied. 'I've been smoking the narcotics you left for me.' She sat at the table next to him.

'Ah yes,' he said. 'Sanang drugs. If it grows, they smoke it.'

'And just what have I been smoking?' she asked. 'The doctors were curious.'

'I gave you a roll of dullweed sticks. Uncut, very strong. I keep a bundle for injuries, or just to pass the time.'

'And the plant it comes from?'

'No idea, I'm not a botanist. There are hundreds of plants out here in the Sanang forest we Holdings have never seen before. I imagine the horticultural department back at the university will have its hands full for a few decades to come.'

Chane sat. 'They have other drugs, then?'

'Oh yes,' Ethan said. 'Keenweed, dreamweed, loveweed, even death-weed. Weed for all occasions. The Sanang are partial towards oblivion.'

'And they drink too?' she asked.

'In copious amounts,' he said. 'A most rancid beverage, made from fermented and distilled oats and honey. Every household has its own still. They have weak versions for glugging down at breakfast, right up to raw spirits that you'd be better off using to remove stains. B'Dang's boys have been knocking that stuff back with a passion tonight.'

'You got any?' Chane asked.

Daphne raised an eyebrow.

'If, like he says,' Chane continued, keeping her voice calm, though with a hint of desperation in her eyes, 'all of B'Dang's mob are already out of it.'

'They are,' Ethan said. 'They know their fun will be coming to an end tomorrow, so they started earlier than usual and have been out cold in their barracks for an hour. Even Agang's lot are having a drink tonight.'

'Is that wise?' Daphne said.

'They've been good boys, and seeing as it's their last night, and B'Dang's crew have already knocked themselves out, they felt they'd earned it. Not sure if Agang will agree, if he catches a whiff of it on their breaths in the morning.'

'He doesn't let them smoke or drink?'

'Well yes, he has to let them cut loose once in a while. Not even Agang can make them give up their habits completely.'

'Well?' said Chane.

'Alright, Lieutenant,' Daphne said, 'if Ethan's sure it's safe.'

The slave smiled and pulled a jug from his bag, and some cups.

Sergeant Weir appeared at their shoulder, pulling out a chair for himself.

'Did I hear mention of a drink?'

'Good to know that the ears of a cavalry sergeant are as sharp as ever,' Ethan smirked as he poured. Across the room Daphne caught sight of Jonnas. He was still sitting on his bed, but he was looking over at the table with an expression of disapproval. Must have been praying, she thought.

'None for me, thanks,' Daphne said. 'Though maybe, if you had something I could smoke, though not as strong as the ones you gave me for the pain. Don't suppose you have any tobacco?'

'It's about the only thing they don't smoke,' Ethan laughed. 'Doesn't grow here. But I do have a few other sticks with me. I'll look one out for you.'

'By the Creator's sweaty crotch, that tastes rank!' Chane exclaimed, holding her cup of Sanang spirits aloft. A couple of sips later though, and her demeanour changed, becoming more relaxed than Daphne had seen her in some time. They were a pair of addicts, she thought, she and Chane, each needing a crutch to get through the day. She took the offered smoke stick from Ethan, and lit it off a taper.

'Dreamweed, it's called,' he said. 'After a while on the dullweed, I'd recommend switching to that. It doesn't kill the pain completely, but hopefully in a while you won't be needing such a powerful drug.'

'And what would happen if I kept smoking the dullweed?'

'Well, you'd be alright, but you'd feel terrible when you came off it in the end. I've seen Sanang drift through their lives on dullweed, looking like the living dead after a while, in their own little worlds. Quite popular among Sanang women. It's not a lifestyle I'd recommend.'

She smoked her dreamweed and relaxed, her muscles loosening. She thought about picking up on Ethan's comment about Sanang women, but found herself lagging behind in the conversation. Weir started to tell tales of the first invasion, and Ethan joined in with stories about the Sanang. She tried to concentrate on what they were saying, but felt herself starting to drift.

'Captain, you alright?' Chane asked her, her hand steadying her arm as she swayed. Daphne looked up, her eyes struggling to focus. 'Come on, let's get you to bed.'

Chane's breath smelled of alcohol as the lieutenant lifted her up, an arm over her shoulder. Weir came to her other side and, without touching her left arm, they carried her to bed, where she was asleep before her head touched the pillow.

She awoke as someone shook her shoulder. 'What?' she whispered, thoughts fuggy, her body cool in the night air.

'Something's wrong, Captain.' It was Delia.

Daphne looked up. Their candles had burned out, but the room was dimly illuminated from outside, a flickering light of burning torches.

By the door, she could she where Chane and Ethan had passed out. Chane had her head on the table, while Ethan was reclining with his legs stretched out, snoring.

'What time is it?' Daphne asked, rubbing her head.

Delia shrugged. 'A few hours after you fell asleep, still a few hours to dawn?'

Daphne reached over to the bedside table to find her dullweed. As she was getting a light prepared, she looked up again. 'What's going on out there?'

'That's why I woke you, Captain,' she whispered. 'I heard Ethan say that B'Dang's crew had fallen asleep drunk, but they're all outside, busy.'

Daphne lit her stick and took a couple of draws.

'Let's go see.' She stood, and put her leather overcoat over her shoulders. She went over to the table, moved Ethan's legs to the side, and stood on the chair next to him. She pulled herself up level to the little window slat, and looked out.

The square in front of the gatehouse was lit by dozens of torches. The right gate was still hanging loose from one hinge, but the bodies had been cleared away. There were about ten large wagons in the square, with oxen attached to the reins, and men were busy loading them with crates and bundles.

'They're looting the camp,' she said, mostly to herself. 'Must be planning to leave before Agang gets back.' She looked down at Delia's anxious face. 'Why are Agang's guards not stopping them?'

She jumped down from the chair, and starting shaking Chane's arm.

'Chane,' she called.

The lieutenant groaned, but didn't wake up.

'Damn,' Daphne said. 'Delia, go and see if Sergeant Weir will awaken. Quietly.'

Delia nodded and went over to the sergeant's bed. Daphne turned her attention to Ethan. No time for subtlety here, she thought, and slapped him across the face.

'Fucking...!' He grunted, eyes shooting open, bloodshot and glaring. 'What the fuck!' He quietened as Daphne put a finger to her lips.

'Take a look outside,' she whispered.

While he got to his feet, Weir walked over, rubbing his stomach and yawning. 'We got trouble?'

'We might have,' she said, glad to see him up.

'That bastard!' Ethan scowled from his position by the window slat. He jumped down and ran to the door. He knocked, and called out in a low voice. There was no response. He started to pound on the door.

'Stop that!' Daphne said. 'Don't draw their attention.'

He turned, a panicked expression on his face. 'We're fucked.'

Others in the room were starting to rouse themselves. Mink was sitting up in bed, while Jonnas and Delia were getting to their feet.

'Everyone, quiet,' Daphne said, hushing them.

Weir climbed up onto the chair to take a look.

'Shit,' he said. 'They're coming.'

As they all stood around frozen, staring at the door, Weir acted. He jumped down from the chair, pulling a knife from under his shirt. With his other hand he shoved Chane over to the ground, where she fell spluttering and groaning back into consciousness. He pushed in front of Daphne, getting between her and the entrance, and at the same time started edging her backwards away from the door.

'Thank you, sergeant,' she whispered.

'I'm your man, Captain.'

Chane got to her knees, holding her head. 'What the...' she began saying when the door burst inwards.

In strode B'Dang D'Bang, a broad grin on his tattooed face. He held a long knife in each hand, and swaggered towards them, warriors crowding behind.

He looked around the room, until his gaze alighted on Ethan. He smiled at the slave, who looked terrified but defiant.

B'Dang spoke to him for a few moments, and Ethan turned to face the prisoners.

'The great B'Dang,' he said, his voice dripping with sarcasm and fear, 'apologises for interrupting the prisoners' sleep, but his men are getting bored, and he promised them some reward before they burn the fort to the ground and leave.'

B'Dang spoke again, and started pointing at the prisoners. Ethan listened, his face lowered.

'He's taking me,' Ethan said in a whisper, then gestured to where Delia and Jonnas were standing. 'And you two.'

'The fuck he is,' cried Chane, still on her knees. She tried to rise, but B'Dang leapt forward and kicked her in the chest, sending her toppling backwards, banging her head on the side of Dreff's bed. The Sanang guards growled and took a pace forwards. About a dozen warriors were now in the room. Two of them grabbed Ethan. He didn't resist, his face absent of any expression. Weir took a step backwards, to be in a position where he could get to Chane if he needed to, but still reach the captain. The lieutenant was on the floor, vomiting under the bed.

Warriors approached Delia and Jonnas, who were huddling together against a wall. Weir stayed still, keeping his knife out of view, covering both Chane and Daphne. She could see his face contort as he watched the Sanang approach the young doctors, but he bit his lip and remained where he was, defending his officers. The other two doctors were sitting motionless on their beds, horror-struck, as was Mink.

Daphne cursed her arm, her luck, B'Dang, the world. Helplessly she watched as warriors wrestled hold of her two doctors, and hauled them away. Delia slapped one of them, who punched her, breaking her nose into a bloody mess. Jonnas reached for her and got a cuff across the cheek that whipped his head back.

There was a flash of movement, and Dreff leapt towards them, landing into the mass of soldiers. He was screaming, his limbs flailing wildly. One hand found the face of a Sanang soldier, and in a fury he plunged his thumb and fingers deep into the warrior's eyeballs. The warrior pushed him off, bellowing, his hands rising to his torn and bloody face, dark weeping holes where his eyes had been. Dreff hit the floor, and the Sanang surrounded him, their clubs, axes and swords hacking and beating down in a frenzy, which continued long after Dreff had stopped moving.

B'Dang shouted, and the mob ceased, and stood back, leaving a bloody pulp of bone and flesh that had been Dreff. The blinded Sanang warrior was on his knees, his screams drowning out everything else. B'Dang slashed his long knives at the warrior's neck, decapitating him in one quick movement, and the room was silenced.

B'Dang D'Bang looked around, nodding. He stooped to wipe his knives on the slain Sanang's clothes, then motioned to the other warriors. Keeping a firm hold of Ethan, Delia and Jonnas, they backed out of the room. B'Dang gave a short bow and the door swung shut. They heard the bolts slide back into place.

Weir let out a long controlled breath. 'Fuck.'

Garrick rolled off the bed onto his knees and threw up over the floor. Chane groaned and tried to pull herself up, but slumped back down heavily. Weir went over to her, and helped her into a sitting position. Daphne sat, her legs shaky, her right hand trembling.

'Why did no one help them?' Manahan said, his voicing cracking.

Weir moved over to Dreff's body, and covered it with a blanket, then did the same for the headless Sanang warrior. If Weir could keep going, Daphne thought, so could she.

She went over to Chane's side.

'Are you hurt?' she asked.

'I'm sorry, Captain,' Chane replied, tears streaming down her cheeks. 'I shouldn't have got drunk. I might have been able to stop them.'

'No, you'd be dead like Dreff.'

'I let you down.'

'No, Chane,' Daphne said, 'you didn't.'

She looked over to where Weir was up on the table, peering out.

'You see anything, sergeant?'

'No, Captain,' he replied. 'Think they've gone up by the main road, but I can't see where they've taken Ethan and the two doctors.'

'We need weapons,' Daphne said. 'Next time, we fight.'

Weir got down from the table. 'We did a quick inventory when we got here. That's when we found the knife.' He slipped it out of his tunic, and passed it to Chane. 'Sorry ma'am, took it from you while you were sleeping.'

Chane nodded. 'Glad you did.'

'Let's get to work then,' Daphne said.

They gathered everything in the barracks they could use. Daphne ended up with a trenching tool, the kind used in the construction of the fort. Its shovel-head was broad and sharp. Chane had the knife, while Weir had a long wooden staff, the end of which he had sharpened into a spear.

'You're wasting your time,' Mink muttered from his bed.

'Either help us, Lieutenant,' Daphne said, 'or shut up.'

Garrick came over to join them. He looked shaky and his shirt was stained with sick, but he picked up a wooden club made from a bedpost, and started hefting it.

The screaming started. It was far away, but unmistakably the voice of Delia. Daphne's nerves burned like fire, and her stomach muscles tightened, as she heard the tormented cries of pain. She glanced at Chane, whose expression mirrored her own. The sound faded.

Daphne sat. 'Dear Creator, mercy.'

'That was nothing,' said Mink, a shadow across his face. 'Last time, they tortured them in the square, where we could see what they were doing.'

The screams started again, this time a male voice, Jonnas, or maybe Ethan. Helpless pity rose in her, and while the screams continued there was nothing else in her mind but the cruel noise of pain being inflicted. The cries of Delia started up again, joining those of Jonnas, and Daphne put her head in her hands. She tried to block it out, but it was futile, every part of her screamed in empathy, and though it made her sick with guilt, she wished for their deaths so that the suffocating noise would end. She thought about smoking some dullweed, or dreamweed if there was any left, but a part of her didn't want oblivion to dampen the sounds of the young doctors dying, as if it cheapened their existence. Bearing witness to their cries was all she could do for them.

***

A sombre, quiet mood lay over the barracks room. No one had spoken in a couple of hours, while the screams had continued, and then finally petered out and stopped.

Daphne lay on her bed. The flickering light from the torches was still permeating the room, and she had no idea how far away dawn was. No one was sleeping. She could hear, if she concentrated, the individual breaths of her five companions, and they sounded far from the relaxed noises made by someone asleep. The presence of Dreff's corpse on the floor acted like a magnet to her eyes. She couldn't help returning again and again to where he lay, though the shape made by the blanket covering him resembled nothing like a human body. Blood had trickled from the edges of the blanket, which was stained with dark patches. What they had done to him was indelibly imprinted onto her memory, inhabiting a place in her mind filled with screams.

Her left arm ached, but she resisted taking more drugs. She would have to hold off until she really needed it, and that would mean getting used to carrying around a higher level of pain, the price of keeping her head clear.

Weir was maintaining his position by the window slat, looking out. He must be exhausted, she thought, but his expression remained alert. 'I'm your man,' he had said to her. She smiled.

The sergeant angled his head, sniffing. 'Smoke.'

Daphne got up and walked over, avoiding where Dreff lay. 'You sure?'

'Yes, Captain.' He squinted through the slat. 'Something's burning.'

Soon Daphne could smell it herself.

'I can see flames up the road,' Weir said. 'The armoury, the granary, Dex's barracks, they're all afire. B'Dang's torching the fort.'

'What about the wagons?' she asked.

'Leaving,' he said, looking back at the gatehouse. 'Last ones are going through the gates now.'

There was a harsh rattle at the door, and it swung open. B'Dang entered, flanked by warriors. One of them held Ethan upright, clutching him round the chest with his huge arms. The Holdings slave was alive, but badly beaten. His eyes were bloody, and his hair looked like it had been held to a fire, the skin on his scalp blackened and blistered. Foam and spittle flecked his broken jaw.

B'Dang called to him.

Ethan raised his head. 'The great B'Dang...' he whispered.

B'Dang said a few quiet words to him. Ethan trembled in fear.

'The great B'Dang D'Bang,' he said again, louder, slurring, his teeth smashed inside his mouth, 'apologises for not torturing each of you, but Agang's scouts have been seen on the road, and he must cut short his stay. He thanks you for your hospitality, and hopes that whatever god you believe in will forgive him for burning you alive.'

B'Dang smiled, and clapped.

Behind him, several warriors hurled lit torches into the room. The brands arced over their heads of the captives, hitting beds, walls, and the floor, and fires started to take hold. B'Dang drew one of his long knives, and stepped over to Ethan. Looking him in the eye, he pushed the blade into the slave's stomach. He twisted the hilt, and pulled the blade out, sending a gush of blood and fluids spilling out over his hand, down Ethan's clothes, and dripping onto the floor.

He nodded. The warrior let Ethan's body drop, and they withdrew, barring the door behind them.

Mink jumped from his bed and ran to the door, pounding on it with his fists. Manahan started wailing, wrapping himself tighter in his blankets. Everyone was coughing as smoke swirled through the room.

'Is there any other way out?' Daphne yelled at Weir and Chane. There were three separate fires now blazing. The largest was near the centre of the room, and was splitting them into two groups. Garrick and Mink were by the door, while the three soldiers and Manahan were cut off at the far end of the room.

Weir looked doubtful. 'Maybe.'

'We have to try.'

Weir moved to the far corner, and knelt amid the piles of human waste that had built up over the days.

'The shovel, please.' He reached out his hand, coughing and retching from the stink, his knees and boots already plastered in filth.

She handed him her trenching tool, and he started wedging it under the floorboards.

'Get down low,' cried Chane, pushing her to the floor. They lay with their faces an inch from the planks, gasping from the smoke, and the sour stench of urine now steaming up from the damp wood. As Weir worked on, Chane crept up behind him, and tied a cloth over his face. Their eyes met for a second. Chane smiled, and was gone into the smoke.

'Chane!' Daphne shouted. She looked up, and realised she had also lost sight of Mink and Garrick. She heard the loud crack of a plank splitting, and saw Weir rip up one of the boards. The barracks was raised above the ground, supported by posts a foot high, and through the hole Weir had made, Daphne could see the dark earth beneath.

Weir kept at it, becoming more frantic in his movements as he tired, and smoke began to overcome him. Chane appeared at her right, dragging a body. It was Manahan, lying unconscious.

'Couldn't leave the old bastard behind,' she shouted, face streaked with sweat and smoke.

She crawled to Weir. Together they worked on, him levering up the planks, and her pulling and heaving, until another split and came free, and they both fell back onto the floor.

'Let's go!' Daphne shouted. 'Weir, you first!'

Weir winked at her, and slung his legs through the gap. It was tight, but he squeezed himself down through the hole, splinters ripping his shirt, angling his legs to fit under the floor. As his hands disappeared, Chane motioned to Daphne. 'You next, ma'am.'

Daphne crawled to the gap. Holding her left arm close to her body, she reached out with her other hand and gripped the side of the hole. She pulled herself down headfirst, closing her eyes as she passed the ripped planks. She felt the edges tug at her shoulders and arms, and her right hand was cut on something, but she reached out again, and a hand met hers, and started to pull. Her leather coat caught on a jagged plank, and she was stuck for a moment, but the pocket ripped and she was freed. She pulled her legs through, and started crawling along the earth, away from the area stained with their waste. She opened her eyes, and in the grey light of dawn she saw Weir pointing the way. She nodded and began pulling herself along with her right arm, trying to ignore the growing ache in her left. After crawling a few yards, her fingers lost their grip, and she scrambled in the tight space, her feet trying to push her on, but only treading dirt. She could see nothing through the smoke, and she couldn't remember which direction she was supposed to crawl. She lay her head down, panting for air. So close.

Fingers felt their way onto her right hand and took a firm grasp. She was aware of being dragged, her left arm protesting painfully at every inch travelled, as she was bumped and jostled between the posts and the stony ground. The pain became all she could think of, a ball of hurt in her elbow that demanded her full attention. She heard voices, and felt herself being carried, and then the pain became too much.

She awoke in agony, groaning. She was lying on the ground, in the open air. She looked up, and saw Weir sitting next to her. He was lighting a smoke stick, and took a deep draw himself, before passing it to her.

She took it and inhaled, almost weeping in relief as the pain receded. She started coughing, and her stomach turned. She tried to get up, and made it to her knees before vomiting onto the ground. As she retched, she felt Weir reach out, pulling her hair away from her face.

She rocked back onto her haunches, spat, and gazed around. They were sitting outside the fortress, on the raised embankment of the outer ditch. Smoke rose in giant waves from the camp in front of her, reaching up to stain half the sky. She could feel the heat of the fires on her skin.

'It burns well,' said Weir. He was smoking something else. To Daphne's nose it seemed like dreamweed, but she wasn't sure. On his left lay Manahan, covered in a blanket.

'Is he...?'

'Dead,' Weir said. 'Smoke got him. He was probably gone before Chane dragged him out through the hole in the floor.' He gestured over to his right side. 'This one, on the other hand...' She looked over to see Mink laid out on the earth, motionless but alive.

'How did he make it out?' she asked in surprise.

'We broke down the front door of the barracks,' Weir replied. 'Was easy from the outside. Doctor Garrick was dead, but the lieutenant was still breathing.'

'Where's Chane?'

'Supply run.'

'She's in there?' Daphne pointed at the fort.

Weir shrugged. 'Looks a lot worse from out here. Once you're inside, the roads are so wide you can avoid the fires if you're careful.'

Chane made her appearance at that moment. She was coming through the gatehouse, dragging a couple of sacks. Weir trotted over to help her, and they carried them back to where Daphne was sitting.

'Good to see you, Lieutenant,' Daphne said.

'And you, Captain,' she replied. 'You're tougher than I thought.'

Chane opened the first sack, and produced water canteens, and they drank liberally, sitting on the grass in the morning light.

'Food.' Chane gestured at the open sack. 'Eat.'

As Daphne pulled out some bread, Chane unstoppered a small jug and took a swig.

'Here,' Daphne said. 'Give me some of that.'

'Yes, ma'am,' Chane said.

'We might as well get drunk to watch the fort burn.' She took a sip. 'You're right, it's rank.'

Weir chuckled.

'What now, Captain?' Chane asked.

Daphne frowned, her mind exhausted and hazy from the drugs.

'We either bolt for it,' she said, 'or wait for Agang.'

'Twenty day's march,' Weir said.

'The Sanang will catch us long before that,' Chane added.

'So we hope Ethan was right,' Daphne said, 'and Agang is different. Did you...?' She turned to Chane. 'Did you find Delia and Jonnas?'

The lieutenant's face darkened. 'I did. I dragged them to the fire, let the flames take them. If I ever see that bastard B'Dang again...' She looked away, eyes blinking.

'Also,' Chane continued after a while. 'I found out what happened to Agang's guards. They were in their barracks block, faces purple, their tongues hanging out.'

'Poisoned?' said Weir.

'Looked like it.'

'Why?' Daphne said.

'B'Dang probably knew he couldn't beat them in a fair fight.'

'And now he's taken all the loot.'

'Look.' Weir pointed south into the forest. 'Movement.'

They turned, and out of the treeline appeared a troop of twenty Sanang.

'They're in a hurry,' Daphne said. 'Wonder when they spotted the smoke.'

She forced herself to her feet, keeping her left arm tucked inside the long overcoat. 'I guess the bolt option is redundant.'

Chane and Weir also stood, and flanked her as the black-clad Sanang approached. She noticed that one of them was running in full armour.

'There he is,' she said.

'Come to see the fort for himself,' Weir said. 'That scout must have told him there was trouble.'

The Sanang troop joined the road forty yards to their right, and turned up it towards them. As they approached they fanned out into a semi-circle, spears pointed towards the four bedraggled Holdings soldiers, three standing, the other lying prone on the ground.

The armoured warrior approached, and removed his helmet. It was Agang Garo. He looked to be in the grip of a mighty rage. He was shaking with anger. His face was blotched red, his eyes bulging.

He got to within a few paces of them, and spoke in Holdings.

'Where is Ethan?'

Daphne met his gaze. 'B'Dang killed him.'

Agang clenched his fists, closed his eyes and bowed his head, veins throbbing. His guards edged away.

He raised his head. 'Show me.'

Daphne and Chane escorted the Sanang leader and half of his guards into the camp, and led them to the barracks building where they had been held. The fires had burnt themselves out in this part of the fort, and what was left was a smouldering mess of blackened posts, ash and debris. Agang kicked his way inside, smoke and steam rising around him. He looked over to Daphne, who pointed to the spot where Ethan had fallen. Agang pushed aside smoking roof timbers, and rooted through the ash. After a few minutes, his hands touched something under the loose debris, and he picked up a round object, blackened with soot. He held it to his breast, and slowly made his way back to the others.

When he reached them Daphne saw blisters covering the skin on his hands.

'You're hurt,' she said.

'So are you.' He pointed at her arm with his free hand, the other clutching the scorched remains of Ethan's skull. 'In Beechwoods, there is a *hidgitch*. He will heal you.'

CHAPTER 7

BEECHWOODS

River Tritos, Sanang – 27th Day, First Third Summer 503

'I could watch this all day,' said Chane over the noise of the trundling wheels. 'It's amazing.'

She was balanced on her toes, leaning out of the back of the cart as far as the ropes would allow, watching the forest move and re-form behind them. A hundred yards in the opposite direction, at the head of the long column of soldiers, walked a Sanang hedgewitch, or at least that's what the Holdings prisoners called him. The word spoken by Agang had sounded something like that. In front of the hedgewitch, the forest was dense and thick, but as he walked, chanting and gesturing with his hands, it parted before him. Branches swung aside, bushes pulled their undergrowth out of the way, and even the trunks of trees bent and twisted to let them through. The passage thus created was narrow, but enough to allow the soldiers to march three abreast. The cart holding the prisoners formed the widest part of the column, and a branch would occasionally swish past their heads as the soldiers marched onwards. Behind them, the forest returned to normal, leaving no sign that anyone had passed.

'The power of their hedgewitches is astonishing,' Chane said.

'I don't know if they're any more powerful than Holdings mages,'

Daphne frowned. 'It's just a different type of power.' She was reclining on the floor on the cart, looking up at the sky through the gaps in the tree cover, resting her head on a leather pack. She was smoking dreamweed. There were thin ropes tied to her right arm and her left ankle, which were fastened to the side of the cart. The ropes were made from a tough fibrous material, with knots so tight they would need to be cut off. There was enough spare in the ropes to allow them to move about the cart, but there was no denying the fact they were prisoners. Soldiers marched in front of them, more were behind, and there were always two up on the cart. One man held the reins of the oxen, while the other sat facing the captives, holding a levelled spear.

Before the journey had begun, Daphne's left arm had been swaddled in thick bandages to protect it. She could feel it throb, now that she had come off the dullweed, and its aching was a constant presence, reminding her of its uselessness, and precipitating the occasional bout of self-pity. She had a few sticks of dullweed left, wrapped in a pocket in her leather overcoat, but she had taken Ethan's warning to heart, and had decided to switch to the milder drug.

They had been on the cart for three days, slowly bumping their way to Agang's place in the Beechwoods, wherever that was. He hadn't spoken to them since they had left the fort the same morning he had arrived. Without Ethan, the prisoners felt isolated and alone, even though they were accompanied by two hundred soldiers. None of the captives spoke a word of Sanangka, if 'hedgewitch' was excluded, and they were sure that the soldiers surrounding them had no knowledge of the Holdings tongue, so they had gotten used to speaking their minds without a care for who was listening.

Except Weir, Daphne thought. Wary old Weir, always cautious, always checking the exits, and always at her side. Picking up Jaimes' role. He had been upstanding, pious, and a little self-righteous, like a supportive but strict elder brother, whereas Weir was more like a coarse uncle that the rest of the family hinted you were better to avoid. He was rough, hardened and brutalised by his seasons in Sanang. Some of his tales of what the Holding soldiers had done on the first year's invasion had made her ashamed of her homeland, and she was unsettled that he could speak of it so freely. However, now that they were in the forest, with enemy soldiers all around, he sat guarded and watchful.

Mink stayed well clear of the sergeant. The lieutenant had withdrawn into himself, hardly saying a word to his fellow captives since being rescued from the barracks. He looked neither surprised, nor happy, to be alive. He kept his gaze out over the forest, and Daphne sometimes forgot he was there.

Chane laughed as she jumped back into the body of the wagon. She landed next to Daphne, making her flinch her left arm away.

'I don't get why you're so damn cheerful,' Daphne said, sitting up.

'I think, Captain,' she said, pulling a water canteen out from under the bench where Weir perched, 'that it's because this is the first time in three years I haven't had forty troopers to look after. And everyone back home will assume we were killed along with the others. I don't know, I just feel... free.'

Daphne looked at her. Add to that the fact that their guards had been supplying her with alcohol, she thought. She kept quiet. Who was she to judge?

'I don't like the idea of people thinking I'm dead,' Weir said. 'Except maybe my ex-wives.'

'What about your kids?' Chane asked.

Weir shrugged. 'They're all grown up now, and not one of them showed the slightest inclination to follow their old man into the cavalry. Got nothing in common with them. Their mothers made them all soft.'

'How many do you have?' Daphne said. 'Children, I mean. And ex-wives.'

'Six and three,' he said, 'though number six was from a fourth woman, who the church wouldn't let me wed. Said I was abusing the sanctity of marriage. You got any kids, Captain?'

'How old do you think I am?' she laughed. 'I'm only twenty-one.'

'Where I'm from there are plenty of girls who get hitched and are popping out their first kids a lot younger than that. My little sister had three by the time she was twenty-one, and I was a father at nineteen.'

'Where are you from, sergeant?'

'Between the rivers.'

Daphne paused. She had never been to that corner of the Holdings, in the far south-east, where their land's only two rivers flowed. The strip that lay between was incredibly fertile, and was the most densely populated region of the Holdings. The majority who lived there were poor and landless tenant farmers or labourers. The River Holdings provided a fruitful source of recruits for the army, filling the lower ranks, while most of the officers, including Daphne, Chane and Mink, came from the rich estate Holdings on the savannah.

'Haven't ever visited,' she said.

'You've been to the capital?'

'Of course,' she said. 'I was at the university, and the academy, for four years.'

'Between the rivers is not much different from the Lower City,' he said. 'Just more spread out.'

Without any warning the column halted, and the wagon rolled to a stop.

'Too early to be camping for the night,' Chane said. 'There's three hours of light left, unless I'm well out.'

Daphne glanced around. Nothing in the dense forest to either side looked any different. She shrugged. 'Let's wait and see.'

About ten minutes later, they saw a small group approach down the path from the front of the column. Among them was Agang, wearing his bright armour. He strode towards them, soldiers bowing as he passed.

The captives turned to face him as he came near.

'Prisoners,' he said in the Holdings tongue, 'until now, I've stayed away from places where we might be seen, but we're close to a river crossing.' He gestured with his left arm towards the north. 'It's always busy there.'

A guard came forward, his big arms holding a pile of rough sheets.

'Put these on,' Agang said. The guard dropped them into the wagon.

Chane lifted one. It had a wide hole in the bottom, arms were sewn onto the sides, and at the top was a hood that would completely enclose the head.

'I'm not wearing a sack,' she said.

Agang's face flickered with disbelief, then hardened.

'If I say you will, then you will,' he said, keeping his tone even. 'The villagers will tear your body to pieces if they see you. Twice as many soldiers would not be enough to protect you from their hate.'

Chane blinked.

'You will put them on,' he said, 'then you will sit down in the wagon, and say nothing, until I tell you otherwise. Do you understand?'

They nodded.

'If you choose to disobey me on this, I will have no choice but to command my men to stand aside, and leave you to the mercy of the villagers. I'm not having them assaulted through your stupidity.'

'Fine,' said Chane. She turned to Daphne. 'I'll help you on with yours first.'

'Won't the villagers find it strange,' said Daphne, 'to see four people sitting in the back of a cart wearing these... things?'

'No,' he replied. 'They'll assume you're captured Sanang women, being carried back to my household. They might stare, but no one will touch you.'

He stood and waited as they pulled the coarse fabric over their heads. The covering went down to their feet, where it flared to allow them movement, and they slipped their arms into the sleeves, which terminated in thick mittens. Daphne kept her left arm tucked inside the body of the garment. Their heads were completely covered, apart from a narrow flap at the mouth to allow them to eat and drink. There was no eye-slit, but the cloth was at its thinnest there and, after her sight adjusted, Daphne could vaguely make out their surroundings.

'Good.' Agang turned and started walking back to the front.

As soon as he was gone, Chane whispered. 'It's going to get a little sweaty in here.'

A spear flashed out and jabbed her in the ribs. The guard up by the ox reins snarled at them, and Chane made a frantic nodding motion, difficult to see under her covering, but clear enough in its intent. The four sat in silence as the column started moving again, and the cart lurched into motion.

They passed a hot and uncomfortable hour rolling through the thick green forest, with nothing but the noise of the wheels rumbling and the soldiers marching to keep them company. After that, the path opened up onto a wide, clear area, carpeted in a lush field of grass. Two hundred yards before them fell the steep banks of the Tritos, the same river that rushed past the fort. Spanning it was a spindly wooden bridge, tiny and fragile compared to the foaming, surging gorge. Between the bridge and the forest, a settlement was laid out. Wooden huts and dwellings, with smoke coming from several chimneys, lay crowded on either side of the road to the bridge, over-hanging it in places. Street traders and a bustling crowd of Sanang thronged the way, bartering, haggling, or just struggling to pass through the thick press.

As they approached, Agang's soldiers took up a new formation, closing ranks into a tight wedge, with spears at half-height. The soldier at the tip, who wore a breastplate to show his rank, started to bellow out a marching song that the captives had heard often over the previous days. The rest of the soldiers picked up the next line, and they alternated back and forth, keeping time with their boots.

Their presence thus signalled, the crowds parted, clearing a wide avenue for the soldiers. As they passed, Daphne began to feel the stares that Agang had talked about. Faces leered at them from both sides of the road. Male faces, Daphne realised with a start. Everyone out in the street was male. Several of the men were making crude gestures at them with their hands, and laughing. The captives huddled closer together on the benches of the cart. This was worse, Daphne thought, than the time those assholes from the academy had tried to grope her in a crowded city tavern. At least she had gained the satisfaction of beating one of them the following day at sword practice. Now, despite the shapeless covering, she had never felt more exposed.

They reached the bridge. It was wide enough to carry two wagons side by side, but the advance soldiers cleared the whole length of it before the rest began the crossing. The planks groaned and creaked, and through the gaps Daphne could make out the foaming torrent of the river far below. They crossed to the far bank, and turned north-west, along a wide clearing cut through the forest. Although they had left the crowds behind on the other side of the river, there were groups of travellers on the road, who made way and watched as the column passed.

The hours trundled by, and evening turned to dusk, and then to dark night, and still the column continued on. Daphne was close to fainting, as she bumped about in the back of the cart. Her brown hair was stuck to the back of her neck, her eyes stung with sweat, and the ache in her arm, which had grown throughout the evening, was becoming unbearable.

Just as she was about to throw up, the wagon stopped. She looked around, and in the darkness saw the flicker of torches. They had passed through a large open gateway, and double doors were being swung shut behind them.

'You can take them off now,' she heard Agang say.

Weir was the first to react. He stood, yanked off his covering, and threw it to the floor of the wagon. He panted, his hand leaning on his knee, his face shining, sweat pouring down his dark skin. He stepped forward to help Daphne, first easing her right arm out of its sleeve, and then lifting the rest over her head.

'Creator's bollocks,' he said, as she swayed on the bench. He turned to Agang. 'Water, please.'

The Sanang chief nodded, and a soldier came forward with canteens. Weir poured water over Daphne's face, then helped her drink.

'Thank you, sergeant,' she gasped.

He turned to help Chane, whose covering had got tangled in her long hair.

Agang moved closer, studying them. Chane managed to rip the garment off her head, and she hurled it away in disgust. Mink had also removed his, and sat alone and miserable.

'Welcome to my household,' Agang said, sweeping his left arm around. They were in a rectangular stockade, a hundred paces on each side, with four wooden buildings in the interior. Agang pointed at the largest structure, a large hall with an attic storey. 'This is my home. This is now your home also.'

'Sorry to interrupt,' said Weir, 'but the captain needs something for her pain.'

Agang looked bemused for a moment, then nodded.

He said something to a guard, who opened the tail-flap at the rear of the wagon, and motioned for the prisoners to climb down. Weir jumped down first, then assisted Daphne, while Chane and Mink scrambled to the ground. The guard pulled out a flint blade, and cut the ropes from them.

'Follow me,' said Agang. He turned and started walking towards one of the compound's smaller buildings, and the captives stumbled after him.

A canopy ran the length of the building, a long, low structure, with half a dozen doors leading off to the left. Agang walked to the second door, and opened it. He turned, watching the Holdings prisoners approach, escorted by six black-clad soldiers.

'You will all require some healing,' he said. 'Captain, you first.'

Daphne followed him as he entered, a guard closing the door behind them.

The room was small, with shutters that opened out onto the main square of the compound. A Sanang man was sitting at a workbench, which was littered with dozens of little ceramic pots containing plants and herbs. On the other side of the room was an examination table, covered in a thin white cloth. The man looked up as they entered.

'This is Badolecht Nang,' Agang said. 'Our healer.'

The man rose from his seat, staring at Daphne.

Agang spoke to the man in Sanangka, and they talked for a few moments. The healer seemed to be disagreeing with the chief about something. Agang was firm, and eventually Badolecht nodded.

Agang went to sit by the desk, while the healer approached Daphne. He gestured to her, and she undid the buttons of her coat, and let it fall to the ground. Her left arm was roiling in agony, and she flinched as he touched the swaddling around her upper arm.

He withdrew his hand. He pointed at the examination table, and walked over to his desk. She hesitated, but the pain in her arm was louder than the fear in her head, and she climbed up.

Once she was lying on the table, a cushion supporting her head, Badolecht returned. He held out a smoke stick, and she took it and inhaled, feeling deep relief as the dullweed spread through her body. With a small flint blade he cut away the bandages from around her arm, and did the same with the splints. He frowned as he examined her injuries. Her arm was bruised all over, and emaciated, and the joint at her elbow twisted unnaturally. Her hand was clutched, and her fingers curled in on themselves. From far away in her dullweed daze, she felt a tear slide down her cheek. No, she thought, no weakness in front of the enemy.

Badolecht said something to Agang, who got up and joined him by Daphne's side. Together the two stood and discussed her, and her arm. The healer pointed, explaining something, something that Agang didn't like the sound of.

He turned to her.

'I will translate the words of the healer,' Agang said. 'He says that the bones in your arm have already set wrong, in the wrong way, and his healing will not be able to undo that. His power enables the body to heal itself. Your arm has already knitted its bones back together, but they were not set properly when they were broken.'

Daphne looked away.

'Badolecht Nang will be able to speed up the healing in your flesh, taking away the pain, and perhaps allowing some movement in your hand, with practice, but the bones in your elbow will never work again.'

The healer stepped forward, his hands stretched over her. She closed her eyes, trying to focus on what he was going to do, rather than let self-pity take a hold of her.

She felt the most life-affirming glow pulse within her body, and a sudden lifting of so many countless aches and pains, and cramps and strains, that she had been carrying for the last third. She took a deep breath, every inch of her body warm and alive, from her toes to the tips of her fingers. Her left hand felt better than it had since the injury, and she managed to move her thumb a tiny bit. She smiled.

The glow faded, but left her feeling whole and right. She opened her eyes, noticing that even her sight had seemed to improve. She swung her legs over the side of the table, and hopped to the floor. Agang stood smiling at her, and Badolecht's lip curled up at the edge.

Her joy faded a little as she remembered that she was a prisoner, and the man facing her was her captor.

'Thank you for the healing,' she nodded to Badolecht, who muttered something and looked away.

'He says you are welcome,' Agang said. 'Now, while the others are examined, I will show you to your quarters.'

Daphne followed Agang back out into the chill night air. She smiled again when she saw the look on the faces of her fellow prisoners.

'You look great,' Chane said. 'What happened?'

'The hedgewitch.'

'Hedgewitch?' Agang said. 'Ahh, a *hidgitch*.' He laughed.

He spoke a few words to the guards. Two peeled off to accompany him, while the others waited with Chane, Mink and Weir. As Agang and Daphne walked towards the great hall, she saw the sergeant enter the room next.

'What happened to your arm?' asked Agang.

'B'Dang did it,' she said, 'when I was trying to save the troopers you allowed him to slaughter.'

His expression hardened. 'There are many things you don't understand. I will punish B'Dang for his betrayal, but do not lay the deaths of those he killed at my feet.'

'I'm sorry about Ethan,' she said.

'As I am,' he said. 'He was my friend for ten years.'

'Ten years?'

'Yes. He was with one of the first Holdings merchant caravans, long before the war, when our nations were trading rather than killing each other. He was captured by a tribe up near the Blackcliffs, and fell to me soon afterwards. And now he is gone.' He looked over at Daphne. 'He taught me much about the Holdings. Your language of course, but also your ways, your history, your devotion to your creator god. He also taught me what he knew about your government, and your army.'

'He was a traitor.'

'No,' Agang said. 'He was not. He taught me out of pride for the Holdings, his love for your nation, and so that I could learn. So that I could change Sanang, end the bitter fighting among the tribes, and unite us. Transform us into a nation that the Holdings will see as an equal, rather than as a barbarous place to loot and pillage.'

'You want to be king of the Sanang?'

He halted. They were standing before the great hall, its tall doors open and welcoming.

'I will lead the Sanang,' he said, 'and you, Captain Daphne, shall bear witness.'

CHAPTER 8
WITH THE ENEMY

Beechwoods, Sanang – 5th Day, Second Third Summer 503

'But what I don't understand,' Agang said in fluent Holdings, 'is why the queen doesn't remove the church from its place on the council, if they are such a hindrance to her rule.'

Daphne sighed. They had been over this before. She picked up her cup of sweet, black coffee. 'As I've said, Chief, the constitution of the Holdings lays out the precise membership of the royal council.'

'Yes, yes,' he replied, 'but why doesn't she just break the constitution?'

Daphne looked out through the supporting pillars of the balcony, where they sat under shade, protected from the hot afternoon sun. She was unsure what to say, wary of her captor's true intent.

'None of the Holders would support her,' Chane said, 'and the church would see it as a great opportunity to play the martyr. The common people of the Holdings are still very religious at heart, and the queen couldn't risk pissing them all off.'

'But she controls the army,' Agang replied, getting exasperated. His two nephews glanced at each other across the table. Daphne wasn't sure how much they understood, but they could sense their uncle's frustration. 'She could crush any noble that disobeyed her,' he continued, 'then round up all the priests and prophets, make a huge bonfire, and throw them on it. The people would respect that. They would understand who was in charge.'

'But the entire basis for rule would change,' Weir said. He was contributing more to these discussions, Daphne noticed. For the first few days he had said nothing, barely grunting if asked a direct question, but as time passed, and their conditions of imprisonment remained free of any coercion, he had started to open up.

'It would change,' Weir went on, 'from having the feeling that you were ruled through consent and free agreement, like a contract, to one where you were being ruled through fear and force alone. The Holdings folk wouldn't stand for it, they're too used to their constitutional freedoms, no matter how illusory they are in reality. They would rise up against the queen.'

'I see,' Agang nodded. 'That makes sense. It is, in a way, what happened here about half a century ago. Following hundreds of years of rule by the *seulitch*, the people finally tired of their excesses and cruelties, and overthrew them. Unfortunately, Sanang has been without any central government since then, and the results are obvious to see.'

He poured himself a mixture of coffee and chocolate, adding a spoon of honey.

'You've never mentioned them before,' Daphne said. 'The soulwitches?'

Echtang Gabo, the younger nephew, choked back a laugh.

A glance from Agang silenced him.

'The *seulitch*,' the chief frowned, 'and they are not a laughing matter.'

Echtang mumbled something in Sanangka.

'In the Holdings tongue, boy,' Agang said, 'so all present can understand. One day, when the Sanang nation is on an equal footing with the Realm of the Holdings, you will be in my court, and I'll need you to be fluent, and polite, when discussing matters of state with their ambassadors.'

'Sorry, uncle,' Echtang said.

'Thank you,' Agang replied, turning back to Daphne. 'We shall not discuss the *seulitch*. They mark a dark time that is best forgotten.'

Daphne wondered why he was so hesitant to explain some aspects of Sanang history and culture to them. While he had spent many hours over the last ten days asking the captives questions, he had been less forthcoming about his own people's ways.

'Back to something you said, Lieutenant Chane,' Agang went on, sipping his drink. 'You claimed that the common people of your land are more religious, yes? That would imply that the upper classes are less so. Why is this?'

'Better education,' Chane said, earning a scowl from Weir.

'You disagree, sergeant?' Agang said.

'Not that the rich can afford a better schooling for their children, that's true enough,' he replied, 'but every child throughout the Holdings is taught to read, it's in the constitution. Every town, village and farm has its own free school, and even the poorest brats have to attend, whether they want to or not.'

'Yes, I can remember Ethan saying this, though I can hardly believe it,' Agang said. 'The queen pays for the nation's children to be literate? Girls too? Seems like a terrible waste of money. What are all these peasants supposed to do with such knowledge?'

'Read the holy book, of course,' Chane said.

'Yes?'

'That's what's written in the constitution,' she said, 'that all subjects must be able to read and understand the scriptures of the Creator, so that they can be living exemplars of his word.'

'Does anyone check to see that this is carried out?' Agang asked.

'Not so much any more,' she said. 'The church used to send out travelling examiners. They toured the Holdings, and anyone could be stopped by one of them, and have to prove their knowledge of the sacred text.'

'And were people punished if they failed these little tests?'

'Yes, but not by the examiners themselves,' Chane said. 'Usually the people of the village or Holdings would take the matter into their own hands, hold some public shaming. Varied from place to place.'

'I once saw a man get whipped naked down the street,' Weir said, 'after an examiner said he was getting his verses all mixed up. Seems harsh now, but was funny at the time.'

'But the examiners did not punish anyone?'

'They're men and women of peace,' Weir said. Chane snorted, but he ignored her. 'It's their first vow that they're never to raise a hand in violence.'

'And you said that these tests no longer take place. Why?'

'The queen,' Chane said. 'She put a stop to them.'

Mink yawned, long and loud.

Agang gazed over at him, looking annoyed at the interruption. He was perched on the very end of the long bench where the prisoners sat in a row, his legs crossed, and his arms folded. He hadn't touched any of the food or drink laid out for them.

'Do you have something to add, Lieutenant?' the Sanang chief said.

Mink said nothing.

'Speak, man,' Agang pressed, growing frustrated. Echtang looked nervously at his brother Gadang.

'I don't have to say anything,' Mink stated. 'You're not my commander.'

'You can answer him, Lieutenant,' Daphne said.

'I no longer recognise the authority of a traitor who discusses Holdings secrets with the enemy.'

'He's your officer,' Agang said, looking at Daphne. 'Feel free to punish him for his insubordination. My guards won't intervene. Or, if you'd prefer, I could do it myself.'

'No. Let him be.' She looked at her lieutenant. 'Mink, best go to your room.'

He got to his feet, looking down at her in contempt. He turned towards the door at the back of the balcony that led to their rooms. A pair of guards escorted Mink on his way out.

'I'd happily assist in adjusting the lieutenant's attitude, Captain,' Weir muttered.

'I can see you're a loyal soldier, sergeant,' Agang said, 'but I can also respect Lieutenant Mink's position. Are you not doing as he says, discussing your secrets with the enemy?'

'Not the way I see it,' Weir said. 'You haven't asked us a single question about our troop dispositions, tactics, logistics, supply chain or anything that might give you an advantage in hitting back at the Holdings. And if you did, then I would, with all due respect of course, tell you to fuck off. But you haven't. How the government works is not a secret. Our constitution is pinned to the notice-board of every farm and village across the Holdings, where everyone is free to read it, and quote from it, which they do, some of them endlessly. Sharing this with you is not betraying the Holdings.'

'Why haven't you asked us,' Chane said, 'about the army's position and defences?'

'It's not my war,' Agang said, 'it has passed from my hands. For this season, at any rate, I will conduct no more fighting. I was just the one destined to show the Sanang that the impossible could be achieved, that the Holdings could be beaten.'

'Do you know how it's going?' Daphne asked.

'Not as yet,' he replied. 'I know the numbers that travelled east to harry the Holdings' retreat, right through the gap in the lines that your defeat opened up, but I've not heard the outcome of any confrontation.'

'How many?' Chane asked.

'Now you ask me of my nation's military dispositions?' he laughed. 'I think not.'

Chane shrugged. 'It's not like we're going anywhere.'

Agang relaxed back into his seat, sipping his coffee and chocolate drink.

Daphne looked at her surroundings. The balcony had a beautiful view over the lush forest surrounding the compound. The road was visible as a faint line in the trees to the south-east. Each of the prisoners had their own room on the attic storey above the great hall, and there was an indoor common room, where they could gather when it rained. There were no stairs down to the main rooms of the hall below, but there was a trapdoor in the floor of the common room, through which they received their daily supplies of food, drink and water each dawn. The guards ascended and descended via rope ladders, and the outside walls had been plastered sheer, with no finger or toe holds to assist in climbing the walls. With her left arm crippled, Daphne knew there was no way she would be able to get down, even if there had been footholds. Her arm had been steadily improving. She could now raise it as high as her shoulder, and she had recently achieved a weak grip between her thumb and index finger. Not enough to lift anything, but it was a start.

'Do you have any complaints about your accommodation?' Agang asked.

'No,' Daphne replied, 'although it would be nice to go downstairs or outside, now and again.'

'Maybe in time,' he said, putting down his cup. He stretched his arms and rose. 'If you'll excuse me, I have to meet with my weapons masters to discuss my new battalion's training, and distribute some swords to a few promoted officers.'

He gestured to a guard, who yelled something down to the ground level.

As the warriors fitted the rope ladders to the top of the balcony railing, Agang turned back to the prisoners.

'Same time tomorrow,' he said. 'I'll be asking you about the prophets. I remembered something Ethan told me, that they hear voices in their head?'

'Tomorrow, then,' Daphne said.

Agang and his nephews leapt over the railing, and climbed down the rope ladders in a few seconds. Once down, the guards at the top shook the ropes from their pegs, and each slithered off and fell back to the ground.

Weir leaned forward, and started to shovel food from Agang's plate onto his own.

'You're going to get yourself a gut at this rate, soldier,' Chane said.

'Maybe, Lieutenant,' he said, picking up a leg of poultry, marinated in rich spices, 'but it'll be worth it. This is the best damn food I've ever tasted.'

Daphne eyed the half-eaten chocolate covered honey, nuts and oat cake sitting on her plate.

'We need to find a way to get some exercise,' she said, 'or, up here with all this food, we'll be out of shape in no time.'

'Combat practice?' Chane suggested. 'In the common room? See if they'll let us use wooden sticks. Two hours a day would do it, and give us an excuse to beat up Mink at the same time.' She grinned over at Weir, who smirked back. 'It would break up the monotony of the day. And it'll help you, Captain, to keep your right arm in shape.'

'Agreed,' Daphne replied, 'although we cannot force Lieutenant Mink to participate if he refuses. We can ask Agang about getting some wooden swords tomorrow, after we talk about the voice of the Creator with him.'

'Crazy old priests,' Chane said, 'with their little voices telling them whenever the Creator farts.'

'Excuse me,' Weir said, 'I happen to believe in the prophets.'

'Really?' Chane replied. 'You been smoking dreamweed again?'

'Well, yes,' he shrugged. 'Passes the time, but that's not the point. I believe that the Creator speaks his words to a few of his chosen people. It's been proved that their words have saved the Holdings from disaster throughout history.'

Chane smiled. 'I'd like to hear that proof.'

'Another time, perhaps,' Daphne said. 'Tomorrow, Weir, you should speak to Agang about the voice of the Creator. You're a pious man, and the only real believer among us. My faith is of little use.'

'I will then, Captain,' Weir said.

'And Chane,' Daphne said, 'keep your scoffing to a minimum. I don't want to have to send you to your room.'

'Yes, ma'am.'

The following evening, Agang acquiesced to their request for practice weapons without any fuss, and a roped bundle was raised up through the trapdoor.

Echtang and Gadang watched as Chane untied the cords holding the package together and removed four blades of polished wood. They were from a willow tree, Agang had informed them. He had decided to stay in the attic with them a little longer that evening so he could watch them practice, and the common room was busy with guards. At a snap of Agang's fingers, they moved back against the walls. Daphne could see what looked like amusement in their eyes as she, Chane and Weir each took a blade. Mink sat in the corner on a chair with his legs drawn up, making a point of not joining in.

Daphne gathered Chane and Weir close to her in the centre of the floor, her back to Agang and his nephews.

'Remember,' she whispered, 'no mention of battle-vision, that's our secret.'

They nodded.

She turned to face Agang, Echtang and Gadang, the chief a head higher than his nephews.

'First,' Daphne said, 'Lieutenant Chane and Sergeant Weir will loosen up, and demonstrate some basic moves.'

She took a few paces back to stand next to Agang, Echtang making space for her.

She raised her hand to clap for them to start, and stopped herself, feeling foolish.

'Begin,' she said.

Chane and Weir touched the tips of their wooden swords together, then backed off, circling around the centre of the room. The Sanang guards watched them, and edged a little closer.

For a few revolutions, Chane and Weir were content to stretch their limbs, and get a feel for their blades, though their eyes never left each other.

Agang said something to the guards in Sanangka, and they eased from their alert attitudes, coming in closer and forming a circle around the duelling pair. Some started to chat and point, especially at Chane as she circled with her weapon, smiling.

'What are they saying?' Daphne asked.

'That they expect this fight to be over soon,' Agang replied. 'A few are hoping that they will be asked to practice with the sergeant once he has defeated Chane.'

There it was again. The Sanang attitude to women. Daphne had yet to see a female Sanang since arriving at Beechwoods. All the guards were male, and so were the workers, merchants and labourers that they saw each day from their balcony. Daphne smiled to herself. She had a feeling that some of them were about to be surprised.

Weir broke from his circling and lunged out at Chane's left. The guards cheered. At the last second he pulled back from his feint and swiped up towards the lieutenant's chest, but she had anticipated him, stepping nimbly to the right and parrying. They circled each other again, both smiling, then began a series of lightning fast exchanges, sweeping, cutting, blocking. The roar from the guards rose in volume, and Daphne could hear passion in their voices as they watched the two Holdings soldiers fight. She felt pride in Chane and Weir's graceful movements, and her heart soared.

'Are these two particularly skilled?' Agang asked.

'No,' she lied. 'Nothing exceptional.'

Sweat appeared on Weir's brow, and Daphne suspected he was regretting the extra ribs he had wolfed down at lunch. Chane lunged low, ducking under a powerful swipe, and sprang up under Weir's guard, striking him on the chin with the hilt of her sword with an uppercut. The sergeant flew back onto the wooden floor of the common room, bounced an inch, then lay still.

The Sanang fell silent.

Chane stepped forward and offered Weir her hand. He groaned, rubbed his chin and took it. As she helped him to his feet he chuckled. 'Damn, you were right, Captain, we do need exercise.'

Daphne stepped into the centre of the room. The faces of the guards were a mixture of amusement, surprise and resentment. A couple of them started to mutter, and she guessed they were telling each other that the Holdings woman had cheated.

'Nice demonstration,' she said. 'Well done, Chane.' She looked over to where Mink was observing. 'Lieutenant,' she said to him, holding out her wooden blade, 'would you care to take part?'

'I'm not dancing for their amusement.'

'They'll get bored after we've been doing it for a while, maybe you can join us then?'

He shook his head.

The guards, while not knowing the words, clearly understood the meaning of this exchange, and started pointing and jeering at Mink. Guilt filled Daphne as she realised what she had done. Mink glanced up at her, hate in his eyes. She needed to remember that he was one of her officers, and it was her duty to look out for him, not abandon him to the braying laughter of the enemy soldiers. She had to be careful, otherwise what he had been saying about them might become true.

'You and me, sergeant,' she said, turning towards Weir, 'but it's time to calm this lot down. It was good to show them what we can do, but we don't want to become a source for their entertainment. Let's do some boring old thrust and parry.'

'Right you are, Captain,' he said, and fell back into his guard stance. Chane strode over to Agang, still grinning over her victory. Several of the men, including Echtang and Gadang, let their glances linger on her.

Daphne faced Weir, and they raised their swords.

'Captain,' Agang said, half amused, 'you intend to fight while injured?'

'I've still got one good arm,' she replied. 'And this won't be the same as before, we're just going to do some slow practice.'

He nodded, watching her closely.

Weir thrust out with his blade, and she deftly parried. She did the same, a controlled lunge, keeping her balance, while he blocked.

They danced back and forth, thrust and counter-thrust, elegantly synchronising their movements with each other. The guards watched but lost interest as the pair went through their sword drills. After a few minutes, Agang sent them back to the walls, where they resumed their guard duty.

Agang stayed and watched, seeming more interested in the training ground exercises than by the earlier full-blooded fight.

Following a good twenty minute session, Daphne raised her right arm and bowed out. Chane took up her position, and she and Weir started going through the same routines, a little faster than Daphne had managed.

She went to the table and picked up a cup of water. Her right arm and shoulder were aching, and would feel worse in the coming days, but it felt good to work up a sweat. She drank the contents of the cup in a single draught.

'Very interesting,' Agang said, approaching her. 'These moves, you learn them in training?'

'Yes,' she replied. 'Lots of practice.'

He laughed. 'If only my warriors had the patience.'

'You seem to have yours well trained,' she replied, 'compared to the others we saw.'

He snorted. 'B'Dang's mob? Believe me, they're worse than most, but you're correct, my soldiers are better trained than any other Sanang force. They could always do with more training though. Especially in sword work. We're still new to metal weapons, and I know my warriors would greatly improve, if they had better trainers.'

Daphne looked at him, an eyebrow raised.

'Is that the real reason you want us here?'

'I have many reasons,' he replied. 'This one however, has only just occurred to me, now that I've seen you practice. But I can see that these two in particular,' he pointed at Chane and Weir, 'could be very useful. A few sessions with my weapons masters to show them the routines, and then we could have an entire sword company learning the moves.'

'Wait,' she said. 'We're getting a little ahead of ourselves. Discussing Holdings religion and politics, I am just about comfortable with, but training the enemy in one of the skills in which we are superior? We'd be hanged as traitors by our own side, and justifiably so.'

He glowered for a moment, then nodded.

'Later this evening,' he said, 'after you have finished your exercise, the guards will escort you out to the balcony. I wish to speak to you further on this.'

'As you wish,' she replied. She raised her wooden sword, and returned to her practice.

Agang had lit several torches, but the balcony was shrouded in shadow and darkness, and the sky was pitch. Furs and extra cushions had been laid out on the low, wide bench, and Agang was reclining on a long divan. His upper body was thick and muscular, and his shoulders bigger than those on any Holdings man she had seen. His arms, like all of the Sanang, were proportionately longer than theirs, and a single hand could comfortably encompass her whole head. He wasn't handsome from a Holdings point of view. Maybe Sanang women, wherever they were, went for his type. He had a powerful presence, and was as intelligent as anyone she had met. He had long black hair, and the rough pale skin on his beardless face shone in the torchlight.

'Smoke?' he said, as she sat.

She had not taken any drugs since Badolecht had healed her arm, and wondered whether that was because she didn't need any, or because none had been offered to her. She knew that Weir had somehow got his hands on some, but she hadn't asked him how.

'What is it?'

'A blend,' he replied, 'half dreamweed, half keenweed.'

'Keenweed?'

'Keeps you alert, stops you falling asleep,' he said. 'Ethan said it was the closest thing we had to your tobacco, only much stronger.'

'I'll try a little.'

Agang poured some drinks, and lit a couple of sticks. He passed one to her.

'Why do you think I brought you here?' he asked.

She lit her stick, and inhaled. Her mind cleared, and she felt nicely relaxed. *He wants me to open up to him,* she told herself. She had to remember that he was not her friend.

'Information, primarily,' she said. 'You learned a lot from Ethan, but from the sounds of it he didn't know much about government or politics.'

'That is true,' he said, laughing, 'though he did know an awful lot about the sugar trade.'

'Fascinating, I'm sure, but not much use to you.'

'Indeed.' He took a drink. 'When I was planning the assault upon your outpost, I was hoping to capture a few officers, even though I knew it would anger the other chiefs, not to mention the soldiers.'

'Why?'

'You need to ask?' he said, anger in his voice. 'You, who invaded my country, committed atrocity after atrocity, and turned miles of forest into a desert wasteland? Do you not comprehend the rage within the Sanang people? You say you want to go outside. If I let you out there without an armed guard, you'd be ripped to shreds within minutes.'

She sat still during his outburst, remembering the slaughter of her own soldiers by Agang and B'Dang's men.

'Then why are we alive? Why are we here?'

'Because,' he said, calming, 'despite all you have done, Ethan taught me the inherent goodness of your people, just as, at heart, the Sanang are good people too. You do not see this, I know. To you we are violent savages, but we are only what these violent, savage times have made us. Give us peace, give us unity, and the goodness within will rise.'

'You want us to help you?' she asked. 'Why should we help you? We will not betray our nation.'

'Ethan was able to help me, without becoming a traitor.'

'Maybe,' she replied, 'but his skills weren't of a military nature. Look, I'm not unsympathetic to your cause of peace and harmony, and we'll continue to teach you about our law and religion, but we have a line that we won't cross.'

There was a long silence.

'Good enough for the present,' he said eventually. 'Now, I know that I haven't been very open with you about my own people. But I want you to trust me and so, if you have any questions about Sanang history or culture, please ask.'

She leaned forward, wondering at this new tact.

'First,' she said, 'how did you know that my company hadn't withdrawn from the fort when you attacked? And how did you know the others had?'

He chuckled, shaking his head. 'Questions about history and culture only, please.'

She sighed.

'My next question, then,' she said. 'Where are the women? Why haven't I seen any? Why are there none in the homestead?'

'There are fifteen females living in this compound,' he replied, 'as well as you and Chane.'

'There are?' she said, astonished. 'Where?'

He pointed down to his left. 'That building is the women's enclosure.'

'The what? Enclosure?'

'Yes,' he said. 'Where they live.'

'A prison?'

He laughed. 'Of course not. It's their home.'

'Then why do they never come outside?'

'They must remain within, for their own safety. It's their place, their domain. Within the enclosure the women rule, as we men do out here in public life.'

'Why?'

'Sanang women know nothing of the world; they cannot lead armies, plan campaigns, or make difficult decisions.'

'I'm not surprised, if they're locked up their whole lives.'

'Their minds are too fragile,' he explained. 'Raising the children of the household is their duty, their calling; it's where they are the experts. Inside the enclosure they have everything they need, food, drink, smoke, fancy clothes.'

'Everything except the freedom to go outside.'

'As I said, that's for their own protection. Any female out in the forest unescorted is liable to be kidnapped by one band of warriors or another. And frankly, if she's out there unescorted, she deserves it.'

Daphne gave him a cold stare.

'And what about us?' she said at last. 'I am a captain in the Holdings cavalry, and the rather capable Lieutenant Chane is my officer. Do we not somewhat disprove this nonsense?'

'You are foreign,' he said, waving his hand. 'I already knew from Ethan that women made up a large proportion of your army, but to most in Sanang that just proves the weakness of your menfolk. After seeing you and Chane with a sword today, and having fought your female soldiers at the outpost, we now know differently. However, Sanang women are not the same as you. To hear them talk, all foolish giggles and gossip.'

'You infantilise them, then complain when they act like children,' she said. 'Is it maybe a difference that I've had about twelve years of education?'

He sat in silence for a while, drinking and preparing a couple of fresh smoke sticks. He passed her one.

'I concede there may be something to that,' he said, 'but first must come peace. For Sanang women to have more freedom, there must be an end to the bands of murderers that plague the forests. This is the task I face. Social change will have to wait.'

She sat smoking, surprised that he had backed down even a little.

'Now I have a question,' he said, smiling again. 'You say you are of the cavalry, but where are your horses? Do such mythical creatures even exist?'

She looked up. 'My father's land holds one hundred and sixty thousand heads of the finest horses in the world. I grew up beside them every day of my youth. I personally own nine: two battle horses, three work ponies, one for general out and about, one stud, and two for travel. I trained in the queen's cavalry for two years, and then,' she sighed, 'at the first sign of war, we had to leave our horses at the border, because they're no good in the forest.'

Agang poured himself another drink, laughing gently.

'One more question, then,' he said.

She leaned forward. 'Who were the soulwitches?'

His laughter stopped, and he sat back, smoking.

Daphne bit her lip.

'I should have guessed you'd ask about them,' he said, 'and forbade it. However, I did not, and so I will keep my word.' He took a long, slow drink.

'The *seulitch*,' he went on, 'were a powerful group of Sanang. Like the hedgewitches, as you name them, only stronger. Hedgewitches can control living things, persuade them to grow or to heal, or in some rare cases, to die. The soulwitches had those same powers, and more. They used them to rule over the Sanang for hundreds of years. They were harsh rulers, but the Sanang lived in peace. The soulwitches had a government, law, and an army of servants to carry out their orders. Farms were organised, and townships built, and roads and bridges, but the people lived in fear of them, especially in the last decades of their rule.

'They became arrogant, and greedy, and cruel, and because no one could stand up to them, they began to behave as if they could do anything. They broke their own laws and took what they wanted, and crushed any who opposed them. It was during this dark time that it became unsafe for girls to go out into the forest without protection. Packs of their servants would scour the countryside, looking for young females. They would enter villages and demand two or three be surrendered to them, or they would burn the place to the ground, and take the girls anyway.'

Daphne shuddered. 'What did they want with them?'

'For their harems, mainly, though the common people still mutter dark words about bloody rituals and sacrifice.'

'What happened to the soulwitches' rule?'

'After a civil war, they were overthrown, and slaughtered. But the war had been painful, and gone on for so long, and so many had died, that the whole country just fell apart. The greatest tragedy is that for the majority of people in Sanang, the way we live now is normal. The violence, the lawlessness, the fear, taking vengeance over the slightest insult, the cheapness of life...' His words tailed off, and he fell into silence, his head bowed.

Daphne watched him, saying nothing.

'Forgive me,' he said. 'It saddens me to dwell upon the condition of my wounded land. I know that the Holdings people look at us and see savages, cruel and barbaric. I look at my own people, and I see the same. Someone must take this shattered nation, hold it close to his heart, and carefully put all the fragile pieces back together, until we are united and whole, and we can walk out into this world with our heads high.'

'And you're taking that first step?'

'Yes,' he said. 'I control over a hundred square miles of forest, thirteen settlements, dozens of farms and orchards, and twelve hundred warriors, including three hundred swords. Another three thousand warriors swear fealty to me as allies, and I sit among the councils of the high chiefs. It is a first step.

'But things are changing,' he went on, raising his cup. 'Soon everyone in Sanang will know it was I who struck the first blow at the Holdings invaders. It was I who dared, and I who was victorious.'

His eyes were lit with a deep fire. 'At the end of summer,' he said, 'the chiefs will come to me.'

CHAPTER 9

THE TURN

Beechwoods, Sanang – 21st Day, Last Third Summer 503

The four Holdings prisoners at Beechwoods passed the rest of the summer in peace. Agang and his nephews visited them on most days, despite the chief having squeezed every last drop of information out of them that Daphne thought possible. The Sanang seemed to enjoy their talks and, to keep the sessions going, they had persuaded the prisoners to learn Sanangka. Chane had shown the most eagerness to pick it up, and often tried out what she learned on the guards, much to their amusement. At the other end of the scale, Mink had refused to attend these sessions. Daphne knew he set himself on the contrary path to whatever she suggested, but in some ways she was grateful for his presence. His barbed comments about treason and going over to the enemy put pause in their minds, no matter how often they might deny it.

With twelve days until the start of autumn, the nephews had informed them that the other chiefs were on their way to Beechwoods to meet with Agang. At last the summer campaign against the Holdings was coming to an end, and the tribal warriors were returning home. Agang had remained tight-lipped about any news from the front but, in their youthful eagerness, his nephews had not been able to resist dropping a few hints. The war was progressing well for the Sanang, that much was clear, but the lack of details left the prisoners on edge.

Two days later, Agang paid them a visit in the early evening, as they were about to begin sword practice. It was raining, so they remained in the common room, and had flasks of hot coffee pulled up from the kitchens below.

'I have a small gift,' he said, throwing a large package onto the table. 'I have come into possession of a share of captured supplies, and I noticed this among the other goods, and thought of you.'

Chane opened it, and let out a small squeal. 'Tobacco,' she grinned.

Weir walked over and held a tightly bound bundle to his nose.

'Stringer Holding's Golden Blend,' he stated authoritatively. 'Not shit at all.'

Agang laughed and sat, pouring himself a coffee.

Only Mink stayed motionless in his chair, wrapped in his blankets, not having bothered to get dressed. He glowered at them. Daphne, Chane and Weir prepared a few cigarettes, and Daphne offered one to Agang.

'Thank you.' He tried a puff, and nodded.

Daphne sat back into her chair's deep cushions, and put her feet up on a stool. She smoked the cigarette, her first in over two and a half thirds, and drank the coffee, for which she had developed a taste. Just needs some sugar, she thought, and this morning would be as perfect as it got.

She couldn't remember when her hopes of going home had faded to the point where she barely ever considered the possibility, but the uncertainty over her future brought her no particular fear. Instead, she felt freed from responsibility, the injury to her arm having provided her with a valid reason for why she hadn't tried to escape. It was continuing to heal, but as Badolecht Nang had predicted, her elbow remained fused at a crooked angle. Through tiring and painful daily practise, the grip in her misshapen hand had improved to the point where she could pick small objects up, and hold onto them, and she was able to dress herself without assistance. Chane and Weir had been helpful and supportive throughout, and she felt closer to them than anyone except her family.

'I have news,' Agang said, 'though I suspect that Gadang or Echtang might have already told you. Can't keep their mouths shut, those boys.'

'The chiefs?' Daphne said.

'Yes,' he replied. 'They are due to arrive here before nightfall, so the messenger said.'

'And then what?' Chane asked.

'There will be a complicated reshuffling of the hierarchy,' he said. 'In other words, I'll be moving up a few places. Next year, I shall command the Sanang defences.'

'Congratulations,' Chane said, raising her coffee cup.

'Thank you, Lieutenant.' He smiled at her. 'I will also be in a position to formally announce your existence. Of course, word has got out that I took prisoners at the outpost, but now I'll be able to assert that you are on my staff, and therefore inviolable.'

'I'm not on your staff,' said Mink.

'You have no say in the matter,' Agang replied, relaxed. He had long passed the stage of getting annoyed at the lieutenant's intransigence. 'Under the common law of Sanang, you will be elevated from chattel slaves to body slaves, and as I am the body in question, you will come under my direct protection, almost as if you were one of my wives.'

Mink looked away, disgusted.

'This means,' Agang continued, 'that you'll be able to leave the attic at last, though you two will have to be dressed appropriately.' He looked at the women.

'Not sacks again?' Chane said, her face falling.

'I'm afraid so.'

Chane glanced across at Daphne, and they frowned.

'Within the compound,' Agang went on, 'and this goes for the men as well, you will at all times be escorted by two guards. You are not to leave the compound without my direct permission, and you must ask in advance, so that I can prepare the necessary force to be sent out with you for your protection. The first time you leave will be in my presence.

After Autumn's Day I intend to visit the new slave market that has opened by the bridge, and you will accompany me there.'

'To a slave market?' Daphne said.

'These particular slaves may be of interest to you.'

'They're Holdings folk?' Weir asked, a vein in his neck twitching.

'They are. It seems I set a precedent at the outpost, and not all Holdings soldiers who were captured this summer were killed out of hand. I'm looking for a slave with metal-working experience, and you will assist me in their selection. And, if you happen to see others who interest you, you can point them out to me.'

They stared at him.

'I am a fair master,' he said. 'Not all Sanang slave owners are like me.'

'How much are they selling for?' Weir asked.

'Anything from a few pigs for the weaker slaves, up to a bundle of swords for those in the best condition, or the most attractive ones.'

Daphne felt sick.

'Think on it,' he said. 'I'm a rich man; I can afford a few extra slaves. But try not to be guided by pity alone. Everyone I buy must prove their worth to me.'

He put down his cup of coffee, and stood.

'Remain out of sight when the chiefs get here,' he said. 'They'll most likely stay for a few days, so I won't be visiting, but I'll send my nephews to keep your tuition going. Enjoy the tobacco.'

He lifted the trapdoor and climbed down the pulley rope, disappearing into the kitchen below.

'So Agang is taking his pets along to see the wild animals?' Mink said. 'So you can each choose a new puppy to bring back to your cage.'

'Shut up,' said Weir.

'And,' Mink laughed, 'just wait until they realise they've been bought by the bitch that betrayed them all.'

Once that would have bitten, but Daphne had heard it before, many times.

'We'll have to save as many as we can,' she said to Chane and Weir.

'But how will we choose?' Chane asked.

Daphne shook her head.

They stayed indoors for the rest of the evening, sickening themselves with tobacco, until the common room was a fug of smoke. They had missed sword practice, and were bored and listless.

Daphne was thinking of going to bed early, when Echtang and Gadang arrived. They looked cheerful, and their breaths were tinged with alcohol as they panted, following their clamber up the rope from the kitchen.

Echtang coughed. 'Such smoke,' he said in the Holdings tongue. 'Give me one.'

He held out his hand to Chane. She looked at him.

'Please,' he stammered, remembering the Holding customs, which he found foolish.

'Of course,' Chane smiled, passing him a cigarette.

'We've been drinking with the chiefs,' Gadang said. He sat, stretching his legs out. 'We heard the whole story from the front.'

'Yes?' Daphne said, her attention fixing on the young men.

'The Sanang have won a great victory,' Gadang said. 'Our warriors surged through the gap in the enemy lines and attacked a big supply base, before the Holdings had withdrawn, and caught them by surprise. There was a battle, and the Sanang captured the base, and drove off the Holdings soldiers, killing and capturing many. The chiefs said that the Holdings were in full retreat, running back to their wall.'

'One supply base?' Mink muttered. 'Doesn't sound like much.'

Echtang looked at him with contempt. 'The chiefs said that more swords and armour were captured, than there was in the whole Sanang army. Uncle Agang's reward is that every one of his warriors, all sixteen hundred, will get his own sword.' He beamed with pride.

'And over two thousand slaves were taken,' Gadang added. 'As many as were killed.'

'The Holdings lost four thousand?' Daphne said.

'Yes. And Uncle Agang is getting much of the credit, after his victory at your outpost. On Autumn's Day, the chiefs will announce that he will be commanding the Sanang armies next year, and if the Holdings do come back, they'll get a big surprise.'

Daphne blinked. This was the first usable piece of information that the nephews had supplied, something that she could take back to the Holdings, to warn them, if somehow she could get out.

'It certainly was a great victory at the outpost,' she said.

'Yes,' Echtang said. 'Everyone in Sanang is drinking to uncle's name.'

'I'm sure,' she continued, while Weir raised a surreptitious eyebrow at her. 'Tactically, it was genius. Were you there at the planning?'

'We were,' Echtang said. 'Uncle showed us the plans the night before he left.'

She nodded along.

'He told us where his warriors would be,' Echtang continued, gesturing, 'and all about the main attack on the gate, and how two hundred of his best would sneak around the side to climb a tower, and about how no reinforcements could reach you in time, because all of the other Holdings soldiers had already retreated.'

'How clever of Agang to have known that,' she said, her heart racing.

'It wasn't his cleverness, well, not that bit,' Echtang said. 'The young war god told him.'

'Really?' she said. She knew a little of the Sanang religion. They had an ancient trinity of old deities, and a new, younger warlike god.

Gadang shuffled in his seat and half raised his hand, but Echtang was in full flow.

'Yes, it's amazing. The young god came to Uncle Agang in a vision, and told him that the outpost was isolated, and vulnerable to attack. That's how he knew he would win, he had the god on his side.'

'That is indeed amazing,' she said.

Gadang said something in Sanangka to his brother, too quickly for Daphne to understand, and the younger nephew closed his mouth, and quietened.

'We'd best be leaving,' Gadang said, standing, and pulling a crest-fallen Echtang up by his elbow.

'Good evening, then,' Daphne said.

The nephews climbed back down to the kitchen, the trapdoor falling shut behind them.

'A fucking god told him?' said Weir.

'Or, at least that's what he told his nephews,' Daphne said.

'So, we're still no closer to finding out how he knew?'

'Looks like it,' she said, but a dark thought was forming in the back of her mind. She tried to dismiss it, but it refused to leave. Being the only captive with any vision skills, she knew she was party to a certain field of information that was deemed secret by the Holdings government, concerning the powers possessed by a small group of mages. These servants of the realm had the ability to put visions into the minds of others, even at a great distance, and their existence was whispered about in the academy. It made sense that the Holdings would place at least one mage with inner-vision in Sanang to monitor the war effort, but that was as far as her logic would take her. To get from there to the notion that one of them had planted an idea into Agang's mind was a leap too far.

'Four thousand,' Mink whispered.

She glanced at him. His face was grey with shock.

'Imagine what they're saying in the capital right now,' he continued, his voice hoarse. 'Imagine the scenes in Holders Square when it is announced that four thousand soldiers will not be returning home. Imagine what the priests will say at the Autumn's Day services, and imagine the queen's face as she has to sit in the cathedral and listen to the prophet denounce the war, and lay the dead at her feet, and at the feet of her advisers.'

The room went deathly silent.

'The church,' he went on, 'and the mob, will be looking for a scape-goat to blame for this catastrophe.' He looked Daphne in the eye. 'Who do you think that will be?'

She stared back at him.

'Who cares what they think?' Chane said. 'They don't know the truth.'

Mink shrugged at her. 'The truth is irrelevant. The church has been waiting to strike at the queen, and the captain has handed them the opportunity. And, Lord Holdfast's good name may not last the season, implicated as he is in his daughter's refusal to obey orders.'

'But I didn't get any orders, Mink.'

'You know,' he said, 'you've stuck to your story so long that I'm starting to believe you, but what I think doesn't matter. The only thing that matters is how your actions are perceived back in the capital, especially as you're not there to deny anything.'

Knowing he had struck home, Mink smiled, but it was bitter, as if the price of victory had been the loss of four thousand, and he took no pleasure in Daphne's defeated expression.

He got up, and left to go to his room.

'Pay that idiot no attention, Captain,' Chane said, standing. 'He's been trying to rattle you all summer, don't let him get under your skin.'

She nodded, putting on her calm officer mask, the first time she had used it on Chane in a long time. 'Of course,' she said.

Chane looked at her for a moment, then smiled and left.

'Weir?' Daphne said, as soon as the door was closed. 'Come to my room. Bring coffee, and something decent to smoke.'

'What are you telling me?' said Weir. 'That you think one of our own high mages told Agang to attack?'

'No,' she replied. 'I don't know. Just that it's a possibility. I can't believe they would have done it.'

'No servant of the crown would. The church?' He shrugged.

'They wouldn't dare.'

'What, bring down your father, embarrass the queen, and tarnish the war effort?' He half smiled. 'It sounds like something they might consider.'

'I thought you were a religious man.'

'I am,' he replied, 'but my humble faith is far removed from the power struggles going on in the upper courts of the prophet's palace.'

'Then you think they might have done it?'

'I don't know. Just because they'd benefit, doesn't mean it was them. It's more likely, I think, that Agang found out some other way, and his whole vision story is just a smokescreen.'

Daphne leant back on her chair, and flicked ash into a saucer on the table. They were smoking some mixture that he had concocted, and it was starting to have an effect on her.

'I have to escape, sergeant,' she said. 'I have to get home to defend my father's name. And my own.'

Weir broke out into a large grin.

She frowned. 'What are you smiling at?'

'About time, Captain,' he chuckled, 'about fucking time.'

'What?'

'I've been waiting so long for this conversation I was starting to think it would never happen, that you'd turn like Chane has.'

'Chane hasn't turned!'

'Come off it,' he snorted. 'You know she has. She'd happily stay here, and Agang would happily keep her. If you weren't here to stop her, she'd already be teaching them our sword drills. Fuck, she'd probably be bedding him by now.'

She doubted that.

'And Mink?' she said.

'He'll be ready to go as soon as I give him the nod,' Weir said. 'I've talked to him, made him understand that I wouldn't leave without you.'

'You've prepared an escape?'

He shook his head. 'Had it prepared for over a third, Captain.' He picked up his drink, coffee with a shot of Sanang spirits, and took a swig.

'And you never thought to tell me?'

'I figured that if I tried to push you, I might end up shoving you into the arms of Chane and Agang, and then they'd find out about the plan, and we'd be screwed. Mink wasn't happy about it but I knew, well I hoped, that you'd come to your senses on your own.'

'You and Mink, you've been conspiring behind my back?'

'Don't get me wrong, Captain,' he replied, 'Mink will never be my best friend, but he's one of us, and he's loyal to the Holdings. We can't leave him behind. And I need him to help me get you out of the forest.'

She looked down at her crippled arm.

'Your injury,' he said. 'To be blunt, it's going to be a problem, but I've thought of a few ways we can get round it. And you're fit and strong otherwise, we all are.'

'And the plan?' she asked.

He grinned. 'The security around here is nowhere near as tight as Agang likes to think. Our guards believe us cowed and obedient, and they've got lazy. I first slipped out at night not too long after we got here.' He looked at her. 'Did you never wonder how I always managed to have something to smoke?' He held up his lit stick and laughed. 'I was a thief in my boyhood, guess some habits never change. Anyway, their entire defence looks outwards, towards the forest, and once you're clear of the main hall you can pretty much sneak about anywhere, as long as you don't get too close to the front gates, which they guard properly. The side gate, on the other hand...'

'There's another way out?'

'Yes,' he replied, his eyes shining. 'A postern door, beyond the low building with the workshops. It's barred from the inside, but not guarded.'

'When?'

'Tonight,' he replied. 'Agang and the chiefs will be drinking for days to come by the sounds of it. The guards will no doubt be enjoying themselves too. No one's going to be paying any attention to a bunch of slaves in the attic.'

'My dear Sergeant Weir. I don't know what to say, or how to thank you.'

'Well,' he said, 'it would be wrong of me to say that I haven't thought of a few ways you could thank me, once we get back and you're exonerated and all. Maybe use your contacts to hook me up with a nice veteran's farm, somewhere warm, some horses maybe? You get the picture.' He winked.

She nodded, and almost smiled, when a thought struck her.

'What will we do about Chane?' she asked. 'We can't leave her here.'

'I'm sorry, Captain, but her heart is with Agang and his cause. She might refuse to come, she might even tell him. We can't take the risk.'

'But she's my friend,' Daphne said. 'When she wakes up tomorrow, and realises we've gone...'

'I like her too, Captain,' he said, 'and to be honest I'd rather have her along than Mink, especially if it comes to a fight. But she doesn't want to go back to the Holdings.'

Daphne lowered her head.

'I get it,' she said, 'I just wish we could say goodbye to her.'

'Write her a note,' he said. 'Say you're sorry and all that. She'll probably appreciate it, after she's finished cursing us.'

'I might do that.'

Daphne felt her eyes starting to close.

'A bit strong for me,' she said, raising the weedstick. 'Not used to it.'

Weir smiled and stood.

'Get some rest,' he said. 'I'll be back for you later. I have a few things I need to be doing, if we're to get this plan in motion.'

After he had left, Daphne reached into the drawer under the table, and pulled out some Sanang paper, lighter and thinner than the Holdings version.

She prepared a quill, and started to write.

To Lieutenant Chane, my dearest friend.

I am sorry.

She paused, a tear forming in the corner of her eye. What could she write? That she believed her friend was a traitor in her heart, and that they couldn't trust her?

She left the paper as it was, and stumbled off to bed.

CHAPTER 10
INTO THE FOREST

River Tritos, Sanang – 22nd Day, Last Third Summer 503

The dead crowded round Daphne in the darkness, saying nothing. They stared, their fingers pointing at her, their ragged cavalry uniforms filthy with blood and dirt. There were so many of them, pushing her, reaching for her, clawing at her with broken fingernails. Please, she whispered. It wasn't her fault, please...

'Hush, Captain,' came a low voice, along with a gentle shake of her shoulder.

She started, and sat up, head fuggy with interrupted sleep.

Weir stood at her bedside, a lit candle in his hand.

'Time to get up.'

She looked around. A pack was sitting on the floor near the little table, and a set of clothes, all dark greens and browns, were hanging off the back of a chair.

'I've taken the liberty of packing some things for you,' he said. 'Hope that wasn't out of order.'

He handed her a knife, with a real metal blade.

'For you.' He looked at the astonishment on her face. 'I've been busy. Get dressed.'

He took a pace and turned away to give her some privacy.

'Weir,' she said. 'I'm not still dreaming, am I?'

'No, Captain, you're not,' he chuckled, 'though you do look pretty sleepy.'

He drew a smokestick from a pocket, lit it, and passed it back to her over his shoulder.

'Keenweed,' he said.

She inhaled, and felt the fog lift from her mind, and her senses sharpen.

'Thank you,' she said. 'How long were you gone?'

'About three hours or so,' he replied. 'Had to make sure all the guards in the attic were asleep first.'

'How did you manage that?' She pulled back her blanket and swung her legs off the bed.

'Wasn't too difficult,' he went on, while she dressed. 'Left some dull-weed-infused booze in the common room where they could find it. They're hardy buggers though, took a while to take effect. Made sure Chane got a drop too. They'll sleep right through. Mink is waiting by the balcony for us.'

'I'm ready,' she said.

He turned. Her dark green tunic hung halfway down to her knees, under which she wore thick brown leggings, and her cavalry boots. He was similarly dressed.

'We look like Holdings farm labourers.'

'One last thing.' He pulled a long black length of cloth from his own tunic. He stepped forward, and carefully wound it around her head, leaving only a slit for her eyes, and some holes for her to breathe through.

'We're all going to wear them,' he said. 'I've seen some Sanang bandits with these on out in the forest, we might get mistaken for them at a distance, if we get spotted.'

He helped her pull the pack on, and blew out the candle, plunging the room into darkness.

They waited for their eyes to adjust to the dim glow coming from under the door, then padded out into the corridor. The light was coming from the candles in the common room ahead, and as they passed it, Daphne saw their Sanang guards, sleeping where they sat, around a table where they had been playing dice.

They slipped back into the shadows on the other side of the common room, and went out onto the balcony. The long table and benches were bare and deserted, but they could hear the sounds of drunken laughter from the hall beneath them. The kitchens and storerooms that lay directly under the prisoners' bedrooms were quiet, but the main hall was echoing with the riotous sounds of a feast, as Agang hosted the chiefs. They found Mink crouching over by the far corner of the balcony. He was wearing the same outfit, and also had a cloth covering his face. He looked up at her as they approached, his eyes expressionless.

Weir crouched down, handed Mink a similar cloth, and the lieutenant tied it round the sergeant's head.

Weir beckoned Daphne over, and she joined them, crouching in the corner. He opened his pack, and took out a set of ropes and blocks.

'I copied this from the trapdoor pulley that goes to the kitchen,' he said. 'Stole all the bits I needed.' He handed her a section of rope.

'Stand,' he said.

'You put your foot in here.' He guided her right leg to a loop in the rope, then wound a further section around her waist. 'And you grip with your right hand, here.'

She grabbed the rope where he pointed.

'I'll go down first,' he said. 'Mink, you know what to do?'

The lieutenant nodded.

Weir moved a crate over to the balcony rail.

'When I get to the bottom, I'll wave,' he said, pulling on a thick pair of leather gloves. 'When you see me, hop over the edge. I'll take the strain, and lower you down. Got it?'

She nodded.

He jumped up to the railing, and took a good long look around the rear of the compound. Satisfied that no one was watching, he attached his pulley mechanism to one of the hooked pegs the warriors used to scale the wall. Holding onto another rope, he descended, the rope whistling through his gloves.

Once on the ground, he took up the other end of the rope attached to Daphne and the pulley, stepped back a few paces, braced himself, and waved.

'See you at the bottom, Mink,' she said, and climbed up to the railing. She tested her weight on the loop where her foot was lodged, and it was steady. She stepped off, fell three feet, and hung there for a moment, swinging gently, suspended at the top of the wall. Weir started to release the rope in short measured bursts, and she was jerked downwards, a yard at a time.

She stepped off with a foot to go, and leapt clear. Mink pushed the pulley from its peg, and Weir stepped forwards and caught it. He packed it into his bag as Mink, using the first rope, descended. Once he was at the bottom, Weir took the rope. He rippled it up the wall like a snake, and it slipped off its peg and fell to the ground.

He picked it up and smiled. 'That'll fox 'em.'

Mink went to the corner of the hall, and peered round. He turned back, nodding.

The three of them ran for the side of the workshops, dashing into the shadows under the wide canopy that ran along its length. The compound was lit with torches and storm lanterns, but they were few, and several had gone out. Looking up at the nearest corner tower, Daphne could make out the shape of a solitary sentry, up on the battlements, gazing out over the forest to the west.

They heard a door opening in the side of the hall, and a warrior staggered out. Weir crouched low into the deep shadow of a workshop entrance, and the others followed, cramming into the booth. The warrior stumbled over in their direction. He stopped a couple of paces to the left of them, leaned against a post, and pulled up his tunic. He unfastened his belt, and unleashed a torrent of piss against the door of the booth next to the one where they were hiding.

Crowded in next to Mink and Weir, Daphne stifled her urge to vomit and run, and made herself as small as possible, shrinking into the shadows.

The warrior belched and grunted, gave his privates a shake, and refastened his belt. He turned, and swayed his way back to the hall.

Weir waited for him to disappear into the building, then gestured, and they sprinted along the side of the workshops to the rear of the fort, away from the direction of the front gates. They reached the corner and halted, staying in the shadow of the low building. Across from them was the palisade wall, rows of boxes and crates stacked up against it.

Weir stole forward, examining the crates. He paused at one, stared at it, then pulled it down and placed it away from the wall.

In the gap where the crate had been, Daphne could see part of a doorframe. Weir kept at it, and had soon cleared the space. There was a short door embedded into the palisade wall. It was barred with a thick horizontal beam that fitted into brackets on either side. Weir lifted the bar up and out, and leaned it against a crate. He put a hand on the door, and shoved. It swung out a couple of feet, then got caught in some undergrowth. Weir squeezed through the gap, and Daphne followed. The trees had been cut back from the side of the stockade, creating a cleared area five paces wide, but bushes and thick brambles had been allowed to grow, filling the space up to the walls.

She pushed herself along the outside of the thick palisade timbers. Mink squeezed out and joined her.

'Wait here,' Weir said to them, and went back inside.

They waited a few moments in silence, then Weir rejoined them, a large pack strapped to his back. He stood at the doorway with his back to them, carefully restacking the crates to block any view of their exit. He squeezed back through the gap, and pushed the door closed. Although there was no bar to lock it in place, it sat flush within its frame.

He pointed towards the forest ahead. They followed him in the darkness through the undergrowth, thorns catching on their tunics, and scratching their legs. Weir went ahead, and Mink followed to the rear.

Once they reached the cover of the trees, the blackness of the night seemed absolute. She heard Weir rummaging about, then saw a tiny spark lit, and for a moment the sergeant's face was lit up by a red glow as he inhaled.

'Pure keenweed,' he whispered, passing the stick to them. 'We'll have to get as far as we can for the rest of the night, then keep going all day tomorrow.'

'Where are we going?' she asked, inhaling. Her eyesight began to pick out the dark shapes of her comrades, and then the faint outlines of the trees.

'We're going to swing round the compound, then join the road back to the bridge. We'll need to be off the road before it gets light, following the line of the river, east.'

He took the stick back off Mink, puffed, then passed it on to Daphne again.

'We've got about four hours until dawn,' he said. 'Let's go.'

'Happy Autumn's Day,' Daphne whispered, coughing as she sat down and shivered in the cold rain. They were under thick branches, but large drops fell onto them through the leaves. She pulled her blanket close. For ten nights they had been running. Stumbling in the darkness would be a more appropriate term, she thought. Each morning they buried themselves deep into the forest's thick undergrowth, and tried to sleep, remaining motionless for twelve hours. At dusk they ate their rations, smoked one of Weir's keenweed sticks, and set off again. She estimated that they were averaging well under twenty miles a night, half that might be a closer guess, but she had no way of telling. So long as they kept the river a few miles to their south, onward they plodded. Keeping track of the river was her job. Each dawn and dusk she would gaze southwards, find the tallest tree, and run a short burst of line-vision. The river was wide, and the gap it created through the forest was easy to find. Each dawn she would discover that they had strayed during the night, either closer to or further from the river, and they would try to correct their way the following night.

After the sixth night, she had seen their old fort in the distance, at the edge of her vision, the clean, straight line of the undamaged rear palisade wall rising above the tree cover. They had stayed well clear of the place, not knowing if any Sanang lingered there.

Four dawns later, when she had looked out at the river, she saw that its line was veering to the south east, towards its source high in the towering mountains that separated Sanang from the Plateau. She knew they would have to continue east, which meant giving up the river as their guide, and increasing their chances of getting lost.

'Well?' Mink asked.

'By tomorrow morning,' she replied. 'The river will be out of sight to the south-east. We're going to have to rely on clear skies, and an occasional glimpse of the seven stars to keep our way.'

'I reckon we need to stay about a hand width to the left of the rising sun,' Weir said. 'We just have to find somewhere where we'll be able to see it.'

He opened his pack, and shared out a portion of their dwindling supplies. Salted pork, dried and shrivelled to the consistency of leather, a handful of nuts, and some bruised and wrinkled fruit. They had lost weight on the journey, but as they had all been on the heavy side while they were enjoying Agang's hospitality, they were in pretty good shape, though always hungry. Each of them parted the cloth binding their heads, to allow themselves to eat.

'Mmmmm,' Mink said.

'You want to supply the food, go right ahead,' Weir snapped at him. 'Sarcastic bastard.'

The lieutenant scowled.

'Wonder what Chane's doing?' Daphne said drinking from her cup of gritty rainwater.

'She's probably commanding an entire company of Agang's swords by now,' Mink said.

'I don't think they'd take orders from a woman,' Weir said, 'no matter how good she was.'

'Savages,' Mink said.

'In a few days,' Daphne said, 'she'll be at the slave market, dressed in a sack, getting to choose who survives.'

'So speaks the woman who was quite happy to stand next to her,' Mink said. 'Right up to your sudden and convenient change of heart, you were behaving as badly as she was.'

'I never said a thing that the Sanang could use against us,' she shot back.

'No?' he said. 'I saw they way the two of you flirted with Agang. Demeaning behaviour, ill befitting ladies of the Realm.'

Weir frowned. 'You had a funny upbringing, Mink, if you thought the captain's behaviour was flirting. Chane though? Maybe.'

'I don't agree,' Daphne said. 'Chane was just being... keen. Anyway, I never once saw the slightest hint of interest coming from Agang, so even if she was, it wasn't working.'

'Maybe he only likes pale-skinned women,' Mink said.

'Never saw him with any,' Weir said, finishing the last of his breakfast. 'Come on, let's burrow under the leaves here and get some sleep.'

***

She awoke with a hand over her mouth. Weir's wrapped face loomed through the leaves beside her, and he motioned with his eyes over to her right. He removed his hand, and she turned her head in the direction of his gaze. Though the bushes and undergrowth, she saw a group of six Sanang warriors, sitting around a fire, in the same little dell where they had eaten breakfast that dawn. The sun was shining overhead, high in the sky.

She lay still, keeping her eyes on the small group. They seemed relaxed, and were talking to each other. She strained to hear what they were saying, and she made out the name Agang Garo, but not much else. They looked thin and underfed, and though they were sharing a drink from a skin, there was no food to be seen.

As the minutes dragged out, Daphne kept herself still, though now she was badly in need of a pee. To her alarm, she saw a large snake slither through the tangled brambles between her and the dell. She froze. The serpent's tiny yellow eyes flickered as it passed, its red diamond pattern glaring out a warning. She saw Weir's narrow eyes follow it, as it glided alongside him toward where Mink lay. It paused at the lieutenant's leg, which was trembling. Its tongue darted out, as if appraising the man, then it started to slither up Mink's tunic.

'Fuck,' Weir whispered, reaching for his knife.

There was a loud yell, and the leaf pile to Daphne's right erupted. Mink appeared amid a shower of forest debris, his arms flapping at his tunic.

She turned back to the Sanang, who were up and reaching for their weapons. One of them shouted in their direction, asking who they were in Sanangka. As she was flexing her right hand, trying to wake it up after hours of inactivity, Weir burst through the undergrowth, jumping over her shoulder towards the fire, roaring like a enraged stallion.

On instinct, Daphne summoned her battle-vision, and pulled herself to her feet, feeling a powerful rush clearing her head and priming her muscles. She scanned the dell. Weir was piling into the Sanang. One was down, bloody hands grasping at a slash to his neck, but in a few moments Weir would be overwhelmed. Run, or fight?

Before the question could fully form in her mind, she was already half way to the dell, knife out, her right arm held back. As she leapt towards the fire she hurled the knife at a warrior who was aiming a blow at Weir, taking him in the eye and knocking him backwards. She ducked a swing from a club, picking up the spear that the first warrior had dropped. She braced its butt into the earth and held it at an angle and the oncoming warrior ran himself through. She dived out of the way as the falling Sanang tumbled down next to her, snapping the spear. She yanked the broken end from the back of the dead warrior; it was a foot and a half long, its serrated flint edge dripping red. She jumped to her feet as another pair of Sanang rushed at her. She slashed at the one on the right, ripping his throat out, while the other aimed a club blow at her head. She twisted and dodged, and the strike glanced down her left arm. She blinked in excruciating pain, as her crippled elbow took the brunt of the blow. With pain overcoming her, she punched out with her good arm, stabbing the warrior up through his left armpit, into his heart. They slumped to their knees in unison, and toppled to the earth.

When she came to, she was propped up against a tree. She realised that her head covering had been removed, and her face was feeling fresh air against it for the first time in days. She opened her eyes to see Weir kneeling next to her, holding a waterskin, and smoking a stick. He offered her one.

'What is it?' she croaked.

'Just a cigarette,' he smiled. She took it, and he lit it for her. 'That was something back there, Captain. When I ran at them, the only thing going through my mind was that it would be better to die fighting. You moved faster than I could see. And with only one good arm.' He shook his head.

She took a long drink. Her arm still throbbed, but the pain was manageable. Her healing and exercise had toughened it up.

'Could you make me a shield, sergeant?' she asked. 'Something light, that I could have strapped to my arm?'

'Could do,' he nodded. 'I'll break up one of their shields, take the wood and the straps, see if I can rig something up for you.'

Mink came over.

'Sorry,' he mumbled.

'About the snake?' Daphne said. 'Not your fault, Lieutenant, I'd have done the same.'

Weir stared at him. 'No toilet to hide in this time?'

Mink looked away.

'What are you talking about?' Daphne said.

'That's where I found him,' Weir said. 'Back at the fort, when Agang attacked, he was skulking in the water closet.'

'Fuck you,' said Mink.

'You're not a bad officer,' Weir said. 'You know how to organise, and plan, and give orders and suchlike. It's just the fighting bit that gives you trouble. I saw you last year, at the battle for the Twinth. You just stood there with a frozen expression on your face, just like you were doing when me and Daphne were taking on those Sanang boys.'

'That's nothing to be ashamed of,' Daphne said. 'Lots of people freeze in battle.' She looked at Mink. 'I know you're not a coward, Lieutenant.'

'You're right Captain,' Weir said, 'about people freezing. Only thing is, when troopers do it, they're dishonourably discharged, but when officers do it...'

'When we get back to the Holdings...' Mink cried.

'We're going to say "thank you sergeant for helping us escape", aren't we?' Daphne said.

Mink snorted.

'If we get back.' Weir sighed. 'I overhead those boys talking. They were on their way to Agang's to see if they could enrol. Said they were four days away from his household. Meaning, that in ten nights, we've only come the distance it would them four fucking days to do. I propose, Captain, that seeing as how we're already up, we should make an early start of it, and run for the rest of today.'

She got to her feet, groaning. 'What I'd do for a cup of tea.'

Weir shrugged. 'I've got every kind of Sanang weed there is, but no tea, I'm afraid.'

Something occurred to her.

'Could I have some keenweed, please, I want to try something.'

'Sure,' he said, rummaging in his pack. He opened a box, extracted a stick, and lit it off the end of his cigarette.

She took it and inhaled deeply. She let its effects clear her mind, and heighten her senses, then drew upon a little of her battle-vision, not turning it on completely as she usually did, but just pulling a small strand of it.

She reeled back as her senses were almost overwhelmed. Her sight, smell, hearing, all were amplified. Every detail of the forest around her was picked out in clarity, and the noises of the birds and insects, which she had started to block out, came shouting and screeching back into her mind. Energy pulsed through her, and she felt strong and fit, and alive.

'They should try this in the academy,' she said, puffing out her cheeks.

Weir helped her on with her pack, and they got ready to leave. He kicked a shield to pieces, and stowed away some of the parts.

'Follow my lead today,' she said.

'Yes, ma'am,' Weir grinned.

She nodded, then started to run towards the east.

<hr>

Daphne finally let her battle-vision slip and fade when she heard Mink stumble again on the dark path behind her. She slowed and came to a stop, the keenweed keeping her standing, where usually she would have collapsed following such a long pull on the vision. It was nearly dawn, and they had been running for sixteen hours, putting more miles between them and Agang's compound than they had for several nights put together.

She gripped the branch of a tree, leaning forwards, panting, as Weir and Mink came up. Mink was retching, and Weir stumbled to his knees.

They crawled to a hiding place, under a thick overhanging bush that was clinging to the side of an outcrop of rock. They pulled the undergrowth in around them.

'Same again tonight, Captain?' Weir gasped, opening his waterskin and splashing his face. 'Can you manage that?'

'You got enough keenweed?' she asked, gulping down the water from her own flask.

'For a while yet,' he nodded.

She felt herself slipping, as the last of the narcotic's effects wore off.

'Wake me up at sunset,' she muttered, asleep the moment the words had left her mouth.

Ten hours sleep was nowhere near enough, she thought, as she stumbled to her feet in the fading light of dusk. She retched, coughed and gagged, then spat. Her head ached.

'Here,' Weir said, holding out a lit stick.

The three of them stood and smoked, passing the stick between them.

She felt her senses awaken, and once again pulled on a tiny strand of battle vision. Energy soared back into her, not as quickly as it had the day before, but enough.

'You need to eat,' Weir said, handing her a bowl. In it was a greasy lump of pork fat, a peeled orange, a few nuts, and a miniscule square of chocolate. 'You get double rations from now on,' he said. Mink looked like he was about to speak, but Weir glared at him. 'With her leading, we can travel at twice the speed.'

'But,' Mink said, 'mixing narcotics with her mage powers, isn't that dangerous? I knew a recruit, a battler, who used to drink a few shots of rum before using his vision. It made him a great fighter, until his heart stopped one day, right in the middle of the training field. Officers gave us a lecture about never mixing the power with anything else. It's dangerous enough, they said, and they asked us to report any battler we saw drinking before practice.'

'I remember being at a similar lecture,' she smiled, barely able to contain her energy. 'You going to report me, Lieutenant?'

'Fine,' he said, shaking his head. 'You do what you like, Captain. Despite everything, I'd still prefer you to be alive when we get back.'

'I didn't know you cared.'

'I don't,' he snapped. 'Neither of you seem to have realised that the moment we step foot back in the Holdings, we'll be arrested, and marched off to the capital. If we don't get our stories straight, and back each other up, they'll hang us as traitors. Avoiding that is what I care about.'

'No, Mink,' she said. 'It's too late. You don't want me to die. That's enough for me.'

Mink almost smiled.

Weir handed her a waterskin.

'It pains me to say it, Captain,' he said, 'but he has a point, about mixing the weed with your powers. All we can do is try it for a few days, and see how you are. If you feel like it's too much, then we'll find some quiet place to hole up for a while and let you recover.'

'Sounds fair,' she replied.

Mink shrugged.

'Also,' Weir went on, 'I have this for you.' He stooped down to where his pack lay, and picked up something. It consisted of two diamond shaped sections of wood, hinged together with leather straps. 'Made it this evening while you were sleeping.'

Daphne held her left arm out towards him, and he buckled the straps of the two-piece shield to her lower and upper arm. She raised her limb as he stepped back, looking down at the wooden armour. It was solid enough to deflect most blows, but wouldn't hinder her running.

She smiled. 'Thank you, sergeant.'

'And,' he said, pulling out a broken Sanang spearhead, 'I saw you fight with this yesterday.' He fixed the spearhead into a low groove on the lower diamond. The flint blade extended beyond her twisted fingers by a good four inches.

She laughed, and took up a fighting stance, holding her knife in her right hand, and swinging out with her left, the spear blade cutting through the air. She carried out a few training ground moves, dancing as she slashed, parried and lunged at an imaginary foe. The two others watched, Weir with an appreciative smile on his face, while Mink smirked.

'When you're quite finished,' the lieutenant said, holding up her pack. 'I would rather we got back to the Holdings before Winter's Day.'

Daphne stood while he slung the pack over her shoulders, while Weir pulled his own on.

She nodded at them both, and started running.

CHAPTER 11

ON THE EDGE

Mya Region, Sanang – 6th Day, Second Third Autumn 503

There was a pounding inside Daphne's head, as regular as a pulse, and she ran to its insistent beat.

She couldn't remember why she was running, but knew it was important. It certainly seemed so to her two companions, although she had forgotten their names, or the reason why they followed her through the forest night after night. She hadn't talked to them for so long she was unsure as to whether she could speak, or ever had. Each dawn, when she stopped running, she would hear the two men argue, about her she was sure. Sometimes they seemed to address her directly, but she couldn't make sense of their words, and was always unconscious within a few minutes of stopping anyway.

Every dusk she was awoken from her dreamless state, and she smoked, and ate, and then she would run again. She had started to believe that this was all her life had consisted of, and all it would ever be; a never ending alternation between running and oblivion. Part of her mind felt like it was screaming in pain, but she tried to ignore the signals coming from every inch of her strained and exhausted body, and found it was easy if she instead focussed on the pounding in her head.

When she had been shaken awake the previous evening, it had

taken her longer than normal to get up, and one of the men had made her have lots to smoke, before she was able to stumble to her feet. The two men were angry with each other, and she had thought that they were going to start fighting, so she ran, and hadn't looked back since.

Running to the pounding beat.

Her conscious mind had long since ceased processing the over-whelming amount of information coming from her senses while she ran, and she was only vaguely aware of her dark surroundings, like running through shadows. Her body kept going however, regardless of what was going on in her mind. She sprinted along boar tracks, leaping fallen tree limbs, ducking under branches, always, somehow, finding the best path.

She registered in her mind that it was nearly dawn. The vague blacks were transforming into hazy greys, and she felt her body auto-matically respond, her senses scanning for somewhere to shelter. She tried to observe her body during this, but the sudden rush of stimuli threatened to break her mind. She almost stumbled, and she pulled her mind back to a safe space, where there was nothing but the pounding.

Just as the first rays of the autumn sun were sending beams through the branches above, she burst through a dense patch of undergrowth, and ran straight into a large pool of water, up to her knees. Her momentum kept her going, and she toppled forward into the cold pond with a splash, her head dipping under. She slowly sank to the muddy bottom, her mind a dull blank, bubbles escaping from her mouth. Then she was pulled back, and up out of the water into a sitting position, strong hands gripping her shoulders. She looked up to see a tall, thin man, with dark hair and skin. He was saying something to her, while shaking his head, but her ears were ringing, and she heard nothing. The other man was behind him, and he was gesturing in alarm over her shoulder.

Still sitting in the pool, she turned to look.

There were a dozen pale-skinned women on the other side of the pool, just twenty paces away. They had armfuls of clothes for washing, and were sitting on the edge of the water, where they had been busy rinsing and scrubbing, until a few moments ago.

Now every one of the pale faces was looking wide eyed at Daphne and her companions.

For what seemed like an eternity, the two groups stared at each other across the pool, neither side moving or speaking.

Then one of the pale women opened her mouth and screamed.

Guards with spears burst through the edges of the forest around the pool, looking for the threat to the womenfolk, and seeing Daphne and the two men.

The shorter man pulled her to her feet, and shouted something in her face as he pulled a knife. She heard nothing, but saw his lips mouth 'run'. He started to push her to the left, away from the guards, who were rushing round the pool towards them.

He gave her a final shove, then turned to stand between her and the guards. She stood there, helpless, her mind disengaged. Run, she thought. Run.

She started to jog along by the side of the pool, the screaming from her body louder now, as she felt the narcotics given to her at dusk begin to wear off. She drew on every last thread of battle vision that she possessed, and her speed increased to a sprint, and she flew off through the forest like a startled deer. Without the drugs, her senses started to shut down, her hearing, her sense of touch, and soon her sight were failing, but still she ran. Although the day was bright, and the sky crisp and cloudless, everything seemed to her as if she were running at night, and all around was cast in silent greys and shadow, but still her body pushed her on and on. The pounding in her head increased, until there was no space for any other thought in her mind, just the pounding, pounding, pounding.

Her foot went over the soft and crumbling edge of a ravine, and she fell, spinning and tumbling down the steep bank, and landing with a crunch on the rocky bottom of the narrow crevasse. Her face was pressed up against the side of a gnarled tree trunk that was clinging to the ravine's shallow soil. Her right ankle felt like it had twisted, and her left arm was in agony. She squeezed her eyes closed. Never had she experienced such pain, never had her head felt under such pressure, like it was liable to explode any second, ending her existence in an instant. She longed for death, to end this pain, to end this hurt, this torture.

Be at peace, child.

A calm flooded through her.

Be at peace, the voice said again.

Terror froze her, the feeling of calm vanished, and the pounding returned. She retched.

'Who is speaking?' she croaked in agony.

Listen to me. Hear my words, child, for I am your creator.

Her panic increased, and the pressure in her mind threatened to send her into oblivion at any moment.

You are at your limit's edge. Be Calm.

This time she felt the calmness within her forcibly assert itself, as if the voice had taken control of her mind. The pounding ceased, and the pain in her head receded. The pressure on her skull seemed to lift completely. She felt as if she were floating.

'You are the Creator?' she gasped.

Yes, I am your creator, He who speaks through the prophets.

I have gone insane, she thought. The endless draw on the vision, and the drugs. I am insane.

No, child, you are not, although you were perilously close to permanently damaging yourself. Yes, I can sense your thoughts; I can hear them in my mind, as I can hear those of your prophets when they call upon me. You, however, I have never heard before until now. I will heal your mind.

She felt her memories and full consciousness return to her for the first time in many days. She remembered who she was, and where she was, and why. She opened her eyes. Her sight had returned.

'My...' she began.

Your friends? The two men are still alive, I can see them. One is injured, the other is carrying him, but they have strayed from the path you took, and are over twenty miles from here.

She focussed on her body. Her left arm had grown numb, to her relief, but pain was still shooting through her ankle.

That, I cannot heal. My powers were long ago limited to mind-to-mind contact with the rare few among your people with the ability, the sole beings I have communicated with in millennia.

'The prophets are telling the truth?'

Yes. I notice they often simplify my words, but my meaning is carried to your people.

'Then the war is wrong?'

It is. Your people's invasion of Sanang is a grave crime, as is the Rahain's treatment of the Southern Clans. Your queen has erred. Her advisors have erred. Your father has erred.

'My father?'

Yes.

'Why are you telling me this?' she said. 'I'm going to die out here.'

You will if you remain on the ground, Daphne of Hold Fast. You are so close, yet you do not realise it. I will help you, and in return you will preach my word.

She hesitated.

Yes, people will say that you have lost your mind, but I will tell the prophets that you speak the truth.

'What should I preach?' she asked.

Peace and Unity. Peace among the five peoples of this continent, and an unbreakable Union to bring them together as one.

'If I agree,' she said, 'how will you help me?'

Are you bargaining with God, Daphne Hold Fast? the voice laughed. *I will do thus; I will make your will unshakable.*

Something within her mind changed, and she was infused with a strong belief that she was going to make it home, even if she had to crawl all the way. So powerful was this urging, that she started to stumble to her feet. Her right ankle gave out immediately, and she fell. She got back up, her right hand grasping onto a thin but sturdy tree branch for support. She leaned against the side of the ravine, and used her knife to trim the branch into a staff.

See Daphne, you are not helpless. Now, watch.

Her sight soared upwards, out of her body, higher and higher, gazing downwards at the Sanang lands below.

The forest spread out endlessly on both sides, and behind her, but ahead the edge was visible as a ragged line, just a few miles distant. Beyond that was the deforested zone, where each year the Holdings had cut back the forest deeper and deeper, carting off the timber. The desert of tree stumps that they had created now spread for miles, all the way back to the frontier forts. She saw carts and wagons dotted about, digging up the great roots of the trees that had been felled. Every scrap of wood fetched a price in the Holdings.

Now look.

Her sight snapped back to her position, then lowered, until it set out a path for her of the quickest route to the nearest cart, inscribing it into her mind.

Now go. I can feel the link between us fading.

'Will I be able to speak to you again?' she asked.

That I cannot answer. It may be that your thoughts only appeared in my head due to your extreme use of the vision powers I bestowed upon you. It may be that we shall never speak again...

The voice faded, and disappeared from her head, but the feeling of irrepressible certainty that she was going to get home remained. She held out her staff, and began hobbling along the base of the ravine, following the path that shone brightly in her mind's eye. She was injured, and exhausted, hungry, thirsty, and probably smelled like horseshit, but her mind was crisp and clear, the pounding a memory only. How many days had she been running, she wondered. She was nearly skeletal, thoroughly emaciated from her legs to her chest and arms. Her bones were showing, and her hair was dank and tangled and stank. She hadn't brushed her teeth in a third, and she prayed she wouldn't need to have any teeth pulled when she got back.

And now she was on a holy mission.

She laughed out loud, and continued laughing as she stumbled the few miles to the edge of the forest.

With her back to the treeline, she gazed out over the devastation her people had caused. Mile upon mile of forest stripped bare and cut down. Nothing lived or moved out here among the sad looking stumps, nothing except the root scavengers. She sighted the closest set, a few miles down a deeply rutted cart track, and continued onwards.

It was mid-afternoon by then, and the weak autumn sun was on her back as she limped down the track. The scavengers' cart grew closer, and she could see a family out working, with shovels, mattocks and picks. There was a middle aged couple, and three teenage children, all Holdings by the darkness of their skin.

She hailed them from a distance, and they turned and stared. The mother, who was closest, raised her pick axe.

'I'm Holdings,' Daphne shouted, her voice hoarse. 'I've escaped from the Sanang.'

The family squinted at her, then the mother approached.

She gasped when she saw Daphne's condition.

'I need food,' she said, 'and water, please.'

'Kids,' the woman called. Her accent was from the River Holdings, like Weir's. 'Bring water, and the food.' She called to her man. 'Sandy, come over here and give me a hand.'

They helped Daphne hobble to the cart, where they set her down. She drank deeply from a water canister, and ate what had probably been intended as the family's evening meal.

'Thank you,' she managed to get out between mouthfuls.

'What's your name?' the woman asked.

'Lieutenant Black,' Daphne said. 'Captured at the third supply camp.'

'We heard the apes took prisoners this time,' Sandy said. 'Didn't believe it myself.'

Daphne nodded. 'I need to get back to the frontier forts, can you take me?'

The family looked at each other.

'We're a poor lot,' the woman said, 'though you probably already guessed that, seeing as how we're out so far, scavenging for anything left behind. We need to be out here for the whole season, to make enough to get through the winter.'

'What date is it?' Daphne asked.

'The sixth day of the second third of autumn,' the woman replied. 'We've still another ten days out here before we're due to head back.'

'I'll see that you're compensated,' Daphne said. 'My family has money. Once we get to the wall, I'll make sure your winter will be a comfortable one.'

The family looked at each other again.

'What if she's lying?' one of the teenagers said. 'And she bolts on us once we get to the wall?'

'You have my word,' she said.

'That might be a lie too,' the teenager shot back.

'Be quiet, Mabel,' the woman said. She looked at Daphne. 'We'll take you,' she said, 'though you'd better be telling us the truth.'

'You have my word,' Daphne repeated.

CHAPTER 12

DOUANNA

Midfort, Sanang/Plateau Frontier – 21st Day, Second Third Autumn 503

Daphne flitted through the dawn crowds of Midfort market like a ghost. A grey, hooded robe covered her, and she kept her head low amid the bustling Holdings traders, peddlers and beggars. She was hungry and tired, but coinless. All her life she had enjoyed easy access to money, but never needed it, and now she needed it she had none. Having escaped with nothing but her clothes and a knife, she didn't have anything she was willing to sell. She slowly made her way across the square to the merchants' quarter.

Mabel had been right.

As soon as the wagon had passed through the gates of Southfort, she had bolted, using a dash of battle-vision to flee down the back alleys. She remembered the layout of the streets from the time she had been stationed there, and had soon lost her enraged pursuers.

She had eaten and drunk and slept under shelter for half a third due to the hospitality of the scavenger family. The thought of them going hungry that winter because of her clawed at her conscience, but the alternative would have been to hand herself in to the army, and she doubted the family would have seen any money if she had done that.

Daphne had ditched her phoney name and assumed another. She now introduced herself as Beth, a merchant's assistant, separated from her caravan and looking for passage home to the capital. She had listened in to conversations, hoping to hear word of Mink or Weir, and had heard snippets of news from the Holdings. The queen was ill, though some swore it had to be poison. More relevant to her immediate situation, she discovered that she had been tried in her absence by the military courts and found guilty of treason. Assumed dead, no sentence had been passed on her, but there was no doubt what the common people felt about the matter.

Bereaved wives and husbands of soldiers killed in the campaign begged on the street corners, and more than a few cursed and spat on the name of that bitch Daphne Holdfast and her leash-holding father. The first time she had heard it she had slipped away through the streets, stolen the robe, and hidden.

The following day, with still no word of her companions, and scared that she would be recognised in the town where she had worked the previous summer, she left Southfort and walked the ten miles up to the larger town of Midfort. The stone fortress was built into the wall itself, and was the biggest castle on the frontier defences. The town that had grown up on the near side of the wall around the fortress was as big as any to be found back in the Holdings, though unlike them, it had been untidily constructed, and was a sprawl of wood. It was large enough to be divided into quarters, with the marketplace in the centre.

This was where the Rahain traders were now based, Daphne had noticed. They worked out of an office in the merchants' quarter, and seemed considerably wealthier than they had the previous year. They were dressed in rich robes and sparkling jewels, with Holdings body-guards lurking at their shoulders.

Her hunger had driven her to stealing food from the marketplace, fruit, bread, anything she could surreptitiously clutch and pull into the folds of her robe. She kept her left arm out of sight, though she realised she would be less recognisable if it were visible.

She had made a deserted warehouse loft her temporary home, as she waited and listened for news of her companions. Twenty miles away, the voice had said. They must be close to returning, even if they had walked the whole way. She stopped herself. The voice? Surely she had imagined the whole thing. In truth, her recollections of the endless run through the trees were vague and hazy, and she believed she had been close to losing her mind in the forest. The further she got from the dark woods of Sanang, the more dreamlike the whole experience seemed.

She felt fully awake now that her mind was free of the forest drugs, and she was terrified. She had thought of no plan other than to wait for Mink and Weir, but as the days had passed, and she grew hungrier and more desperate, she had decided to act.

She entered the merchants' quarter, staying close to the shadows under the overhanging eaves of the timber buildings. They were packed tightly together, with little thought for planning, and wagons squeezed through the streets amid the crowded bustle. All around her were the voices and accents of her homeland, sounds that she had longed to hear for thirds, and now she stayed hidden among them, afraid to reveal herself to her own people.

She found a small tea house close to the offices of the Rahain Trading Company, an opulent building faced in stone. On a search of her warehouse, she had found a few odds and ends left behind that she had peddled for a handful of coins. She knew she needed to buy food, and her stomach complained at the injustice it was suffering, but she handed over her money for a tiny pot of tea, and sat at a table by the roadside.

She waited a full hour before catching sight of a Rahain merchant. With a waiter hovering by, she slipped out of her chair and crossed the street.

'Excuse me,' Daphne said.

The merchant turned. She was dressed in a long blue gown, with silver tracery down her arms, to accentuate her subtle scaling. Her eyes were a light green, flecked with yellow, and her vertical pupils widened as she appraised Daphne.

'I'm looking for a Rahain merchant,' she continued. 'Douanna. Do you know her?'

The Rahain's tongue flickered in and out. Daphne tried not to stare.

'No,' the merchant replied, and started to turn.

'Wait, please!' Daphne said. 'Are there any records that I could look at? Maybe I could ask around, to see if anyone knows her? It's urgent.'

The Rahain considered. Looking like she wanted to avoid a scene, she nodded to Daphne, and strode towards the front door of the office.

She knocked, and a slit opened at eye level. A few seconds later, the door swung open, and the merchant went in, Daphne a step behind. They walked into an entrance hall.

A Rahain doorman put a hand out to stop her.

'Is she with you, ma'am?' he asked.

'No,' the merchant replied. 'She was asking after a Douanna. Give her ten minutes in the saloon to make enquiries. If she's still here after that, you can throw her out.'

'Yes, ma'am,' the official replied, his tongue flickering.

The merchant disappeared through a side door.

'Your name, please?' the Rahain asked Daphne, going to a lectern with a ledger balanced on top.

'Beth of Hold Down.'

He wrote for a moment, then handed her a ticket.

'Welcome to the Rahain Trading Company, Beth of Hold Down,' he said. 'This paper marks you as a visitor, and states that you are permitted to be in here. Show it to anyone who asks.'

'Thank you,' she said, putting on a smile. 'The saloon?'

'That door,' he pointed. 'Then first on the right.'

She went through and heard the saloon before she saw it. The room was large, smoky, noisy, crammed with Rahain, and impossible to miss. Standing on the polished wooden floor, she noticed a few other Holdings people present. They fell into two types: the rich, and the waiting staff. The rich were dressed similarly to their Rahain hosts, in long flowing robes, while the young serving men and women were in plain brown uniforms of tunic and trousers, of the same type as the doorman was wearing. There were tables covering the floor, and booths along three of the walls, but the place was crowded, and many were standing. A long marble-topped bar stretched by the wall to the left, serving alcohol openly, presumably under a special license, Daphne guessed. No wonder it was packed.

She walked to the corner on the left, and started there. Three Rahain men sat, drinking some wine imported from their homeland.

'Please excuse me,' she began.

'No beggars,' one of them growled in the Holdings tongue.

Daphne was stunned, but only for a moment. 'If I were a beggar, sir, then I hardly think I would have got through the door,' she said in her best aristocratic voice. 'And to think I had considered the Rahain a most polite people.'

'My apologies,' he spluttered, while one of his companions laughed. 'My lady, how may I be of assistance?'

'You are most kind,' she said, sitting down at their table. 'Gentlemen, last year, I enjoyed a quite profitable business with a merchant by the name of Douanna, from the city of Jade Falls. I am looking to enquire whether the same merchant has returned this year, and if so, where I may be able to locate her.'

'What line of business was this merchant involved in?' asked one.

'Tobacco,' she replied. 'Some tea also.'

'I can introduce you to an excellent trader,' he said, 'who happily for you deals in both of those commodities. I think he might be in here today, I'll just...'

'My apologies for not making myself clearer,' she cut in. 'I promised Douanna that I would always deal with her first, and,' she paused, 'I'm a woman of my word.'

The merchant sighed. 'Very well, you can make me a promise too.' He pointed across the table at her. 'That if you cannot find this Douanna, you will come back here and I'll set you up with all the connections you'll ever need.'

'Then you don't know the woman?'

He shrugged, and looked at his companions, who shook their heads.

'Thank you very much for your time, gentlemen.'

Daphne made the rounds of the large room, long out-staying her allotted ten minutes, but no one came looking for her. She spoke to drunk Rahain, bored Rahain, excitable Rahain, most of whom tried to buy or sell or introduce her to someone or something. She found she slipped back into the role of young noblewoman easily, and, despite the poor quality robe she was wearing, realised not for the first time that it was all about the tone of voice, how one carried oneself, and confidence. She surprised herself at being able to laugh at the merchants' poor jokes, and she flattered them, and ingratiated herself. It was a role she hadn't played since her teenage years when, as the youngest daughter of a member of the Queen's Council, and an heir to one of the richest families in the Realm, it hadn't been a role at all, but her life.

It was well into the afternoon before she found someone who recognised the name of the merchant she was looking for.

'Yes, she's in town,' the old man said, 'or rather, she was the last time I looked, a while back.'

'Please, I don't suppose you could write down her address for me?'

She passed a scrap of paper and a thin charcoal pencil across the table.

He picked up the pencil, then eyed her for a moment.

'It's a little late in the season for business, is it not?'

'Indeed it is, sir,' she replied without hesitation. 'That's why it's so important I find her before the season ends altogether.'

He pursed his lips, his tongue flickering, then scratched out an address on the scrap of paper.

She took it from him, scanning it.

'My thanks, sir,' she said, rising.

He looked regretful, so she disappeared into the thick crowd before he could have second thoughts.

A different doorman was on duty, and she handed him her pass. She had read it while in the bathroom of the saloon, one of her many trips there, due to the endless mugs of filtered water she had drunk. The pass hadn't mentioned anything about a time limit that she could see.

The doorman took the ticket, read it, then marked it with a rubber stamp. He stepped forward, and opened the door.

'One last thing,' she said. 'If you would be so kind as to tell me where Daryon Road is?'

'Go left for half a mile, then ask around,' he replied, before closing the door in her face.

She stood on the doorstep, her sight dazzled by the low sun over the wall to the west. The crowds in the streets had thinned, and some of the shops had shut up for the day. The tea house was still open, and she recognised the waiter who had served her earlier. He glanced over at her and paused in his stride as their eyes locked for a second. He looked away, but Daphne felt troubled and started to hurry down the street. As she neared a corner, she risked a look over her shoulder, and saw that the waiter was talking to another man, and pointing at her.

She froze. Through instinct, she drew upon her battle-vision and took in the scene. The man the waiter was talking to looked vaguely familiar, medium height and build, short brown hair; he could have been one of the many officials or soldiers she had met the previous year. He was squinting at her, and she saw his expression change from bafflement to profound realisation, and his mouth opened in amazement.

Daphne turned and ran as fast as she could, barrelling through the winding streets, eking strength and speed from her vision well of energy. After ten minutes, she entered a poorer part of town, and slowed down. The shadows were lengthening, and the narrow streets were cloaked in the gloom of early evening. She slipped into a dark alleyway, her robe wrapped around her, and watched the road.

She chanced a quick line-vision, using the top of a nearby building to latch her sight to, from where she scanned the streets. Satisfied that she had lost her pursuer, she pulled her vision back to her body, and immediately fell to her knees and vomited up the water she had drunk at the saloon, letting it splash down into the gutter.

That was stupid, she thought. She had eaten little in days, and needed food and rest. But first she had to find Daryon Road.

It took her several more hours of following vague and misleading directions from the inhabitants of Midfort before she found the road and the house halfway down it, that she had been seeking.

It was a modest four-storey timber tenement, cheaply built. She entered through the entrance lobby and climbed the stairs to the top floor. She was exhausted, and had to stop several times on the way up, gripping onto the rough wooden rail, urging herself onwards over the complaints from her body.

She reached the top and knocked on the door. After a few moments, it opened a crack, and the face of a Rahain man appeared.

'Yes?'

'I'm sorry,' she panted. 'I'm looking for Douanna.'

'And who shall I say is calling at this hour?'

'Beth of Hold Down,' she said without thinking.

He turned to go. 'Wait!' she said. 'Say that it's her student from last summer, come for a lesson.'

He raised an eyebrow, but said nothing, and closed the door.

She leaned up against the wall, taking in long deep breaths, trying to steady herself.

What if the Rahain woman couldn't be trusted? Too late for that, she realised. In her condition, she was going nowhere.

The door opened again and the Rahain man, dressed in a simple brown uniform, beckoned for her to enter.

He closed the door behind her as she walked into a small entrance hall, lacking in the opulence she had seen associated with the other Rahain in town. She followed the man through to another, larger room, with a roaring fire, and comfortable chairs. Standing by a dining table to the left stood the Rahain merchant from whom she had learned their language the previous summer.

'My word,' Douanna said, her face suppressing a smile. 'My heart leapt when Jaioun delivered your cryptic little message. This Beth girl, I would have sent away, but my old student?'

Daphne stood on the carpet, trembling with exhaustion.

'It really is you, then?' Douanna said.

'I'm sorry, I didn't know where else to go.'

'Yes,' the Rahain replied. 'Well, here you are, though I can't quite bring myself to say your name, for fear the neighbours hear it through these thin walls and a mob arrives to burn the place to the ground.'

'You've heard, then?'

'Heard, my dear?' Douanna replied, arching her eyebrows. 'The whole town is speaking about nothing else. Talk of your trial has filled the streets since the news arrived here a half third ago. I could hardly believe they were talking about the same girl that I'd tutored last summer. You certainly didn't seem like a wicked traitor back then.'

'I'm not a traitor,' Daphne gasped, putting her hand out to steady herself.

'My child,' Douanna said, 'are you ill? Please sit.' She looked over at her butler. 'Jaioun, my dear fellow, please have some hot food and drink prepared for our guest.' He nodded and started for the door. 'A guest,' she said, 'about whose presence here I would rather we be discreet, don't you agree?'

'As you say, ma'am.' He bowed and left the room.

Douanna helped Daphne sit, then poured a brandy from a glass decanter on the table.

'Drink this,' she said, handing her the glass.

Douanna sat on the arm of the chair next to Daphne, and examined her closely.

'You've certainly changed,' she said. 'So much thinner. But stronger-looking too. Hmmm. And what's this? Your arm! Oh my poor dear.' She put one hand to her mouth, while the other peeled back the robe to reveal the extent of the damage to Daphne's left arm and hand.

'The Sanang?'

Daphne could only manage a faint nod, as she lifted the glass to her lips and sipped the brandy. She nearly retched again, but then felt a warming glow spread through her.

'Those damn savages!' Douanna said. 'What were they like?'

Jaioun walked back in, carrying a large tray, which he set down on the table. On it were plates of steaming hot food, meat and vegetables, and bread. There were also two pots, a tall one for coffee, and a squat one for tea. There were cigarettes laid out by an ashtray and a tiny table lamp. On a side dish were a few small pieces of chocolate.

'Food and drink from the Realm of the Holdings, the Rahain Republic, and the anarchic Sanang,' said Douanna. 'Come on, girl, you must eat.'

Daphne struggled to the table, sat, and ate all of the chocolate from the dish.

Douanna raised an eyebrow. 'You had better manners last year too.'

'Sorry,' Daphne said. She poured herself a coffee and for the first time experienced it with Holdings cane sugar. She lit a cigarette, drank her sweet coffee, and leaned back into her chair, sighing.

'A woman of simple tastes, I see,' Douanna said, pouring herself a tea. 'We have no hot drinks in my homeland, and I must confess it seemed a ridiculous notion when I first heard of it. However, I have learned the error of my ways, and am now a devout tea worshipper.'

'I used to love tea,' Daphne said, smoking. 'Prefer coffee now.'

'Spend some time with the Sanang, did we?'

Daphne hesitated.

Douanna raised her hand. 'Later,' she said. 'You will tell me everything, but after you have eaten. And taken a bath. And sorted your hair. And just where did you get those clothes? Dear me.'

The following morning a clean and freshly dressed Daphne told her story to Douanna, leaving out nothing except her encounter with the

Creator, if indeed it had happened. She ate her way through an enormous breakfast while doing so, as Douanna sat behind her brushing her hair and braiding it into pleats.

'That was most fascinating,' she said, once Daphne had finished. 'Now, I happen to have an account of your trial. It was posted up throughout the town, and my butler has kindly provided me with a copy.' She reached into a small bag that she always carried around with her. 'Ah, here it is. Now let me see. Yes, this part. It says that the clinching evidence against you was the presence of a signed receipt of the withdrawal orders that the messenger deposited with the army, once he had returned from your outpost. Mmmmm, what do you say to that?'

Her tongue flickered.

'May I see it, please?' said Daphne.

'Of course,' she said, handing over the single sheet of thick fibrous paper.

It was a simple report. She had been charged with disobeying orders, and remaining in the fort when ordered to leave. Her motive was stated to be the vainglorious influence of her father's political ambition, and though this did somewhat temper her guilt, she was still found responsible for the loss of her entire company, and the consequent collapse of the Holdings withdrawal. For any doubters, the proof was in the receipt for the orders, clearly signed by Daphne's own hand, as testified by the only survivor of the fort's personnel, the company priest, Father Rijon.

She gasped and dropped the paper.

'My dear?' Douanna said.

'The bastard,' she growled.

'Who?' The Rahain swooped down and picked up the document. 'The priest? He's the only one I see named here, except yourself and your father of course, and I assume you're not referring to him.'

Daphne shook her head. 'He's lying. I didn't sign any receipt, because the damned orders never arrived.'

Douanna sat back and folded her arms.

'Do you know what happened to my father, to my family?' Daphne asked.

'There has been no specific word on them,' Douanna said. 'I imagine they'll be lying low. I didn't hear anything about your father being charged with any crime, but I would guess he is out of favour as it were. He is, or was, close to your queen, no?'

'He's a member of her council.'

'Does Holdings law have any procedures for removing troublesome councillors? Or is it like in Rahain, where those in power are there for life?'

'It would be at the queen's discretion,' she replied, remembering tutoring Agang not so long before on the same topic. 'Unless found guilty of treason.'

'Well then,' Douanna said. 'If he's as cunning a politician as the mob here take him for, then he'll go back to his estates for a few years, let the whole thing be quietly forgotten about, and then make his return. Of course, much would depend on whether your queen is still alive by then. She is said to be very ill. I believe her brother is next in line, no?'

'Prince Guilliam, yes.'

'A pious man, I hear?'

'So it is said.'

Douanna nodded.

'And so, my dear,' she said. 'I must ask you, what is it exactly that you want from me? I am already endangering myself and Jaioun by hosting you here. At the very least the town officials would revoke my licence to trade. And, as you can see by my simple dwelling, business this year has not been as good as I'd hoped.' She gestured around the sparsely furnished room.

'By sheltering and feeding me, you have already helped enough.'

'Come now, you must have a plan.'

'Just to get back to the capital,' she said. 'Somehow try to clear my name.'

'Excellent,' she said. 'I've always wanted to see the Holdings. I will take you, for no more than expenses and a small fee, which I am sure your father will be happy to honour once he sees his youngest daughter alive.'

Daphne stopped eating. 'You would do this for me?'

'It's nothing,' she said, waving her hand. 'We'll have to hide you of course, until we've left the town far behind us. It'll take a few days to organise, but my business in Midfort is almost wrapped up for the year, and to be honest, the winter here is horrid, all that mud. I hear it's warmer in the Holdings, no?'

'Yes,' Daphne said. 'Especially up in the north where my family's estate lies.'

'Excellent,' Douanna smiled. 'I shall pack appropriately.'

Daphne was forbidden from leaving the apartment, but she felt safe, and there was plenty of food and drink to be enjoyed as her strength recovered.

On her third day in Douanna's home, she sat alone at a small table next to a window overlooking the street. Her host was taking her after-noon nap, while Jaioun was out shopping. Daphne was relaxing with a book, smoking and sipping her sweet coffee, when she started to hear shouting from the road below. There were lace curtains over the window, which she left open while smoking, and she peered through them to see what was causing the disturbance. A news-seller was on the street, holding sheets of the daily journal. The top half of the paper was dominated by a picture of someone's face, but she was too far away to tell who it was.

The people in the street were crowding around the seller, grabbing copies from his hand in exchange for a few pennies. Groups huddled together, reading shared copies.

A few moments later, Jaioun came through the front door, carrying nothing but a copy of the news-sheet. He ignored Daphne, and walked straight to the door of Douanna's chamber.

He gave it a sharp knock.

A sleepy and annoyed looking Douanna pulled the door open.

'Yes, yes, what is it?'

Jaioun held up the news-sheet. She snatched it from his hand, scanned it, glanced up at Daphne for a moment, then resumed reading.

'Oh dear,' she said. 'Jaioun, I'll be needing tea before we depart, if you would.'

The butler nodded and left by the kitchen door.

'Is something the matter?' Daphne asked.

'Not at all, my dear,' Douanna said. 'We may have to slightly bring forward some aspects of the plan.'

She handed Daphne the news-sheet.

The top third was covered by a sketch of a woman's face. Who was that supposed to be?

Fugitive Seen In Midfort! the headline blared. She read on.

Daphne Holdfast, Notorious Traitor – Not Dead.

The criminal responsible for the losses in the Forest this summer, Daphne Holdfast, 21, has been seen at large in Midfort. Eye-witnesses say the most hated woman in the Holdings was seen at Brokers Tea House in the Merchant's Quarter. Town sheriffs say she is dangerous and not to be approached, if seen...

Daphne put the paper down onto the table's polished surface.

'Damn.'

'Quite,' Douanna said. Her tongue flickered.

'By "bring forward", did you mean...?'

'We leave today, yes,' the Rahain replied. 'I imagine the fine sheriffs of this town will have already visited the Rahain Trading Company where that little tea house is located, and if you used my name there, then, well... Luckily, that picture looks nothing like you, and there's no mention of any injuries to your arm, so I still have hope. So yes, we'll be leaving immediately. Once I've had my tea, of course.'

Within the hour they were ready to go. Daphne's nerves were slowly shredding, as she waited for a knock on the door to come at any moment. Douanna had supplied her with a clean brown tunic and trousers to wear. The simple tunic was short-sleeved, and Daphne was worried about her crippled left arm being on display.

'Of course people will stare, my dear,' Douanna had said, while adjusting her hem. 'But no one who does will think of Daphne Holdfast.'

Jaioun carried the trunk down the stairs, while Daphne and Douanna followed. She was given a few brief instructions regarding the behaviour of the Rahain serving classes, and she kept her eyes low and said nothing as they walked out onto the street.

Douanna went in front, with Daphne at her elbow, while Jaioun pulled the trunk along on a trolley. They garnered plenty of stares, and a few loud tuts at the sight of a crippled Holdings girl so reduced that she had to work for the Rahain, but no one challenged them. After a few turns they entered a wagon marshalling yard. A few men and women loitered near the gates, which were used as a place to pick up casual labour. Daphne caught eyes looking at her arm, but she kept her head down.

Once in the forecourt, Douanna reached into her bag, and passed an inscribed metal token to Jaioun.

'Please locate our wagon, there's a good chap.'

The butler left the trunk with Douanna and Daphne, and strode off to the yard's office.

The Rahain woman gave Daphne a wink, but her stomach was churning with nerves. She hated her useless arm.

Jaioun emerged from the office, and came back with a key.

They walked through the quiet yard to a row of sheds by the far wall, and Jaioun unlocked a door. Inside the dark and dusty old shed was a wagon, with a high canvas canopy. The butler undid the cover's straps and buckles, and opened the rear doorflap. He removed a long coat, which he handed to Daphne. She pulled it over her shoulders, glad her arm was no longer on display.

'I'll get the horses,' he said.

Daphne started to smile.

Douanna walked to the rear of the wagon and flipped a latch on the underside. A panel fell open, revealing a false bottom. The hatch was as wide as the cart, but less than a foot high.

'So Beth,' Douanna smiled. 'How do you feel about enclosed spaces?'

CHAPTER 13

ARRAIGNMENT

Outside Holdings City, Realm of the Holdings – 30th Day, Last Third Autumn 503

The quickest that Daphne had ever managed to get from Sanang to the Holdings capital had been sixteen days, switching horses at every way station, and galloping the exhausted beasts for hours at a stretch.

With two Rahain and a wagon, the pace had been half as quick, and her growing impatience had been almost tangible. It had taken them ten days alone to reach the border of the Holdings. Although the windswept stretch of land between Sanang and the Holdings had been ceded to the Realm following the conclusion of the Rahain wars, it was sparsely populated, and wild treeless country still. Everything seemed more ordered and civilised once they had crossed the border into the Holdings, and the wide cultivated plains started to open up.

For a few days they had kept the western spur of the Barrier Mountains to their right, then, at the road junction leading to the coal-mining city of Blackwater, they had taken the north-easterly branch, and started to cross the savannah.

Several more days had passed before the mountains to the south disappeared over the horizon, and there was nothing but vast wheat fields all around; no hills to break the endless monotony.

'I find all this mildly disconcerting,' Douanna had commented, her arm sweeping across the land. 'There is not a single spot in the whole of Rahain where one cannot see mountains, and of course, all seven cities are buried deep within the hills, closed in on themselves like little worlds. This land is the very opposite. It's like someone has taken the lid off.'

For hundreds of miles around there were no geographical features to disrupt the flow of the plains, excepting the Greater and Lesser Rivers. The course of the Greater had gouged a wide channel through the savannah, and where the current ran against anything harder than soil or sandstone, the erosion had formed several rocky outcrops, especially on the western bank. The capital of the Holdings was built around the highest of these free-standing rocks. Nine-tenths of the city was on the lower, eastern bank, where a large urban sprawl had been built from yellow and white sandstone mined from the local quarries. It was laid out around several elegant boulevards, and was the largest settlement in the Holdings.

On the western bank, which towered a hundred feet above the river, sat the walled Upper City, comprising the royal palace, the council house, the cathedral and the prophet's citadel. Sheer cliffs ran almost all the way round the outcrop, but on the eastern side, facing the Lower City, two sets of switch-backed steps had been cut in the side of the cliff, leading to the summit. At the northern end, where the slopes of the Upper City were less steep, a wider ramp had been dug out of the rock, to allow more stately, horse-driven processions to take place. At the lower end of the ramp, the bridge over the river led to the enormous cavalry grounds, home of the city garrison.

It was almost a third since they had left Midfort, and they were in sight of the city at last.

'There it is,' said Daphne, pointing along the road.

'That little hill?' Douanna said.

'That's just where the queen and prophet live,' she said. 'You can't see the rest of the city yet, it's all spread out on the other side of the river.' She pointed again. 'That spire there belongs to the university. It's the highest point in the Lower City.'

'So we'll arrive in good time for tomorrow's Winter's Day celebrations?'

'Yes,' Daphne replied. 'But as I've said, here in the Holdings it's a religious festival. There will be no parties, just lots of praying.'

'Dear me,' Douanna tutted. 'How dull.'

'Maybe, but it'll be perfect cover for visiting a few of the people I trust.'

'Your father's agent?'

'Yes, she's one of them,' Daphne replied. 'My father will most likely be at the Holdfast estate. Even if it weren't for the difficulties I've caused him, he always avoided the city during religious festivals.'

'Another sign of his wisdom,' Douanna said.

Daphne turned to her. 'Are none of the Rahain religious?'

'Oh certainly a few of the lower orders hold to their superstitions.'

Jaioun turned his head just a fraction, a mild look of amusement fleeting over his usually expressionless features.

'But,' Douanna continued, 'among the educated, that sort of thing is mostly frowned upon. We are a nation of science and knowledge, and, occasionally, enlightenment.'

'Are you not at war with some clans or tribes somewhere in the south?' Daphne asked, remembering a snatch of her dreamlike conversation with the Creator. 'Doesn't seem very enlightened.'

Douanna stared at her for several seconds, an unreadable look on her face.

'My, Daphne,' she said, 'you are unexpectedly well informed. And just where did you learn that little snippet of information? No, wait, don't tell me. Some drunken Rahain forgetting who they were speaking to, no doubt. Dear me.'

They rode along in silence, drawing closer to the city.

'And have you told anyone else about this?' Douanna asked after some time.

'No,' Daphne replied. She was beginning to feel a deep sense of disorientation. It made her dizzy to think that a fragment of that strange, barely remembered exchange in the Sanang Forest had been confirmed as true.

'Good,' Douanna said. 'Now, what I am about to tell you is strictly in confidence, upon your honour, agreed?'

Daphne nodded. 'Agreed.'

'It's true the Rahain are at war,' Douanna said, 'and a greedy little war it is too. The war coalition has gone too far, I think, acting out of pure avarice. They invaded another's land to plunder its resources, and are dressing it up as a defensive action against a few poorly-behaved barbarians.'

Daphne blushed. Had Douanna just described what her own nation was doing? She had never considered it in such harsh terms before.

The Rahain woman seemed to catch the irony at the same time, for she also blushed. 'Apologies.'

'None necessary,' the Holdings woman replied, as she looked ahead to the city. 'It seems, Douanna, that our nations might have more in common than we'd thought.'

The road ran alongside the river for the last few miles, before sweeping over a broad, stone bridge, carried above the water on seven enormous piers. Traffic was busy, and continuous. Carts, wagons, people walking, people on horseback, and herds of sheep and cattle filled the wide, paved road.

Daphne was now Sally, a servant to Douanna, who was arriving to cultivate business contacts for the coming season. They earned a few passing glances from others on the road, but it was the Rahain that people were staring at, not Daphne. She wore a long robe, with a hood, and kept herself hidden in the back of the wagon.

Across the bridge was a large crossroads, and they took the left turn, towards the great southern gates of the Lower City. Jaioun steered their cart into the long queue lining the road to the gates.

'Daphne, dear,' Douanna said. 'We may have a little problem. Didn't you say that these gates were always open to traffic? There are guards stopping everyone as they enter, asking them questions.'

Daphne looked up. Holdings soldiers were gathered round the entrance to the gate in far greater numbers than she had previously seen. She noticed that while most people on foot were admitted into the city without difficulty, all carts and wagons were being searched.

'Can we turn the wagon around?' she asked.

Douanna glanced at the queue, which continued on behind them. 'Not without bringing rather a lot of attention upon us, I'm afraid.'

'What should we do?'

'Well,' Douanna said, 'let's not panic. We don't know that it's you they're looking for.'

'If they've heard I'm coming, they might be looking for me in the company of Rahain.'

'Yes my dear, good point,' Douanna said. 'Best you slip off the cart, mingle in with the pedestrians, and try to get in on your own. Follow us once we're through, we'll catch up after a couple of streets.'

Daphne nodded, and shuffled her way to the back of the wagon. She unfastened the rope knots and opened the rear canvas.

'Halt!' a soldier shouted. He was standing three feet from her, holding his spear up, as were several others alongside him.

'Captain!' he yelled. People on the road were starting to take an interest. Daphne dropped the rope and raised her right hand into the air.

'Douanna,' she called back.

'Stop that cart!' cried another voice. Within seconds, the wagon was surrounded by a bristling wall of spears.

'You Rahain up there,' someone with an officer's accent shouted. 'Down from the wagon!'

'My dear Captain,' she heard Douanna say. 'Am I to assume by this that we are under arrest?'

The officer didn't reply, and Daphne heard steps come round to the rear of the wagon. A tall, thin man approached, a captain of the city guard, his breastplate gleaming in the sunlight.

He stopped in front of her, eyed her up and down, a half sneer on his face.

'Saved us the trouble of coming to find you,' he smiled. 'Most considerate.'

He gestured, and a pair of guards ran forward. Each took a shoulder and pulled Daphne down from the wagon. Pain flared in her arm, but she remained steady on her feet. She looked the captain in the eye.

A noisy crowd had formed around them, and curious citizens jostled in to get a better view.

The captain glanced up, as if sensing the potential for a mob developing. He motioned to his troopers, and without another word they started to jog back to the gate, Daphne herded into their midst. Douanna and Jaioun were also being escorted by the soldiers. The Rahain woman looked furious.

Daphne was bundled through the gate, and into a guardhouse to the side. The captain turned to her. He held a sheet of thick paper in his hand, and was scanning it and her alternately.

'Miss Daphne Holdfast,' he said in a low voice, 'I am placing you under arrest for disobeying orders.'

A few soldiers gasped.

The captain turned on them. 'Not one fucking word of this gets out, understood?'

The guards nodded.

'"Miss"?' Daphne asked, raising an eyebrow.

'Yes,' the captain said. 'The courts stripped you of your rank. You didn't think you would be permitted to remain in the Queen's Own, did you?'

Daphne said nothing.

'I have strict instructions, right from the top,' the officer went on, raising his voice so the room could hear. 'We're to escort her to the palace, immediately, and preferably without a lynching or a full scale riot taking place. We'll take two squads. Keep her in the middle with a hood up at all times, and get hoods for the two Rahain. They're coming too.'

'Yes, sir,' they replied.

'And what about my wagon, Captain?' Douanna interrupted. 'My entire livelihood rests upon it.'

The captain glared at her as if she was nothing more than a nuisance.

'You two, go back out and retrieve their wagon,' he said to the closest soldiers by him. 'Lock it into the sheds behind the guardhouse, and set a watch on it.'

They nodded and ran off.

Douanna and Jaioun were pushed close to Daphne, and given long cloaks with hoods.

They were moved into a long, low hall, where the squads were arming themselves. Most were avoiding all eye contact with Daphne, though a few stared, slack jawed.

The captain nodded as he walked past. 'We're going to be moving fast, so keep up.'

'Just remember that I'm a citizen of an allied nation,' Douanna said, but he ignored her and continued to the front of the hall. Soldiers closed in on either side.

The captain turned when he reached the doors.

'We're transferring these three prisoners directly to the palace, via the Royal Steps,' he said. 'Stop for nothing.' He put on his helmet.

The double doors at the end of the hall swung open, and the squads started jogging out into the road. The sergeant in front yelled at people to clear the way, and they followed her down the middle of the hastily emptied street. Eyes stared at them from the houses and shops lining the way. Daphne kept her head down.

They stuck to the main, wide thoroughfare that led from the gates to the Royal Steps, and reached it within a few minutes. The soldiers didn't pause as they bounded over the long bridge to the foot of the stairs.

The short day was ending, and shadows clung to the eastern side of the rocky outcrop. The Royal Steps were wide, and climbed up the cliffside in a regular zigzag. At each turn a turret had been built, and the stairs had a stone banister running up its entire length. Workers with long poles were starting to light the lanterns set into the cliffside above each stairway.

'I need a drink before I'm climbing that,' Douanna wheezed.

The captain motioned to a soldier, who approached with a water-skin. The guards maintained their perimeter around them, despite the steps being quiet at that hour.

'Quite frankly,' Douanna said, 'this treatment is unacceptable.'

'Up we go,' cried the captain, and they moved off again, jogging up each long flight. There were seven in all, Daphne remembered from climbing it in earlier years, each with one hundred steps.

She was barely out of breath as she reached the top. She had been eating well and keeping herself fit, and her left arm apart, was probably the strongest she had ever been.

Douanna nearly fell over as she got to the final step, and she gasped for breath.

Daphne held her steady as she panted.

'What,' she breathed, 'a stupid... place... for a palace.'

They had emerged onto a broad plaza. On three sides great walls rose up from the perfectly set paving stones. In the centre of the middle wall, facing due east, was an enormous set of gilded gates, marking one of the formal entrances to the palace complex beyond.

The squads advanced along the main processional way towards the gates, passing pedestals and plinths with towering statues of ancient kings and queens.

Before the gates stood a company of the Queen's Household Cavalry, and the Lower City squads halted twenty paces from them on the road.

'What are you doing, bringing your squads up here?' shouted a voice from the cavalry.

'I'm under orders sir,' the captain replied, 'to bring the prisoner directly to the palace.'

An officer emerged from the ranks of the cavalry, and strode towards the captain.

'And who might that be?' he asked, a major from his lapels.

The captain approached the major.

'Daphne Holdfast, sir,' he half-whispered, 'and two Rahain who were accompanying her.'

'That rumour from the frontier was true then,' the major said, a look of satisfaction appearing on his face. 'Who'd have thought it?'

They walked towards Daphne.

'Hood off,' the captain barked at her.

She pulled it down.

The major leaned forward and squinted at her.

'Yes,' he said. 'It's her all right.' He shook his head as he paced around her, staring. 'Before I take you in,' he said, 'let me just ask, why the blazes have you come back?'

'To clear my name.'

He snorted, amused.

He turned to the younger officer. 'Thank you, Captain, we'll take it from here. I'll make sure your name is mentioned in the report. Good work.'

The captain nodded, a doubtful look in his eye. He about-turned his squads and they jogged back towards the steps. Soldiers from the ranks of the cavalry ran forward to take their places around the prisoners.

The major smiled to himself.

'Take them to the Tower.'

The Old Tower was the most ancient, as well as the tallest, building in the entire city. Legend told that its stones had been raised by the first king, with the first prophet by his side, at the founding of the Realm. It lay to the north of the compact, blocky palace. Piled up in tiers of clashing architectural styles, the palace suffered from the lack of space on the summit of the promontory, and had expanded haphazardly upward and outward. In contrast, the tower next to it was simple and severe. It may once have been the seat of the monarch, but for hundreds of years it had housed cells. For a long time it had been the only prison in the capital, but nowadays there was a new brick jailhouse in the Lower City for common criminals, and the Old Tower was reserved for enemies of the Realm.

When Daphne, Douanna and Jaioun were led inside, they were separated, and each taken to a different floor. Aside from the guards and the three prisoners, the rest of the building appeared empty and quiet.

Daphne was escorted into a cell, and the guards closed and locked the door without a word spoken.

She looked around.

There was a deep opening on the thick wall opposite her, barred at the far end, and even though it was evening, the light coming from the Lower City below lent the cell some dim illumination. A wireframe pallet lay to her left, and she sat down on the stained mattress. It smelled fusty, and the blanket on top hadn't been washed in a long time. There was a small stone bench built into the wall under the window, and a cracked old chamber pot. She shivered. It was the last day of autumn, and although the day's sunlight still held some warmth, at night the temperature would dip dramatically.

She pulled her robe around her, and eyed the blanket. The Creator only knew what insects and biting fleas dwelt within, just waiting for an opportunity to taste her flesh.

The footsteps of the guards outside trailed away and she was left in silence and gloom.

Why had she come back? What a fool. All she had gained by fleeing Midfort was a more comfortable journey to the capital than on the back of a prison wagon. Was that worth getting the two Rahain into such trouble? She was also disturbed by the lengths the soldiers had gone to keep her arrival a secret. Was it so they could quietly get rid of her? No witnesses, just a couple of unfounded rumours, and no body. Once again she was helpless in the hands of others.

The evening dragged. After some hours, footsteps outside her cell woke her from her melancholy stupor. In the darkness, her breath was the only thing she could see.

The door to her cell opened.

Squinting her eyes from the harsh torchlight, she saw two guards enter, followed by three others. Two of them she recognised. The uniformed woman was from the army, Field Marshal Howie, and the old man in black robes was from the church, Archdeacon Bruit. The other man was dressed in the finery of a queen's steward.

She stood and faced them.

'Stay where you are,' a guard shouted, levelling his spear at her.

'So it's true,' Bruit said, in his strangled voice. 'The traitor has returned.'

She made no reply.

The royal steward pulled out some paper and charcoal sticks, and started writing.

'Miss Daphne Holdfast, this is your formal arraignment,' Howie said to her. 'As you have already been found guilty in your absence, you are required to attend a hearing where you will be sentenced.'

'I wish to appeal,' Daphne said, her heart thundering.

The field marshal raised an eyebrow. 'I would advise against it. The court may show some leniency if you plead guilty, and throw yourself upon its mercy. If, on the other hand, you decide to fight the court's judgement, and you fail, then you can expect the sentence to be as severe as the law allows.'

'I plead not guilty,' she said, 'and I appeal.'

Howie nodded, while Bruit looked scathing.

'She just wants to spread her poison in front of an audience,' the archdeacon said. 'I will seek the judicial quashing of any appeal, and demand that sentencing be held in private, in the name of public safety.'

'That is your right,' Howie said. She gazed around the bare cell. 'In the mean time, let's not have our prisoner freeze to death. Guards, make sure she gets blankets, candles, food and water. Tonight, please. Also, if any of her close family turns up looking for her, let them talk to her.'

'What?' Bruit spat. 'She's a traitor, why should we show her kindness?'

Howie shook her head. 'It's not for her benefit. The entire Holdings will be watching us, as soon as we announce we've arrested her. I don't want even the slightest hint of mistreatment to arouse any sympathy for her.'

Bruit snorted, his arms crossed.

'Be patient,' Howie said. 'After sentencing...'

Bruit frowned. 'Very well.'

'Steward,' Howie said to the man writing. 'No need to record that last exchange. Stop at the part when I offered to allow her family to visit.' She leaned over to see what the steward was doing. 'Yes, perfect.'

Howie nodded, and they left. A few minutes later the guards came back in. They lit a candle for her, and piled blankets and cloaks on the pallet. They also left a small sack of food, a large jug of water, and a ceramic mug.

She threw the dirty old blanket to the far corner of the room, and pulled the new blankets around her, feeling warm for the first time in hours. She sat on the bed, and ate her way through the contents of the sack: bread, cheese, beef strips, tomatoes.

'As severe as the law allows,' Field Marshal Howie had said. Death, then.

In the morning, not long after she had awoken, she heard footsteps again. A large metal hatch in the upper half of the cell door was opened, and Daphne could see someone through the wire mesh. She stood to get a better look.

'Jorge!' she cried.

He came forward, his mouth hanging open, a look of nervous curiosity on his face.

'What are you doing here?' she asked.

'The news of your arrest is all over town,' he said, looking through the grille into the cell. 'It was announced at dawn.'

'But how did you get past the guards?'

'I lied,' he whispered. 'I told them I was your brother. Showed them the old Holdfast ring you gave me, and they let me through the crowds. Still searched me, the buggers.'

'Well, it's good to see you,' she said.

He shook his head. 'You should have stayed away.'

'I'm innocent, Jorge,' she replied. 'I had to come back.'

'Oh Daphne,' he said, 'it's too late for guilty or innocent. In a city riven in two by pro- and anti-war factions, you have succeeded in uniting the populace into believing that you're a filthy traitor. You are the only thing both sides agree on.'

'And which side are you on?'

'My eyes have opened,' he said. 'As you know, I used to be pro-war, but after reading about what happened this summer, and seeing how much money the greedy merchant classes are making from war profiteering, I've changed my mind. So have most. There have been fights on the university campus, real fights, Daphne, between the pro- and anti-war types.'

'So you're siding with the church?'

'Enemy's enemy and all that.'

'And who is the enemy, Jorge?'

'The immoral merchants who are stuffing their pockets with the wealth of Sanang, while the common soldiers are being killed and wounded. It's not a war, it's armed robbery!'

'My father, then,' she said, 'and by extension me, I suppose. We're the enemy.'

'Listen,' he whispered through the grille. 'I know what you should do. Come out and say it was all your father's doing, that he put you up to it. Tell them that he forced you to ignore those orders and, you know, turn on the weeping, If you can gain the sympathy of the people, the judges won't be able to touch you.'

'I'm not guilty,' she said, 'and I'm not going to lie in court.'

He looked pained, as if hurt by her unreasonable obstinacy. He glanced up at her, his eyes widening.

'What happened to your arm?'

'Elbow got smashed up,' she said, holding up her withered hand. 'Crippled.'

Several emotions swept over Jorge's face in a flash, before he could assert control. There was horror, confusion, calculation, and a hint of disgust.

Ashamed, he looked away.

'Thank you for visiting, Jorge,' she said.

She held out her hand.

'The ring, Jorge.'

He put a hand to his pocket, hesitated, then withdrew the ring she had given him. He pushed it through the grille, and it dropped into her hand, the Hold Fast crest glinting in the torchlight. He looked as if he was going to say something, but instead just nodded, turned, and walked back down the passageway. A guard approached her cell. The door-hatch was closed with a clang, and she was alone again.

She dried her tears.

CHAPTER 14

APPEAL

Holdings City, Realm of the Holdings – 11th Day, First Third Winter 503

Each morning in her cell when she awoke, Daphne scratched a notch onto the cold stone wall above the pallet where she slept.

She had seen no one bar her jailers on the days of the first four marks, but on the fifth, just after dawn, she had been visited by her father's agent in the city, who took care of the Holder's business interests in his absence.

She was a middle-aged woman, an accountant by trade, before being sought out and employed by her father. She had been curt and professional when she had visited, her questions revolving around what Daphne was going to say in court about her father. The agent had assured Daphne that a messenger had been sent to the Holdfast estate as soon as her arrest was announced, but due to the distances involved, it would take her father at least a third before he would arrive in the capital.

On the day of the sixth notch, a tailor arrived, who took her measurements with a tape, in a hasty exercise that had taken less than three minutes.

Now it was the tenth day, and she remained alone in her thoughts.

Jorge had not returned, but Daphne felt relieved that their relationship was over. So much had happened to change her, while he had remained the same. She had hung the ring round her neck on a piece of string, and often found that her right hand was clasping it, drawing comfort from its provenance, a frail thread reaching back home. A reminder of who she was.

There was a thump on the cell door. Daphne remained on her pallet.

'Stay back from the entrance!' cried a voice, and the door opened.

It was the tailor again. She strode into the room, without sparing Daphne a glance. She had a long package folded over her arm, and she set it down on the stone bench by the window. The tailor turned, and walked back out.

As the door slammed shut, Daphne got to her feet.

She opened the package, and saw that she had been given a dress, presumably something to wear in court. She picked it up in her right hand, running the withered fingers of her left down the coarsespun material. It was black, high-collared and ankle length, the dress of a penitent, a shamed criminal. By putting the dress on, it would signal to others that she was admitting her culpability, but as she had already been found guilty, she assumed the court had felt it was appropriate.

It was a struggle to get the outfit on, and her left arm was sore by the time she had succeeded, but she had been loath to call upon the guards to come to her assistance.

The hem of her dress brushed the floor of the cell, hiding her prison-issue hide slippers. The rough fabric was loose over her arms, down to the wrists, but seemed to emphasise the crookedness of her left elbow, and accentuate her crippled hand.

She slept in her new dress that night, an uncomfortable and fitful sleep, interrupted by shouts echoing up from the city. Shadows flickered across the walls of the cell, from light coming through the window. Something was happening in the city. Was it connected to her? Mink had been right. She was being made the scapegoat for the disaster in the forest. Was the mob down there calling for her blood? She neared despair several times throughout the long dark night.

At dawn, she was awoken by loud footsteps outside her cell.

'Back from the door!' came the usual cry.

The door opened, and three soldiers walked in. At their head was a young captain.

'Up,' he said.

Daphne rose from the pallet, trying not to look as nervous as she felt.

The captain looked her up and down for a moment, then nodded.

'You're dressed, good,' he said. He motioned to a guard behind him, who came forward. He had chains slung over his shoulder, which he began attaching to Daphne. One set joined her ankles, giving her a pace of slack, and the other set were fastened to her wrists. She stood without complaint while being manacled, maintaining eye contact with the captain.

'You are being moved to the courthouse,' he said, once the chains were secure.

'Why?' she asked. 'Is my appeal being heard today?'

The captain gestured towards the door. She sighed and followed them out. Daphne and her escort went down to the hall on the ground floor, where a further twenty soldiers were waiting in a double line. She was placed between them, and they marched round the edge of the circular wall to a door on the far side. There they halted, while one soldier opened the door and peered out.

'Courtyard clear, sir,' she said, 'but a crowd has gathered on the other side of the gates.'

'Very well,' the captain replied. 'Escort! Listen! We will be taking the prisoner directly across the yard to the courthouse. Right flank, keep your shields high, in case the crowd get it into their heads to start throwing things.'

He nodded to the soldier at the entrance, who pushed the door open. The column started moving at a brisk walk. As the soldiers emerged from the Old Tower, a roar bellowed out from the crowd to the right, who were prevented from entering the square by an iron gate. When Daphne herself came outside, blinking into the bright winter day's sunshine, the roar grew. She could see the people on the other side of the gate, their faces contorted with rage, reaching their arms through the metal bars towards her. Several were hurling obscenities at her, or threats, and she almost halted, and had to be cajoled along by the soldiers.

The courthouse was ahead, on the western side of the square, and Daphne kept her head lowered for the rest of the route, jogging to keep up with the soldiers. Stones were thrown over the gate at them, which skittered off the cobbles. One soldier was hit on the head, and went down. Two others picked him up by the shoulders, and hauled him along with the rest of the column.

Guards were waiting for them at the fort-like entrance to the courthouse, and the column rushed under a large arch and inside. Heavy doors were swung shut behind them and barred with a loud clang. The soldiers relaxed, and some kneeled to tend to their injured comrade.

A group of court officials and guards had been waiting, and now approached.

'Thank you, Captain,' said one. 'We'll just need your signature, if you please.'

The officer took the offered quill, and scrawled his name on the sheet. 'She's officially yours now.'

The court official looked at Daphne with undisguised contempt.

'She may well be yours again by this evening,' he said to the captain. 'This shouldn't take too long.'

'I'll keep the squads here, then,' the captain said. 'In case we're needed.'

The official nodded to his own guards. 'Take her to the holding cell.'

Daphne was escorted down a set of stone steps to the basement under the court, and locked inside a tiny cell. Up by the ceiling, a barred slit opened onto the courtyard outside, from where she could hear the menacing roar of the mob, calling for her blood.

She sat down on the cold bench, and shivered. Fear was stretching her nerves to breaking. She tried to relax, but the events of the last six thirds flooded her mind. She put her head in her hands.

Her thoughts were interrupted as the door to the cell was opened. Two guards gestured for her to follow, and she was led up the stairs and through a hallway into the main courtroom. It was a large chamber, but the sheer mass of people who had crammed inside made it seem small and claustrophobic. There were three seating areas for the public, one on the ground level, and two tiered above. Every seat was taken, and people sat or stood in any available space. As she entered, there was a single intake of breath from the crowd, and the volume rose as shouts and curses filled the air. There was violent hatred in many of the faces she saw as she scanned the seats looking for anyone she recognised. She lowered her eyes, unable to cope with so much rage. Her chains clanked as she was led to a seat on the right, halfway between the public gallery and the judges' table that ran the length of the rear wall. Between her and the crowd, a thin line of guards stood, their shields raised.

She sat down, and closed her eyes. The noise was deafening. Through the open doors of the main entrance, she could hear a larger mob outside.

A door in the wall opposite was opened by a guard, and the five appeal judges entered, and made their way past the clerks' desks to the high table, where they sat. They were all dressed, like her, in black. The judge in the central chair was one she recognised, though had never met. He was Chief Justice Barker, a figure not known in the Realm for his tender qualities.

He picked up his gavel, and glanced around the room. His expression as he gazed at the rowdy audience was cynical and amused. He brought the gavel down, and the noise simmered away.

He waited for silence.

'This appeal hearing is now in session,' he announced, his voice filling the room. 'Daphne Holdfast, identify yourself.'

She raised her head. The judges were all looking at her, every eye in the audience stared, and she felt her mouth dry.

'I am she,' she croaked.

'What was that?' Barker snapped. 'Speak up!'

Courage, Daphne, she said to herself. Don't let them win so easily, don't let the mob see you're beaten.

'I am Daphne of Hold Fast,' she said in a fine, clear voice. The crowd gasped.

'Young Holdfast,' Barker said, 'this appeal hearing has been granted due to your absence from the earlier trial, at which the first high court found you guilty of disobeying orders, leading to the loss of the forward fort under your command, the consequent breach of the Realm's defensive positions, and the subsequent losses at the second supply station, and further associated losses of personnel, and sundry materials. You have now entered a plea of not guilty, and this hearing will determine if you are in possession of any evidence sufficient to overturn the aforesaid verdict.

'Furthermore, there are three new witnesses, who shall provide testimony, according to the set rules of appeal hearings...'

Daphne stopped listening. She started to scan the rows of people in the audience again. Many in the crowd were looking at the judge, but a few were staring in her direction. Several of them made slitting motions across their throats. Finally, she saw someone she knew. It was Ariel, her older sister. She was dressed in a long, hooded robe, but was looking at Daphne, and their eyes met. Ariel had a sad smile on her face. Daphne looked away before she could start to cry, and to avoid drawing attention to her sister as she sat in the crowd.

Barker banged his gavel again, and she turned to look at the judges.

'First witness,' he called.

The door in the opposite wall opened again, and Weir walked in. He was wearing civilian clothing, and didn't look at her as he went to the witness stand. It was a small raised platform to the left of the judges' table, just in front of the clerks' desks, where they were recording every word and gesture.

'State your name,' said the judge to the left of Barker.

'Weir of the River Holdings,' he said, his hand trembling, 'formerly a sergeant in Daphne Holdfast's company, under Lieutenant Mink's command.'

'And you were in the forward fort when it was attacked?'

'Yes, ma'am. I was.'

'And you were captured with former Captain Holdfast, and then escaped from the Sanang in her company?'

'Yes, ma'am.'

'And did Daphne Holdfast ever speak to you about her reasons for not retreating from the fort?'

'Yes, ma'am,' Weir said. 'She said it was because the orders didn't arrive.'

'And did you believe her?'

'Well yes, I did,' he said. 'Sure she was inexperienced, she made mistakes, but she's loyal.'

'I see,' the judge replied. 'Do you have any evidence of this loyalty?'

Weir paused. 'Yes,' he said. 'When we were with the Sanang warlord, he was always asking us about the Holdings, but she never once told him anything secret.'

'And this was under torture?'

'No,' he replied, 'we were treated fairly enough.'

'Did she say anything else about her thoughts on the matter of the fort being attacked?'

'There was one thing,' he said. 'A theory she shared with me. Made sense at the time.'

Oh no, Daphne thought. Her stomach clenched and she could taste the bile rising in her throat.

'Yes?' the judge prompted. The courthouse fell silent.

'She suggested to me that the church might have set her up,' Weir said at last. The noise level rose, as people cried out in disbelief.

Barker banged his gavel, and slowly the noise abated.

'The church?' the judge went on.

'Yes,' Weir replied, looking like he wished he had kept his mouth shut. 'The Sanang warlord was telling everyone that the idea for attacking the fort had come to him in a dream…' He hesitated, looking over at Daphne.

'A dream?'

'A dream, yes,' Weir said, his voice a little over a whisper, 'and the captain suggested that perhaps one of our high mages had implanted the image into his head.'

Pandemonium broke out, as everyone shouted at once. Daphne closed her eyes, unable to look at the regret on Weir's face.

It took some time to calm the crowd down. Extra guards were brought in, and a double line now separated the mob from the rest of the courtroom.

Finally there was silence and the judge continued.

'And how was the former captain's state of mind at this time?'

'What?' Weir said, looking blank.

'Let me clarify,' the judge went on, 'was Daphne Holdfast under the influence of anything that may have clouded her judgement while she was being held captive?'

Daphne looked up.

'Do you mean like alcohol and narcotics?' Weir said.

'For example,' the judge said.

'Yes,' Weir said. Again the crowd gasped, its attention focussed on the red-faced ex-sergeant. 'But she was in a whole lot of pain, what with her arm being crippled. She needed the drugs to get through it.'

'Quite,' the judge replied. 'That will be all, Weir of the River Holdings, thank you.'

Weir got up, his head bowed, and walked from the courtroom.

'Next witness,' Barker announced.

It was Mink, smartly turned out in his cavalry uniform. The tall lieutenant strode to the stand, and turned to face the judges' bench.

'State your name,' said the old judge to the right of Barker.

'Lieutenant Mink of Hold Getram,' he replied, 'formerly of Captain Daphne Holdfast's command.'

'And you were with Sergeant Weir and Captain Daphne, both

formerly of the Queen's Own, during the attack on the fort, and subsequent captivity and escape?'

'Yes, sir.'

'And were you ever present when Daphne Holdfast spoke about her reasons for not leaving the forward fort?'

'Yes, sir,' Mink replied, 'she often talked about it. She always maintained that the orders never arrived. However, I was not in her confidence like Lieutenant Chane or Sergeant Weir, and I was not privy to her real thoughts on the matter.'

'Were you not being held together?'

'We were all kept on the same floor, but had our own rooms. I was often sent to mine by Daphne, not to her discredit, after all she was only trying to protect me whenever I stood up to the Sanang. Every time I angered them she would send me away.'

'I don't understand,' the old judge said, 'were you the only prisoner to defy the Sanang?'

'Yes,' he replied, glancing over at Daphne. 'Much to my regret, but to be frank, the others were quite friendly with the Sanang. They feasted in the warlord's company, held long discussions with him about the politics and religion of the Holdings, and they drank alcohol and smoked the forest narcotics together.'

There were gasps, and shouts of 'shame' from the crowd.

'We heard earlier from former Sergeant Weir that Daphne only took these narcotics for her pain.'

'At first, yes, that was the case,' he said, as if it hurt him to go on. 'But afterwards... I hear they can have an addictive effect.'

'You never partook?'

'No sir,' he replied. 'I did not wish to dull my senses in front of the enemy.'

'Thank you, Lieutenant Mink, that will be all,' the old judge said. 'It's good to see that the Holdings still have some officers capable of exercising restraint and common sense under pressure.'

Mink flushed, and nodded. He got up and left the courtroom, avoiding Daphne's eyes.

'Final witness,' Barker announced.

The door opened, and Douanna walked in. There was a murmur through the crowd, many of whom had never seen a Rahain before. She was elegantly dressed, and looked confident, regal even.

'State your name, please,' said the judge on the far left.

'I am Lady Douanna, of Jade Falls in the Republic of Rahain,' she smiled.

'Let the records show,' Barker interjected, 'that Lady Douanna is protected by the diplomatic immunity of the Rahain ambassadorial delegation, and thus cannot be prosecuted under Holdings law. Also note that she is here at her own request, and that this court has allowed her presence as a courtesy to our Rahain allies. Please continue.'

'Thank you, Chief Justice,' the younger judge said. He turned to Douanna. 'My lady,' he said, 'what is your connection to Miss Daphne Holdfast?'

'I had business dealings with your towns along the Sanang frontier the summer before last, and Lieutenant Daphne, as she was then, was the liaison officer for the Rahain merchants. And then, about a third and a half ago, I encountered her again in Midfort. The poor thing was in a terrible state, half-starved to death, and her arm all broken.' She shook her head. 'The very idea that she had somehow enjoyed captivity...'

'Please,' Barker said, 'restrict your testimony to facts of which you have direct experience, rather than supposition.'

She gave him a look, and her tongue flickered.

'I agreed to assist her on her journey to this city,' Douanna said, 'as she is innocent of her alleged crimes...'

'Daphne Holdfast has already been found guilty, may I remind you,' stated Barker.

'...and I was with her when she was arrested at the gates,' Douanna went on, ignoring him. 'Throughout my time with Daphne, I found her to be unstintingly loyal to the Holdings, and...'

'Yes. Thank you,' Barker said. 'That will be all.'

'...and I do not believe that she is a traitor,' she finished. The courtroom was in silence, and there were many angry glares being aimed in the Rahain woman's direction.

Douanna spoke into the quiet. 'I ask that the court show mercy.'

The Rahain got to her feet, and crossed the floor. Before she slipped out of the door, she turned to glance at Daphne. She gave a slight nod, and left.

'Quiet,' Barker growled, banging his gavel as the noise started to increase again.

'That concludes the witness testimonies,' he said, when silence returned. 'I will now put questions to the appellant.' He turned his head to face her. 'Holdfast,' he said, 'is it your assertion that you never received the orders to withdraw from the forward fort?'

'It is,' Daphne said, her heart racing faster than ever.

'And do you have any new evidence for this hearing to support your assertion?'

'Only my testimony, Chief Justice.'

'Clerk,' Barker said, gesturing at one of the court's aides, 'present to the appellant the two pieces of material evidence from the earlier trial.'

One of the aides stood, and picked up a tray from under his desk. He walked past the other clerks and approached Daphne. There were two items on the tray, both documents.

'Please describe this evidence as you understand it,' Barker said.

'This,' Daphne said, pointing at the book on the left, 'is the Queen's Cavalry Command Logbook, opened to the page dated the twenty-second day of the last third of spring, year five-oh-three.'

'And is there anything on that page relevant to this case?'

She scanned the paper. 'Yes, it states that orders were sent to all forward fortresses to withdraw. I can see the Holdfast name in brackets in the list that follows.'

'And what would you conclude from this?'

'That the orders were sent.'

'Thank you,' Barker smiled. 'And the other item?'

She studied it. She had known what it would be, but still stared at it in disbelief.

'It's a receipt,' she said.

'Yes, saying what?'

'That the orders to withdraw have been received, dated the eighth day of the first third of summer, year five-oh-three.'

'And is the receipt signed?'

'It is.'

'By whom?' Barker asked, his impatience rising.

'By someone who has forged my signature.'

The crowd roared at this, and it took several bangs of the gavel to quieten them.

'I see,' Barker said. 'As Father Rijon, the witness who positively iden-tified that signature as belonging to you, is not currently present in the Holdings, he cannot be summoned to refute your allegation. However, as he has entered his testimony into the written record, we do not require him here in person in order to proceed.'

He gazed around the courtroom.

'As the appellant has disputed the evidence, it now becomes a ques-tion of her reliability and honesty; in short, we must judge her character. Holdfast,' he said, turning to her again, 'it has been alleged that you freely partook of narcotics and alcohol in the company of the enemy Sanang, and held feasts, parties, and discussions with them about aspects of Holdings life. Do you deny any of these allegations?'

'We spoke only about things that every Holdings child learns in junior school.'

'Drugs, Holdfast?' he pressed. 'Alcohol, feasts?'

'The drugs because I was in pain from my injury,' she said, to calls of 'liar' and 'shame' from the crowd. 'Alcohol and feasts, yes, occa-sionally.'

Barker just shook his head, and allowed the crowd to vent its anger at her for a few long moments.

'Tell us, Daphne,' he continued once the room had quietened again, 'about your theory that the church conspired against you.'

'It was nothing but an idle thought,' she said. 'Forgotten in a moment.'

'Brought on by your dependency on potent hallucinogenic drugs and powerful painkillers?'

'No!'

'It was the alcohol then that clouded your judgement?' he smirked, as the crowd laughed.

Daphne sat back, her chains clanking, her eyes smouldering.

'A couple of final questions, Holdfast,' he said, a half-smile at the corner of his lips. 'When you returned to Midfort on the frontier, why did you not hand yourself in to the authorities, if you were innocent?'

'Because,' she cried out, 'I discovered that there were mobs everywhere who would tear me to pieces before I could tell them the truth. The disaster needs a scapegoat,' she was shouting now, above the growing noise of the crowd, 'and I'm it.'

'Silence!' Barker shouted at the angry crowd, banging his gavel.

'Another outburst like that Holdfast,' he said, glaring at her, 'and you'll be removed from the courtroom.'

She nodded sullenly.

'And, finally,' Barker said, 'can you please tell us how much influence your father had over you when you chose to ignore direct orders?'

'I did not disobey orders,' she spat back, 'and my father had zero influence over me in my capacity as an officer in the cavalry. He never once advised me on military matters, and even if he had, I wouldn't have listened.'

'Then,' Barker said, 'we are being asked to believe that the convergence of his designs with your actions was merely a coincidence?'

'I did not disobey orders,' she repeated.

He sat back in this chair, and conferred quietly with the other judges.

Daphne caught her sister's eye for a brief second. Ariel was smiling at her, her hood framing the dark oval of her face. Daphne wondered where the rest of her family were, and what would happen to them because of her.

After a few moments, the judges finished their whispered conversation, and they turned to face Daphne.

'The judgement of this appeal hearing,' Barker began, 'is that no new evidence has been presented that overturns the previous verdict. The character of Daphne Holdfast has been tested, and found wanting. In captivity it appears that she abandoned the decent norms that guide the people of the Holdings, and fell into the abominable sins of alcohol, narcotics and gluttony. According to eyewitness testimony, she regularly held or attended parties and feasts with the enemy, and seems to have been more friendly with them than with some of her own officers. Her judgement has been, frankly, poor, and yet she asks us to discard all of the evidence from the previous trial, and put our sole trust in her word. The court hereby rejects the appellant's argument as to the trustworthiness of her character, and consequently, the appeal fails.'

He banged his gavel, as excitement built.

'Daphne Holdfast,' Barker said, 'this court finds that the original verdict stands, that you are guilty of disobeying orders. The court shall now proceed directly to sentencing.'

The crowd roared again, louder than before, revelling. Daphne lowered her eyes. A chant of 'death! death!' started, and was allowed to go on for several minutes, the chamber echoing to the cacophony.

Barker banged his gavel, and the whole place fell silent, every ear straining to listen.

'This court,' he began, 'sentences you, Daphne Holdfast, to death by hanging.'

The room erupted in noise, loud cheers reverberated around the large chamber, and a great roar echoed from outside.

'The sentence will be carried out at dawn tomorrow, in Holders Square,' Barker shouted over the noise, his gavel banging uselessly. 'Does the condemned have anything to say?'

She looked up.

The frenzied mob was hurling abuse at her, many miming choking gestures, while others just pointed and laughed. She tried to find Ariel among them, but her sister's seat was empty. On the other side, the judges looked satisfied with their day's work, and Barker was smirking at her. So that was it, then. Death by hanging. Anger at the unfairness of it rose within her, and she clenched her right hand. She wanted to speak, but what could she say that would make any difference?

'Yes,' she said. 'I do.'

Silence was achieved in a heartbeat, as every leering face turned to her.

Daphne stood. She held her head up, straightened her back and faced the mob with no sign of fear in her eyes.

'When I was fleeing the Sanang,' she said, 'I was close to death.' She paused, waiting for the crowd to crane their heads even further towards her.

She drew out the silence for as long as she could.

'There,' she continued, a smile on her lips, 'I, Daphne Holdfast, heard the voice of the Creator, and he saved me.'

Someone laughed; a short laugh that choked off into an awkward silence as the crowd gaped at her in disbelief. A voice called 'Blasphemer!' and the whole crowd exploded in a terrifying crescendo of noise. Men and women charged the guards separating them from Daphne. Swords were drawn, and chaos threatened to overwhelm the court.

Another door opened, and more soldiers ran in. Some of these had uniforms marking them out as battlers, a company of which were kept stationed by the palace.

The crowd surged forward, ripping up chairs, and hurling them across the chamber.

'This hearing is ended!' Barker shouted, getting out of his seat. 'Get the prisoner back to the tower!'

As the judges filed out the back door, guards surrounded Daphne, and together they ran back through to the entrance hall where they had arrived that morning. Other soldiers joined them, and they closed ranks, with shields forming a wall to their left. The doors were opened, and they charged through. Outside, the volume of noise from the crowd behind the iron gate was deafening. Bricks and stones were hurled at them, and Daphne heard several bounce off the shieldwall. They rushed into the Old Tower, and closed the door behind them. The captain walked up to Daphne. He looked her in the eye, shaking his head, then turned to his squads.

'You're going to see a proper riot now,' he said. 'Full armour everyone, we'll...'

He tailed off as a new set of guards entered the hall from the far door, their cloaks the dark blue of the church wardens. Their commander walked right up to the captain.

'I am Deacon Lessing,' she said. 'This prisoner is now under my authority.'

'Why?' the captain asked.

'Her sentence has been suspended,' Lessing replied, 'until the church can test her story.'

'Come on,' the captain said. 'She's obviously lying.'

'She may well be, Captain,' Lessing said, 'but anyone confirmed with vision abilities who claims to have heard the voice of the Creator must be tested by the church. In all likelihood, she'll be returned to secular authority in a few days. You can hang her then.'

'Very well,' the captain said, 'though I'm going to need to see some paperwork.'

'Of course,' Lessing said, handing him a folded document.

The captain scanned it, nodded to his soldiers, and they stood back.

Lessing turned to the wardens. 'Take her.'

The wardens surrounded Daphne. Lessing signalled to them, and they set off at a jog through the hall. They went under an archway into a tunnel that skirted the outer palace wall, in the direction of the southernmost corner of the flat-topped promontory, where the church had its ancient and labyrinthine headquarters.

Lessing jogged alongside the prisoner.

'Thank you,' Daphne whispered.

Lessing spat at her.

'Don't thank me, you blaspheming bitch,' she snarled. 'You'll get what's coming to you.'

CHAPTER 15

IN HER HEAD

Holdings City, Realm of the Holdings – 9th Day, Second Third Winter 503

Were it not for the twice daily delivery of food and water, Daphne would have believed that she had been forgotten about. For almost a third she had been held in a long, narrow cell somewhere in the bowels of the enormous complex of church buildings, the headquarters of her religion. The citadel of the prophet took up almost half of the Upper City, and was several times larger than the palace. Its roots burrowed deep into the rock of the promontory, and Daphne guessed she was several levels below the main floors, about halfway down the cliffside. There was a square shaft cut into the thick wall at the end of her cell, ending in a small barred opening. Every morning the sun's rays would pierce the shaft, illuminating the cell, and for a couple of hours Daphne enjoyed the light. Then the shadows would lengthen, and the cell existed in a low gloom for the rest of the day, while the sun reached its apex, and fell to the west.

The other end of her narrow cell was taken up with a barred iron door, which afforded her no hiding place if anyone was outside. This had led her to build a little tent-like shelter from a chair and some blankets, behind which she could get a little privacy when she needed it.

Through the bars she could see lines of other cells along the passageway to her left and right, but they all appeared to be empty. There were usually no wardens present, except at dawn and dusk, when food, water for washing and drinking, and a clean chamber pot were brought to her. Her provisions were generous, and she had been provided with plenty of bedding, which kept her warm during the cold winter nights. She presumed her captors did not want to risk upsetting the Creator if it turned out she had been telling the truth.

She often wondered it herself.

Her memories of the escape from the Sanang forest had become vague and hazy mere days afterwards. Now, more than three thirds later, she had no idea if what she remembered had been hallucinated or real. Had it not been for Douanna verifying that the Rahain were at war with the Southern Clans, whoever they were, she would have discarded it as an effect of drugs and exhaustion. Now she hoped with all her being that it had been real. If she had imagined it, she would surely be sent back to the Old Tower for execution.

What the church would do if she had been telling the truth intrigued and scared her. And if Rijon had been the one to engineer her downfall, then how many others were complicit? What would they do with her if they knew she suspected them?

She found herself worrying less as the days went by. She reflected on her life, and how hollow much of it felt. Her cavalry training, the passionate political discussions through the night with fellow students, their hopeless idealism about the war, all of it had soured, and it was with some surprise, after several days of solitude, that she realised she was ashamed of the Holdings and what they were doing in Sanang.

She had idolised the queen since she was a little girl, and had taken her side in every argument, especially against her old foe, the church. Never had the Holdings felt so free from the suffocating clutches of their stifling religion than in the last thirty years, yet Daphne was faced with the horrible realisation that, in this instance, the church was correct. The war was wrong.

She remembered her father coming home one day to their family's apartment in the city. She had been studying and living there at the time, and had tagged along with him for the few days of his visit. He had been summoned to the Queen's Council, and Daphne had arranged to meet him afterwards. When he had arrived at the apartment, her father's mood had been grim, and he had been shaking with rage. The family had lost a large portion of its fortune, he had explained. Their entire stake in the most recent trade caravan to Sanang, all the goods, and the lives of the merchants transporting them, had been lost. A savage attack by the barbarian tribesmen had slaughtered them, and taken everything.

Hold Fast had been one of the first and largest investors in the short-lived, but highly profitable trade with the Sanang tribes on the edge of the forest. Metals for wood was the primary and original exchange, but the Holdings merchants had soon adapted, and before long sugar, coffee, chocolate, tobacco and dozens of other items were changing hands, and the money started to pour in.

The exorbitant price of a tiny, sugared chocolate bar in the Holdings capital had caused a scandal when they had first appeared one morning in the marketplace, but the entire stock had sold out in record time.

But now, her father told her, they were facing massive debts. He had borrowed heavily on this latest caravan, and unless they could recoup some of their losses, the family would be forced to sell much of their property.

Their evening out had been cancelled, and her father sat and glowered in silence by the fireplace, working his way through a bottle of fine white rum. He had still been sitting there when Daphne had gone to bed, though when she arose the next morning, he had gone.

When she saw him the following evening, his mood had improved considerably. The queen had listened to his arguments, and had been won over. A punitive expedition would be sent, to show the Sanang that acts of violence against Holding citizens would not be tolerated, and Hold Fast were going to be the main beneficiaries. Firstly, he had negotiated prime rates and percentages of all appropriated materials, and secondly, the army would require thousands of the estate's horses to transport the vast army and its supplies all the way to the Sanang frontier, where the ancient wall would be re-occupied.

Now, as she lay on the mattress in her cell, she tried to balance what her father had told her, with what she had since learned. How had a single punitive expedition turned into a sustained campaign of systematic pillaging and looting? Her father's greed seemed the inescapable answer.

No, Daphne. Not greed, power.

She started, and bolted upright. Not the same voice, she thought. Then who? It had almost sounded like...

Yes, Daphne, it is your father.

You're in my head? This can't be happening, this cannot be right, get out!

This may make it easier for you, the voice of her father said.

He appeared before her, and she nearly screamed.

'I am not really here, Daffie,' he said, raising his hand. 'Calm yourself.'

'Wha... what? How?'

'I am using inner-vision to enter your mind via your sight,' he explained. 'Once in your mind, I can make your eyes see things that are not really there.' He smiled. 'Really, Daffie, I do hope that all the money I spent to keep you at university wasn't completely wasted. You are familiar with the workings of inner-vision, are you not?'

'Inner-vision?' she cried.

'Keep your voice down,' he frowned.

'I do remember, father,' she said, trying to calm herself, 'but hearing about it in a lecture is a little different from it actually happening inside your own damn head. Especially as you've never told me you possessed it.'

'Apologies for that, my dear,' he said. 'I tend only to tell people if I absolutely must. The uses of inner-vision can be very subtle if no one is aware you can do it.'

'So the church doesn't know?' she gasped. 'But what about when you were tested?'

'It hadn't manifested itself at that age,' he said. 'Yet a further example, if one were needed, of the church's short-sightedness and wilful stupidity. They have blinded themselves to everything except their scripture, and ignore the fact that some people don't fully develop their powers until after they have conducted their tests.'

Daphne started coughing. Her heart was pounding, and she thought she might faint or vomit.

She took a drink of water, and controlled her breathing.

'Is inner-vision taxing?' she asked.

'It varies by distance,' he replied. 'I could have used it to contact you before; I wanted to, but I was so far away that any conversation would have been over in a few seconds. And right now, for the first time, I happen to be quite close to you, geographically speaking.'

'You're in the palace?'

'I am,' he said. 'I arrived back in the capital a few days ago, and after several days trying, have just had an audience with the queen. While she is sympathetic to you personally, she cannot interfere with the workings of the law. Not openly, at any rate.'

'No one has spoken a word to me since I got here,' she said. 'What is the church saying about my case?'

'Very little.' He raised his eyebrows. 'They are using the excuse that an unplanned communion with the Creator may offend him, and have added your claim to the agenda of their next scheduled meeting of minds.'

'You don't believe them?'

'Of course not!' he shot back. 'They're just playing for time. There is no creator, Daffie. I know I have never openly said this to you before, but the Holdings religion is nothing but foolish nonsense, a collection of ridiculous dogma that a child could see through.'

Coming like that from her father, she felt certain he spoke the truth. But if that were the case, then why hadn't the church just called her a liar, and sent her back to be hanged?

'Father,' she said. 'I think the church set me up.'

'Then you really didn't get any orders?'

She lowered her eyebrows and glared at him.

He shrugged. 'Apologies, Daffie. Please, carry on. Do you have evidence of your claim?'

'None,' she sighed, 'but I know for a fact that I didn't sign any damned receipt, therefore I have to believe that the priest Rijon is involved. And the way the image of the fort was put into the head of the Sanang who led the assault...'

'Didn't you deny that theory at your appeal?'

'I did,' Daphne said, 'but what Weir said about the dream was true. That's what the Sanang leader told us. It could have been done with inner-vision, couldn't it?'

'It's possible,' he said. 'It would have needed a mage of great power, as the distances involved would have been immense, so if there were a conspiracy, it went very high up indeed.'

He paused for a moment, pondering.

'It if were them,' he said, 'then they achieved their aims most beautifully. Hold Fast has been shamed throughout the Realm, and I have been told to stay away from the council. I am in the city secretly, as you have probably deduced, and this is the first chance I've had to speak to the queen since news of the disaster arrived. Furthermore, the war has been thoroughly discredited in the eyes of the common folk. Before, we had great support from the masses. Now they are truculent, and riot at the first sign of a recruiting sergeant. Yes, the church has done very well indeed out of your misfortunes, my dearest Daffie, and the coincidence, if it were such, of the queen's illness has tightened their grip on power.'

'How is the queen?'

'Poorly,' he said, looking depressed. 'She was always so strong, so full of energy, and this dreadful wasting sickness has her confined to her bed, where she dictates her commands to her advisors in the dark, as the light hurts her eyes. I doubt she will last much longer, and I fear that her brother will soon be king. When that happens, the church's victory will be complete, and they will lead us back to the dark ages.'

'Was it really that bad?'

'Ahh Daffie,' he said. 'You're too young to remember what it was like, how the priests would poke their noses into every part of your life, and tell you what you were allowed to wear, or say or do, and what would cause you to be punished. It was only twenty years ago that the right for the church to jail, torture and execute heretics and atheists was removed from them. I do not want to live like that again.

'Plans are afoot, Daffie,' he went on. 'Today's meeting with the queen went very well in that regard. Unfortunately, while you are being held here, I cannot get you out by force, but be assured, now that I'm back in the city, I will move mountains to set you free.'

'Thank you,' she said, not knowing if she wanted his help.

'I heard the rioting lasted five days,' he went on, oblivious to her feelings, 'after your execution was commuted. The city has calmed down now, though the people haven't forgotten you. Most seem to trust the church to do the right thing. Fools. There may be some more unfortunate disruption in the streets, once the queen announces her news a few days hence.'

'What news?'

'That the Sanang campaign will continue for a final, fourth year,' he said, smiling at her in triumph.

'Is that wise?'

'This year will be different,' he said. 'I have presented my proposal to the queen. It involves a more considered approach, advancing only to the Twinth, and then fortifying and holding that line. We went too far last summer, I realise that now. The queen has also assured me that she will consider my idea of continually occupying the region up to the river, and transforming it into a permanent province of the Realm. A final and fitting payment for the crimes of the Sanang, I think.'

She opened her mouth to warn him about Agang and his battalions, but hesitated. He wasn't paying her any attention, appearing preoccupied with his plan.

'What do you think the church will do?' she asked instead.

'What?' he replied, snapped out of his reverie. 'The church? What can they do? More fulminating from the pulpit, all useless froth and pompous verbosity.'

'Father,' she said. 'How is mother?'

He looked down. 'Not taking it well, I'm afraid. She blames me, of course.'

'I saw Ariel at my appeal.'

'Yes,' he said. 'I have spoken to her since. And your brothers. They are all prepared to help in any way they can.'

Daphne didn't argue.

'We'll start looking into the priest Rijon first,' he said. 'I will spare no expense investigating your claims, Daffie. If there's anything that implicates the church in any of this, we'll find it. My reach is long.'

'I need a favour, father.'

'Name it, dear.'

'In my haste at the frontier,' she said, 'I left a debt unpaid. A family helped me, at great cost to themselves.'

'Show me everything you remember of them.'

She concentrated, thinking of their faces, and names, and where they said they had lived while staying in the wall forts over winter. She felt a strange pressure on her mind, a shadowy presence pushing at her thoughts.

'I see them,' he said, and she felt the pressure disappear. 'I'll have my agent send someone to find and reward them. You always were a thoughtful girl.'

'Thank you, father.'

'I must go now,' he said. 'I still have much to accomplish today.' He came closer. 'Stay strong Daffie, my dearest daughter of Hold Fast. Do not let them see you weaken. Hold to your story about hearing their god's voice, it was very clever of you to think of it.' He smiled, and disappeared.

All my love, the voice in her head said, then it vanished, and Daphne was alone again.

One dawn, several days after the vision of her father, she began to hear a roar of raised and angry voices drifting over the river from the Lower City, just as he had predicted.

The queen must have made her announcement, she thought, and the people of the capital were letting her know what they thought of her decision. There had always been a steady supply of willing recruits from the capital's poorer quarters, and indeed from all over the River Holdings, but she wondered if the protests meant that a draft had been called.

Her breakfast didn't arrive that morning. Instead, four armed wardens approached her cell. They stood before the barred doorway, and she rolled out of bed onto her feet to face them.

'Daphne Holdfast,' a warden called to her, from behind an iron helmet, 'you are required to be in the holy prophet's blessed presence.'

They opened the door, and entered her cell. The chains that had been removed upon her arrival were refastened to her ankles and wrists, and she let herself be shackled without resisting.

She was taken to the end of the long passageway, and up a spiral staircase that ascended all the way to the main levels of the citadel. While in her cell she had remembered her captivity in Beechwoods, and had exercised daily, and was barely out of breath by the time they emerged into a large hall. A couple of the wardens were out of shape, and were panting, and she smiled the tiny smile of a small victory.

The giant hall was empty. The walls were hung with massive tapestries and paintings, depicting scenes from the life of the first prophet, back at the founding of the Realm five centuries before. In each the prophet was centre-field, usually in the light of the sun's rays, benevolent and mighty. There were no windows in the hall to give Daphne a clue to her whereabouts, and the wardens, once they had regained their composure, led her off again.

Her prison slippers glided over the polished marble floors, and they passed through lavishly decorated rooms and corridors, passing the occasional guard at their post, but no one else.

At last they came to a large gilt door, which was guarded by four armoured wardens. They swung it open for Daphne to enter, and she went into a dark chamber. Daphne could see little once the door was closed behind her, but gradually her eyes adjusted to the dim candlelight.

The room was small, with a black throne on a raised pedestal against the wall across from where Daphne stood. To either side ran long tables, and sitting behind were figures dressed in black, five on her left, and six on her right. Wardens lined the walls, and flanked the throne, their armour glinting in the flickering light. A spear nudged her forward until she was standing in the centre of the room.

To her surprise, she realised that someone was sitting on the high throne a few paces before her. She had thought it empty, but she saw that a thin, black robed figure was hunched over in the great chair.

The sound of gentle murmuring reached her ears from either side of the room, though it was so dark she could see none of the figures moving.

'Daphne of Hold Fast,' a man's voice called out to her, though she couldn't tell from which direction, 'you have claimed a vision skill that was not apparent at your testing.'

'No,' she said, 'I possess battlefield and line, but none other.'

'You claimed at your appeal to have the ability to commune with the Creator, did you not?' the voice asked, a slight rise in temper showing.

'No,' she replied. 'I said that I heard his voice, and that I spoke to him, once, but I could no sooner do so again than I could fly.'

'Your claims are false, Holdfast,' another voice said. 'We have communed with the Creator, and humbly petitioned him about your boast. He does not recall you.'

Daphne had tried to think of all the things they might say to her, but it still shook her to be called a liar, by people she knew were themselves lying.

'I believe I did hear him,' she said, her voice faltering. 'He told me that the war was wrong, and that we should unite the peoples.'

'You could have learned that from any sermon,' a third voice replied.

Daphne paused. 'Do you intend to send me back to be hanged, then?'

'Oh Daphne,' the second voice said, 'we are not the villains here. You said it yourself, the war is wrong. It is a disgusting, immoral, savage attack on a disorganised and poorly defended people, purely for greed and material gain.'

'And it's about to escalate into an outright occupation,' the third voice said, 'starting this coming spring. The queen has today announced the formation of the greatest invasion force yet seen, and drafting sergeants are scouring the townships as we speak. As is always the way, it is the poor who suffer in war, as the merchants grow wealthy on their sweat and blood. Can you, after all you have seen, deny a single word of this, Daphne?'

She said nothing. She knew they were lying about the Creator not remembering her. She felt more certain than ever that the meeting had truly occurred, and that it hadn't been an illusion caused by mental exhaustion. However, as much as she hated to admit it, they were right about the war. It was a shameful stain on the Holdings, and it looked like it was only going to get worse. She imagined Agang confronting the Holdings along the River Twinth. No matter who came out as winners, there would first be great carnage on both sides.

'Do you want to live, Daphne?' asked the second voice.

She shrugged, not caring if they could see her in the dim light.

'It's in our power,' the first voice said, 'to not only commute your sentence, but to quash it utterly, if you agree to repent and make things right.'

'By doing what exactly?' she asked.

'You can end the war, Daphne,' the first voice continued. 'You. If you denounce your father as the influence behind your treachery, you will bring down the entire war-making apparatus with him. Once Holder Fast is prosecuted, the impetus behind the war will suffer such a blow, that there will be no campaign this spring. And, as the health of the queen deteriorates, that means there will be no more campaigns. The war will be over, and you will have helped end it.'

'But, my family…'

'A sacrifice, Daphne,' the second voice said, with soothing compassion. 'For you, a great sacrifice. We understand child, we sympathise, but there is no other way to end this war. Think of the thousands of lives you will save, the children who will keep their parents, the husbands and wives whose lives will not be ripped apart. Peace, Daphne. Imagine peace, and do the right thing.'

'What will happen to the rest of my family, and to me?' she asked, her thoughts paralysed.

'No one but your father will pay the price,' the first voice replied. 'You will be pardoned, and they will be safe.'

Daphne's mind was wheeling and turning. Give up her father to end the war. After seeing what he had become, his greed for wealth and power, maybe he needed to be restrained; maybe he deserved to be punished. But her family would be homeless, as the estate would fall forfeit to the crown if its head were convicted of treason. She imagined trying to explain to her mother why she had betrayed her family. For the greater good, she would say.

The greater good.

She raised her head, her eyes on the dark throne in front of her.

'I know you're lying.'

'Child?' the first voice said.

'About the Creator speaking in my head. I know it happened. The only thing that's puzzling me is why you would deny it.'

'Please, Daphne,' the second voice said. 'Desist with your delusions.'

Daphne ignored her. 'Either you haven't spoken to the Creator to check. Or you have. Either way you're lying. The only reason I can think of why you would lie, is that it was you who betrayed me, by putting the vision in the Sanang leader's head, and getting Rijon to intercept the orders and forge that damn receipt.'

The room fell into silence.

Daphne pushed a long strand of hair back from her face.

'She must die!' a voice cried out in anger.

'The church cannot touch her,' another said.

'Then hand her over to the secular authorities, and let them hang her!'

'We cannot allow her to repeat to others what she knows...'

'She knows nothing,' the first voice said. 'She is obviously deluded, perhaps insane. But you raise an interesting point. It would perhaps be best to keep her fantasies away from the ears of the gullible. Wardens,' he said, 'take her back to her cell. We will devise another way to deal with her.'

Daphne glared at them as wardens approached her.

'You have the power to end the war, Daphne,' the first voice said as they dragged her away. 'Think on it.'

Daphne spat on the floor.

CHAPTER 16
CONFESSION

Holdings City, Realm of the Holdings – 30th Day, Second Third Winter 503

The first sign that her conditions had changed was that the guards did not remove her shackles when she was returned to her cell.

The second sign was the food. Whereas before she had been given two meals a day, this had been cut to one small portion, supplied each dawn. Her water ration had been halved, and in the sixteen days since, she had often been forced to choose between drinking and washing. She wasn't sure if the wardens had been ordered to be pettier towards her, or maybe they had just picked up a feeling from their superiors, but they had begun to treat her with disdain and contempt. She was never physically hurt by them, but they went out of their way to make her life miserable. Some days they refused to take away her chamber pot, or when they did, they wouldn't return it when she needed it. They jeered at her, especially when she tried to get some privacy, and they would awaken her in the middle of the night by banging on the bars of her cell. Once, during a cold spell, they came in and took away half of her blankets, and left her shivering on the bed, while they laughed.

Every day she felt weaker, dirtier, and her clothes stank. Her left arm ached in the chill air, especially around her elbow, and in the joints of her curled fingers. Under the iron bands around her wrists and ankles, the skin was rubbed raw, and oozed. Relieving herself had become a torment. The wardens would leer at her while she squatted behind the screen she had made from a blanket hanging over the back of a chair, and it felt like her body was burning up in pain when she peed. She hadn't had a period in many thirds, and began to wonder if she would ever be allowed to fully recover. In six days she would be twenty-two, but she felt like an old woman.

She knew they were trying to break her, but perversely it made her stronger. She had been through so much that she took a strange satisfaction in refusing to let the wardens see that they had got to her. She would gaze at them with a blithe smile on her lips, which seemed to annoy them more than anything else. She took pleasure from imagining beating them up, day-dreaming about surprising them one day, switching into battle-vision, and pounding their thick skulls off the walls.

Never let your enemy see you weaken, her father had said. Show them only what you wish them to see. You are the master of how you appear. Forget the smell, forget the dirt, and the ripped and filthy clothes, your attitude and demeanour is all they will perceive if you hold yourself proudly, and keep yourself above their petty cruelty. They cannot hurt you if you do not let them.

The wardens had gone for the night, and she lay curled up on her bed, wrapped in every blanket she had. It was dark and silent inside the cell block, and she let her mask drop. She treasured the moments when the wardens left her. Before she had met the prophet, she had been glad to see them, but now, when they hung around most of the time, she wanted nothing more than to be alone.

From outside, she had occasionally heard shouts from the city below, but over the previous couple of days the noise had risen, and become continual. She could hear the massed roar of hundreds of raised voices, the ringing of steel, and the cries of the injured. The unmistakeable sound of horses' hooves on cobbled streets echoed through her narrow cell, and she was driving herself mad with frustration at not knowing what was happening.

The reflection of a light flickered through the window shaft. Daphne lay still and watched the shadows dance across the walls. Something in the city was burning, she realised. She had thought that everyone in the city hated both her and the war, but if that was so, then who was doing the fighting? Had the people risen against the Queen's Household Cavalry, the permanent garrison based in the north-west of the Lower City? The cavalry were fiercely loyal to the crown and, as a consequence, were inclined to be ill-disposed towards the church. In the lower ranks of the army, religious devotion was more common, but among the Household Cavalry there was an ingrained hostility to the monarch's only rival for power.

However, any uprising against the garrison would be over by now, if it had taken place. The troopers would slaughter the crowds, if let off the leash by the queen, who would surely only do so as a very last resort. But if the cavalry weren't fighting, who was?

A lamp appeared in the passageway outside her cell, and a woman approached the door.

'Holdfast,' she said. 'Get up.'

She got to her feet, her chains rattling off the bed. She held her blankets round her, and put her confident face back on. Staring at her was Deacon Lessing, the woman who had escorted her to the citadel. Wardens crowded the corridor behind her.

'We need something from you,' she said.

'In the middle of the night?'

The deacon beckoned to the wardens. 'Open the door.'

One came forward with the key, and unlocked the gate. 'Stand clear!' he yelled, and Daphne took a small step backwards. The door swung open, and Lessing entered, the wardens following. Each was armed with a short baton.

Lessing looked around, her nose wrinkling in disgust.

A warden brought the lamp into the cell, and hung it on a wall-bracket above her little table and chair.

Lessing gestured. 'Sit.'

Eight wardens, Daphne thought, as she walked over and sat by the table. They closed in behind her, and she could smell their smoky breath over her shoulder.

Lessing crossed to the opposite end of the table, and pulled a sheet of paper from an inside pocket. She studied it for a moment.

'You will sign this,' she said, not looking at her.

'And what is it?'

'Your confession, of course,' Lessing said, turning to face her. 'A full and forthright admission of your treachery.'

'May I read it first?'

'Is there any need?' Lessing sneered. She placed the paper down on the table in front of Daphne, and set next to it a thick old-fashioned quill, and a pot of ink, which she unstoppered.

She pointed to the bottom of the sheet. 'Right there.'

Daphne kept her hands under the table, and started reading.

I, Daphne of Hold Fast, freely confess...

Lessing was right, she thought. What did it matter? She wasn't going to sign it.

'I think I'll decline, thank you all the same.'

Lessing smiled.

'We discussed this, you know,' she said, 'that you'd probably refuse. We've been too kind to you, that's the trouble, and we've set some unrealistic expectations. For example, you believe that we would not inflict physical pain upon you.'

'The church is forbidden from...'

'Yes, yes,' Lessing said. 'We all know that.' She squatted down onto her haunches, so that she was level with her.

'Thing is, Daphne,' she said, 'down here, who's going to know?'

Daphne sat back in the chair. 'Why don't you just get someone to forge my signature, like you did for the receipt?'

Lessing stood again.

'It astounds me,' she said, shaking her head, 'how you can lie like that, Daphne.'

'While I'm not surprised in the slightest that your superiors would hide the truth from you.'

Lessing laughed, but her eyes held nothing but hatred. 'It's all a big conspiracy, eh? Is that what you would have me believe? Poor little Daphne Holdfast, persecuted by the prophet. That's the story your father's been spreading through the city, poisoning foolish minds against us, and setting the citizenry at odds with each other. I know what you are trying to do.' She started to rant. 'The last twenty years have seen the godless spread among us like rot! Without the righteous hand of the church the Holdings is falling to fire and ruin, while the queen encourages it all! Well, Daphne, the queen's days will soon be over. King Guilliam will put this nation back onto the right course, and the people will once again live under the guidance of holy scripture, shunning the evil of immoral and worldly distractions, living as a pious people should. Prepare for that day, Daphne, for it will be coming soon.'

Daphne held Lessing's gaze, but said nothing.

The deacon relaxed, and rolled her shoulders.

'I'm going to ask you one more time, Holdfast,' she said. 'Sign the paper.'

'No.'

'Sign it!' Lessing screamed, a foot from her face.

'Fuck you.'

The deacon banged her fist down onto the table, knocking over the inkwell, and sending the paper fluttering like a leaf to the floor.

'Take her arm,' she said.

Hands reached out and took a firm grip of Daphne's left arm, lifting it up from her lap and pinning it to the surface of the table. Pain shot through her like fire. She clenched her teeth, but refused to flinch.

Lessing bent over and retrieved the confession. She put it down onto the table, and set the inkwell back into an upright position. Spilled ink had spread over the surface of the table, a thin black fluid seeping away into the cracks. Lessing dabbed the quill into the puddle, and inspected the end. Satisfied that there was enough ink for a signature, she set it down next to Daphne's right hand.

She came close, right up to Daphne's ear.

'Sign,' she whispered.

'I will not.'

Lessing nodded to the wardens. A heavy arm came over her shoulder and round her throat, restraining her and pulling her back against the chair.

The hands holding her crippled arm started to twist and bend it upwards, and Daphne gasped and closed her eyes, the pain almost over-whelming her. She gritted her teeth and bore it, trying to shut off her mind. Without meaning to, she found herself drawing on battle-vision, and though it couldn't deaden the excruciating agony coming from her ruined arm, it allowed her to view it more passively, as if it might be happening to someone else. She opened her eyes and looked into Lessing's face.

The deacon was staring, her mouth open as she watched the wardens inflict pain on her.

Daphne's fingers edged towards the quill.

Lessing nodded again, and the wardens released her arm.

Daphne picked up the quill, and threw it to the floor.

Lessing slapped her across the face. 'You stupid bitch! Do you want to die?'

Daphne gathered the blood in her mouth, rolled it around her tongue, and spat at the deacon, spraying her chest in red-flecked saliva.

Lessing stared at her, any qualms she may have felt drowned out by rage. She nodded at the wardens.

'Again.'

That second time, Daphne had lasted right until they had struck the crooked bones of her elbow with their batons.

When she came to, with her head on the table, the only thing in her mind was pain, but she drew deep within herself and pulled on a thread of battle-vision, the way she had learned while on the run in the Sanang forest, just enough to keep going.

She heard voices. The wardens.

'This is fucked up, if you ask me,' a man said.

'I know,' a woman said. 'Torturing a cripple ain't what I joined the church for.'

'You were fine about it when we took the piss out of her before, stealing her blankets and that,' a third voice added.

'Come on,' the first man said, 'this is different.'

'But she's a traitor,' the other man said.

'Shush,' the woman said. 'The deacon's coming.'

Daphne heard the wardens get to their feet, the bed frame creaking.

Footsteps came into the cell. With her eyes open a crack, Daphne could make out everyone in the room. The deacon approached the table.

'Has the prisoner stirred?' she said, glancing down at Daphne.

'Nope,' a warden replied.

Lessing tapped her feet on the stone floor. 'We're wasting time,' she said. 'The high priests are getting impatient.'

'Why is it so important?' the same warden asked.

'The fighting in the city is finely balanced. Her confession may tip it in our favour.'

'Then why don't you just forge it, like she suggested?'

Lessing hesitated. 'The church can't...'

'The confession is what? Going to be flashed up in front of a mob?' the warden said. 'Who's going to check the signature? Our supporters already believe she's guilty, while her father's would say the confession was forged even if it was real.'

Lessing was silent.

'Look,' the warden said, 'no one here will say a thing, just put the quill in her hand like this...'

Daphne felt the thick quill pushed between her fingers, and her right hand was rearranged so that it sat poised over the sheet of paper. She kept her limb slack and limp.

'Then, you know,' the warden went on, 'you just move her hand, then you can say she signed it, and you won't really be lying.'

Lessing stepped close.

'I do this for the greater good, you understand?' she said to the wardens, as she leaned forward.

Daphne clenched her hand around the quill, and plunged it deep into Lessing's left eye. The deacon fell backwards screaming, her hands reaching for her face. Daphne kicked the table over, and ground her heel into the confession.

Batons hit her from behind, and she went down under the rain of blows, which continued even as she curled up into a ball on the floor. Her head exploded in pain as a baton struck her left temple.

Her eyes closed, and she felt herself be dragged over to the wall.

Daphne lay bleeding and bruised on the cold cell floor, hearing nothing but an intense ringing in her ears. She opened her eyes, and glanced up at the deacon.

Lessing was propped against the opposite wall, her mouth open in a silent scream, a look of horror on her face as she stared at the quill in her hand. Her left eye-socket was a bloody mess, and the side of her face was red and swollen. The wardens helped her up, and half-carried her from the cell, locking it behind them.

Daphne started to crawl towards the bed. The wardens had neglected to take the lamp with them, and she used its light to guide herself across the floor. She longed for some dullweed, if only Weir were around, she thought, as she grew dizzy. She lifted her hand to the bed, but slipped into oblivion.

She awoke when a ray of sunlight from the shaft in the eastern wall reached her face. She opened her eyes, blinking and dazzled. Her mouth was dry, and she ached all over. Her back, her legs, her head, but most of all, her left arm. She fought back tears, and struggled up into a sitting position.

Nothing was broken at least, she thought, though bruises covered her body. Her left ear was still ringing from the baton blow she had received, but she could hear the faint rumble of shouts and fighting from the city below.

She noticed the confession lying on the ground where she had earlier trod on it. She picked it up, and ripped it to shreds. Amateurs.

She crawled up onto the bed, and remained there for the rest of the day.

When it grew dim, wardens appeared at the door, led by a robed priest.

'Daphne Holdfast,' he said, gazing at her through the bars, 'the prophet has come to a decision in your case. You have spurned every chance the church has offered you and therefore, following your assault upon the deacon, the prophet has been left with no choice but to return you to the secular authorities for due punishment.'

Daphne said nothing.

The wardens unlocked the door, and entered the cell. Daphne got to her feet, clutching a blanket.

They led her out of the cell and along the passageway to the spiral stairs. This time it was Daphne who was struggling and panting long before they reached the top.

She stumbled as they arrived at the landing leading to the Old Tower. The wardens pulled her back to her feet, and they continued on, her chains dragging.

They wound their way through the underbelly of the Upper City, until they reached the ancient foundations of the Old Tower. There, two squads of Household Cavalry were waiting in ranks. The priest nodded to the cavalry officer, and the captain frowned back.

Daphne was handed over. The captain looked at the condition she was in, and raised an eyebrow at the priest. He shrugged, about-turned his wardens, and they departed the way they had come.

'Miss Holdfast,' the captain read to her, holding up a paper, 'the crown hereby resumes custody of you. Know that your sentence still stands, as confirmed at your appeal hearing. You are to be executed in Holders Square at dawn.'

He slipped the paper back into his jacket's inside pocket.

Daphne looked at him.

'I am Captain Summel,' he said. 'Please come with me.'

He turned and walked between the ranks of heavily armoured troopers, and Daphne followed, her head held high despite her rags and shackles.

They marched through the building until they came to a comfortable officer's room, where two aides were preparing tea. The guards remained outside the main entrance while Daphne and Summel went in. The only other door was open, and led to a small bathroom. A large bed sat against one wall, and chairs were laid out in front of a large hearth, where a fire was roaring.

Summel gestured to a plush couch, and Daphne sat upon the edge of a cushion, conscious that she was filthy.

'Would you care for a cup of tea, miss?' the captain asked her.

'Please,' she replied. And a bath, a meal, and how about getting these shackles off, she wanted to say, but instead took comfort from this unexpected kindness.

An aide placed a tray with cups and a teapot onto the low table in front of the couch, and Summel sat down in the armchair opposite, next to the warmth of the fire.

'Sugar?' he said, as he poured tea into two cups.

'Thank you,' she replied. She picked up her cup, and sipped the hot liquid. 'Do you have anything to smoke?'

'Of course,' he said, taking out a silver case. He opened it, lit a cigarette, and passed it to her.

She smoked and drank her sweet tea, a smile resting on her lips.

'So,' she said, rattling her chains. 'Hanged tomorrow?'

He grimaced. 'Maybe not, Holdfast.'

'Oh?'

'There's a rumour going round that the queen is going to pardon you.'

Daphne laughed. 'Really? And why would she do that?'

'You have no idea what's going on in the Lower City, have you?'

'Lots of shouting,' she said.

Summel snorted, and a faint smile came to his lips.

'It's practically civil war down there,' he said. 'The city is split between the followers of the church and the crown. While up here the queen and the prophet struggle to stay neutral, down on the streets their supporters are at each other's throats.'

'What about me?'

'No offence, Holdfast,' he replied, drinking his tea, 'but you're just a piece on the gaming board, played by both sides. But to the people, what happens to you matters. If the queen allows you to be hanged, then everyone will think she's weak, and the church will be exonerated from all the accusations being spread about them by the royalists. Her supporters will all go home, and your father?' He shrugged. 'He's been promising the people that they'll have shares in the Sanang invasion this time, and that every soldier will be rewarded handsomely. That seems to have won many of them over, but if you're executed, and this year's campaign is cancelled, they'll desert him like rats fleeing a burning stable.

'On the other hand, if she pardons you, then I expect that the supporters of the church will try to burn the city to the ground, and the cavalry will be ordered in to quell them. That's the queen's choice. Capitulate to the church, or fill the streets with blood.

'To be honest, Holdfast,' the officer went on, 'I think the queen would have preferred it if the church had hanged you, then she could have blamed them. But now that you're back under her authority? Let's just say that I imagine the queen won't have much else on her mind right now.'

'And in all of this,' Daphne said, 'where does the truth fit?'

'I believe what the queen tells me to believe,' Summel said, 'and though by tomorrow it may have changed, right now you remain a convicted traitor in the eyes of the crown, and are in the custody, but also under the protection, of the Queen's Own. I have two armoured squads up here, and the cavalry have closed the great ramp, to keep the public away. All to make sure no harm comes to you between now and your appointed time with justice in the morning.'

He offered her another cigarette.

'Tonight,' he said, 'you'll be confined to these quarters. We'll get those shackles off, and you can get cleaned up, have some dinner, and sleep in a decent bed.'

'Why are you being kind to me?'

'I figure that if you're executed,' he replied, half smiling, 'then there's no harm in making your last night comfortable, but to be honest, and at the risk of making a fool of myself, I confess that I believe you to be innocent. As a captain in the cavalry, I don't believe for a moment that you disobeyed orders.'

'Thank you,' she said, her face flushing from surprised gratitude.

He got up.

'I'll leave you,' he said, then pointed at the two white-aproned aides. 'These gentlemen will see to your needs. Bath, food, drink, and so on. There are fresh clothes in the trunks over by the alcove, and someone will be along soon to remove your chains, and to treat any wounds you have. Remember, there are two full squads outside the room, so I wouldn't recommend trying to escape.'

He walked to the door.

'Until the morning, then,' he said. 'We'll see what justice brings.'

CHAPTER 17

HOLDERS SQUARE

Holdings City, Realm of the Holdings – 1ˢᵗ Day, Last Third Winter 503

In a warm, deep and comfortable sleep, Daphne dreamt she was flying. No, not flying. She dreamt she was being swept about by the winds, buffeted by gales pulling her one way then another, almost tearing her limbs from their sockets with the ferocity of a storm. The noise felt like thunder, a violent and discordant eruption of sound, clashing and shouting in wild anger.

It grew louder, enveloped her, then faded and grew quiet.

She awoke and sat up, water sloshing from the sides of the bathtub. A small lamp was burning from a hook on a wall, and the hearth was glowing a dim red. She was alone. She listened, and heard nothing. Just a dream, she thought, then she heard it again, the sound of raised voices, somewhere in the Old Tower.

She got to her feet, bleary from her sleep being interrupted and stepped out of the tub, soapy water spilling from her. She dried herself, and pulled on the fresh clothes that had been laid out for her, then rummaged in the trunks until she found some decent boots, and a spare leather cuirass. After putting them on, she strapped her left arm to her side, with padding round the elbow. It throbbed from the baton blow, and she was still carrying the bruises and aches from the beating the wardens had given her, but she was clean. She pulled back her wet hair and tied it up. She drew on a little battle-vision, and her head cleared.

The sounds were getting louder, echoing down the stone corridors and halls of the ancient tower. Someone was fighting.

Who?

The Household Cavalry hadn't been negligent enough to leave any weapons in the room for her, but she found a good-sized iron poker by the fireplace, and hefted it in her right hand.

Heavy thudding sounds came from above her, where a cellblock was located, and the ceiling shook, dislodging particles of dust which floated down through the air.

She stole over to the door, and placed her ear against it, listening. Nothing. She reached out and grasped the handle, then paused. Maybe she should stay where she was, she pondered, a tight knot of fear growing in her stomach. However, if someone were looking for her, they must have bypassed this room on their way up to search the cells. Would they be as careless on their return journey?

She opened the door a tiny crack, and peered out. The corridor was lit with regular and frequent torches, and was bright compared to her room. She snuck out, poker in her right hand. There were four bodies lying sprawled across the flagstone floor. One was a member of the cavalry, her uniform bloody, and her sword missing, while the other three were dressed as civilians, and were armed with long knives.

Judging by the mess in the corridor, a crowd had passed from right to left, where the stairs to the upper floors began. Daphne crept along to her right, stepping over the bodies on the floor. The large door at the end of the passageway had been battered off its hinges, and was lying broken on the ground. A large marble statue of an old king was lying headless next to it, having been employed as a ram. Beyond was a cross-roads of passages, and Daphne tried to remember the way that led to the courthouse, and the public area where the ramp down to the Lower City began.

There were a few bodies by the junction, all dead, except for one.

Smeared bloody tracks on the floor led to where a young trooper was dragging himself.

The soldier was on his front, and had been pulling his body along with his arms. There was a large dark bloodstain on his side and back. He saw her, and looked confused. He tried to speak, and blood bubbled on his lips.

'Holdfast?' he gasped at her.

Daphne lay down the poker, and knelt beside him. She unfastened his water canister, and gave him a drink, holding it to his mouth.

He spluttered, spilling water and blood down his leathers.

'Someone has to summon the garrison,' he whispered. 'The church...'

'What?'

'The church,' he continued, wheezing for breath. 'Priests opened Cathedral Steps, and let the mob up.'

'Why?'

'They heard the queen was going to pardon you,' the trooper said. 'They're here to make sure that doesn't happen...'

'Have they entered the palace?'

'That's where most of them are now,' he wheezed. 'They only sent a few dozen to get you.' He reached out his hand and gripped her arm. 'Holdfast,' he said in a hoarse whisper, 'if you're not a traitor, if you are loyal to the Holdings, now would be a good time to prove it... Get the garrison...' He started to retch, and blood spilled from his mouth, then he slumped, his lifeless eyes staring at the wall.

Daphne pulled the man's sword from its sheath, and left the poker where it lay. She stood. What was the right thing to do - go to the palace to help the queen? Try to alert the garrison in the city below, and bring them charging up the ramp to repel the mob? Or just escape? Every decision she made seemed to end in disaster, and she stood frozen to the floor, staring at the dead trooper at her feet.

The thud of boots on stone sounded from the officers' quarters. They must have realised that she was not in the cells. She could hear rooms being broken into, and tried to start moving, but her limbs were unresponsive.

'There she is!' a jubilant voice cried. 'There she is!'

She ran.

With angry shouts behind her, she bolted down a corridor, in the direction of the courthouse, and the ramp down to the Lower City. She leaped over the body of a dead civilian, and ran along the curving passageway. She saw the door ahead of her. It had been barred from the inside with a heavy crossbeam. With the noise of the crowd getting closer, she dropped the sword and pulled at the beam with all her strength. It clattered to the ground, and Daphne pushed open the door.

The courtyard outside was silent in the cool night air, and she sprinted for the iron gate separating it from the ramp. She jumped, reaching for a thick bar with her right hand, and swinging her foot onto the crossbeam. She tried to pull herself up with her good arm, but she was weak, and was only halfway up when hands started to grab at her feet. She kicked out, but the hands hauled her down off the fence, and she fell to the ground. She rolled herself into a ball, as feet lashed out and kicked her, and blows landed on her from above.

Something struck her arm, which she had brought up to protect her face, and she could hear the enraged screams of the mob surrounding her, shoving and pushing each other to get close enough to hurt her. Someone yanked at her hair. Her head was pulled back, and she was kicked in the face.

Pain exploded, her sight flashed and sparked, and she heard shouting, but it seemed to come from far away.

The blows stopped.

Barely conscious, she felt herself be dragged by her good arm, then someone picked up her feet, and she was carried, her left arm still bound to her side.

She could see nothing, then realised that her eyes were clenched shut. Her hearing came back in a great rush, and the sound of a large crowd engulfed her. Shouts and cheers, and jeers and screams surrounded her, and she felt herself be carried up some stairs. She was lowered to the ground, where she lay still, her right hand instinctively reaching for her face. Blood was pumping from her nose, and some of her teeth were loose. The pain pounded through her skull, and she crawled into a small space inside her head, and tried to shut everything else out.

She sensed fingers touch her throat, to feel if she had a pulse, and then she heard a whisper.

'She's alive.'

'Good,' a male voice said.

Hands gripped her by the shoulders, and pulled her up. The roar from the crowd settled, and quietened. She stayed limp, but opened her eyes a crack. She was on a flight of steps, facing an enormous crowd under the night sky. They were staring at her, their faces twisted by cruel victory in the flickering torchlight. Priests were scattered among the crowd, looking satisfied. Daphne could feel the anger and venom emanate from the mass of people, and it was no different from the hate she had felt from the Sanang.

'We have her!' the man bellowed.

The crowd roared and cheered. The man let them continue for several moments, then he gestured for Daphne to be lowered back to the ground. The guards did so, and she settled onto the step, listening, her eyes closed again.

'We have the traitor and warmonger Daphne Holdfast,' the man cried, raising his voice as he addressed the crowd. 'A criminal of the worst kind, and the queen was going to pardon her, to please her lover, this bitch's father. Well, I say no! She pays for her crimes, and she pays for them tonight!'

Lover? Daphne smiled amid the roars from the mob. They thought her father and the queen were lovers?

She started to laugh as the man ranted on, and realised that her fear had vanished. She lay on the ground, beaten, and ready to be executed in front of a baying mob, but she was without fear. She relaxed her mind, and thought about Chane, and whether she was happy, and Agang, with all of his plans. She hoped Weir didn't feel too bad about the appeal. What was her father doing? Was he plotting and scheming in the Lower City, unaware of the coup that was threatening the reign of the queen, his lover? She laughed again, the absurdity of it making her giggle.

She breathed in and out, stilled her aching body, and opened her eyes a tiny bit, letting battle-vision permeate her.

'The queen has shown herself to be incompetent,' the man was saying to the crowd, 'and unfit for office. I do not blame her Majesty as others do, as her terrible illness has ravaged her body, and she barely clings on to life. No, I blame her advisors, and principally the arch-warmonger, Holdfast the elder, and the chief instrument of his perfidy,' he pointed at Daphne again, 'his daughter, Holdfast the younger. We must eradicate the corruption eating at the heart of our nation, and we demand that Prince Guilliam immediately becomes Regent. Let the poor queen die in peace, in her sickbed! But, for all our sakes, let Prince Guilliam rule!'

The crowd roared their approval. Daphne saw that they filled Holders Square, the largest open space in the Upper City, and that she lay on the great stone steps leading up to one of the formal entrances to the palace, the massive doors of which lay open. To her right, several dozen troopers of the Household Cavalry were sitting bunched together at the foot of the steps, unarmed, with their hands on their heads. Civilians with a variety of weapons stood encircling them.

To her left, on a large platform, used whenever the monarch was required to address their subjects on ceremonial occasions, a gallows had been constructed, and a huge man with a black hood stood ready.

Seeing this, her mind focussed, and she knew she would not be led to the noose without a fight.

'This woman,' the man was continuing to rant, 'having been given an officer's commission, and the command of a forward fortress, only through corrupt nepotism...'

Fair enough, Daphne thought.

'...she proved herself incompetent on countless occasions...'

A little harsh.

'...and she betrayed her company, and the Holdings' people, being a coward at heart...'

He was right, Daphne thought, she had been a coward. She had tried to do the right thing, but had always found herself helpless in the hands of others. She had submitted each time to their plans, and had been a thorough coward. She had been used by the church, and by the queen. Well, no more. She had allowed events to happen to her, trusting that the inherent goodness within people would protect her and keep her safe, and it had all been for nothing.

She looked up. No one noticed, her head was angled downwards, and the crowds' attention was on the speaker.

She took in her immediate surroundings, noting the people, their weapons, and the exact location of where the cavalry troopers were being held. She was going to need a full and sustained burst of battle-vision, one that would exhaust her physical reserves, but the time for saving for the future had gone, and all that mattered was now.

There were three men guarding her, civilians dressed in dark hoods.

She drew in all the battle-vision she could take, and her mind nearly exploded in sensory impact. She rode the storm, and used its power. Her right hand dashed out quicker than anyone's eyes could follow. She pulled a knife from the first guard's belt and rammed it into his crotch, doubling him over. As she pulled the knife free, she turned, aimed and threw, and the blade struck the speaker in the side of his neck. He staggered, his hand reaching up to his throat, and he turned to look at Daphne, who was now on her feet. He gave her a look of stunned surprise, then toppled over.

The crowd roared in confusion and anger, and many started rushing towards the stairs.

Daphne ran up the steps, ducking and rolling under the flailing swipe of a guard. Another tried to grab her from behind, his big arms reaching for her, but she slipped out of his grasp, weaving and dodging. When she reached the top step she turned about, and leapt through the air, landing on the back of one of the civilians guarding the penned-in soldiers, knocking her off her feet. She snatched the woodaxe from the woman's hand, and threw it at the next guard in line, cutting him down. The troopers of the Household Cavalry gazed at her in amazement, and a few reacted, getting to their feet. Daphne registered this without pausing; leaping, rolling, and killing the poorly armed and untrained civilians that were surrounding the troopers. In a few moments, half of them were down, and Daphne was armed with a six-foot stave.

The Household Cavalry rallied, and attacked their remaining captors, pulling weapons from the bodies of those Daphne had slain. Soon all the remaining troopers were up and fighting, and had created a buffer between Daphne and the rest of the mob.

Daphne raced back up the steps, having bought herself a few moments. She upended a man who ran at her, and took the purloined cavalry sword from his hands. She ran through the great doors of the palace, and into the main entrance hall. The room was in disarray, tables overturned, chairs broken, paintings pulled from the walls. Ignoring all of it, she raced for the door in the corner of the hall, which led to the guardhouse and the stables.

She felt her energy flagging with each step as she hurtled along the passageways, and she was almost on her knees by the time she reached the dark stableyard. Staggering, she sliced off the bonds that held her left arm close to her body, and stretched out the crooked limb as far as she was able. She gasped in pain, but it was manageable, and it felt good to have some movement in her arm again.

She heard the low sound of horses, and saw some gazing at her from within the nearest stable-block. She smiled, and went through the open entrance. Apart from her and the horses, it was deserted. Even the stable-hands must have run, she thought. Though she wanted to linger, she chose a short but sturdy chestnut mare. She entered the mare's stall and, holding her neck with her good hand, ran the fingers of her withered left hand down its flank, the smell of the animal filling her, and giving her heart. The mare snorted, and bumped her nose against Daphne's shoulder, making her smile.

She pulled down the saddle and reins from a peg on the wall, and got the horse ready. Having no sheath, she left the sword behind, taking instead a long knife she found near the door. She placed it down the inside of her boot.

Daphne led the mare out of the stable-block, her hooves clip-clopping off the flagstones. The sound of the mob was more distant here, but she knew they would be looking for her. She reached a set of gates that led back out into the Upper City, halfway between Holders Square and the top of the ramp.

Stepping forward, she removed the bar, slung it to the ground, and pushed the gate open. She put her foot in the stirrup, and pulled herself onto the mare's back. The horse shifted its weight a little, its breath steaming up into the night air. Daphne wrapped the reins around her left hand and wrist, and nudged in with her ankles. The mare responded, and Daphne smiled again. It was nearly a year since she had been on a horse, by far the longest time since she could walk. It felt like she was home again, back where she belonged. She had been nervous about this moment ever since she had been injured, but she could feel her left arm control the mare as if there were nothing wrong with it. She circled for a few moments, feeling out her nature, speaking soothing words, stroking her neck with her right hand.

'Hah!' she shouted, kicking her heels and aiming the mare at the open gate, and the horse took off through the archway and into the lane, its hooves clattering. Daphne pulled the reins, and steered the mare to the left, and they raced up the street. The road came out onto a large thoroughfare, used for processions from the ramp to the palace, and the people there turned to stare.

Daphne kept her head down, and urged the mare into the crowd at a gallop. People dived to each side, yelling. Over to her left, the larger mob in Holders Square was turning their attention to the commotion she was causing on the road to the ramp.

Daphne kept the mare at a canter, but the crowds were starting to press around her as they sped past. Someone grabbed the reins, but she drew her knife and slashed at the hand, and the mare careered down the street. Up ahead of her, people were pulling a cart into the road to block her way, so she pulled on the reins, and guided the mare down a tight alley, and into an area of narrow lanes and walled gardens. They cantered on for a few turns, and the sounds of the crowd faded behind her. She pulled back on the reins and the mare came to a halt, next to the gates of an ancient cemetery.

'Good girl,' Daphne said, patting her flank. 'Thank you.'

Daphne gazed up, looking for a high point, and spotted a spire close by. Gripping onto the reins, she drew on her line-vision, and her sight shot up to the top of the spire. She controlled her sense of dislocation and looked at the city laid out wide before her. To the right, in a flickering glare of torches, a sea of people flooded Holders Square, while the Old Tower stood high and proud to her left. Beyond was the wide ramp down to the bridge, and the garrison. The ramp was empty, and there were no sign of movement from the bridge. Across the Lower City, flames and smoke were rising, and she could see people on the streets. Did any of them realise what was happening in the Upper City? Although the mob in Holders Square looked large, it was a small fraction of the masses of people living in the capital.

She turned her focus back to the Upper City, looking for a way down. Both the Royal Steps and the Cathedral Steps had been commandeered by the mob, and only the ramp lay clear. She checked the location of her pursuers, and quickly mapped out a route. She closed her eyes and switched back to battle-vision upon re-opening them. She was getting better at this. She grinned, the dry blood on her face cracking.

'Ready?' she whispered to the mare, and dug in her heels.

The horse took off, and Daphne raced her through the narrow twisting lanes. At one corner they had to jump over a handcart, sending civilians diving to the ground, and at the crossroads just before the ramp started, she had to gallop out in full view of the crowd, gathered only a few paces away. The mob roared and surged towards her.

Daphne pulled the mare into a tight turn, while hands reached out for them, stretching and almost touching. She kicked her heels and the mare burst out from the mob, Daphne hanging on, and they raced down the ramp, hooves clattering, an angry roar echoing in her ears.

There was one switchback in the ramp, halfway down, and Daphne struggled to control the mare in the turn, they were going so fast, and sparks flew as horseshoes skidded off the flagstones.

'Come on!' Daphne screamed, as the mare made the turn, and they careered down towards the river.

As they approached the bridge, on the far bank she saw cavalry troopers pointing at her. They were guarding the entrance to the city garrison, which stood on the Lower City side of the river.

Daphne slowed the mare to a walk as they crossed the bridge, while the soldiers stared at her.

She pulled on the reins, and came to a halt before them.

'Tell your commander,' she said, her speech slurred from the bruising on her face, 'that she should get up to the palace, if she wants to save the queen. The church are about to put Prince Guilliam on the throne.'

'It's Daphne Holdfast!' one of them shouted.

'Get down, Holdfast!' their sergeant yelled. 'You're coming with us!'

'No,' she said. 'I'm done. Just do your job, and pass on my message. Can you manage that?'

The sergeant looked blank for a moment, then frowned. 'Off the horse, Holdfast.'

Daphne pulled her feet from the stirrups, and untangled the fingers of her left hand from the reins.

The soldiers approached. They reached out their hands.

Before they could touch her, she sprang up onto the mare's back and jumped, leaping through the air and diving over the side of the bridge into the cold dark waters of the river. She heard yells and curses from above as she resurfaced, then she kicked out with her feet, and drifted away into the night.

Hours later, near dawn, Daphne perched on the tiled roof of a tenement, in a pleasant residential district of the capital. Wearing clothes she had stolen from an open window, a dark hood shadowed her face as she watched the building opposite.

A faint light was growing to her left, the east, where the first glimmerings of sunrise were approaching. Over to her right, the Upper City was ablaze, and she could see flames coming from the Old Tower, and from part of the citadel. The streets below were silent. She had ghosted through areas of the Lower City where riots were still going on, but none had reached this neighbourhood, filled as it was with more upmarket, and guarded, mansions of the merchant class.

The particular mansion that concerned her looked no different from the others, but she knew it was where her old friend Douanna was residing.

A bedroom lay opposite Daphne's position and through a narrow crack in the shutters she could see a bed, where someone was sleeping. She smiled at the thought of what she was about to attempt. Though she had read about the power in books, she had no idea how it was done, but something within her was urging her to try. After all, if her father could do it, why couldn't she?

She made herself comfortable, resting against the stone blocks of a chimney, and focussed her line-vision, shooting her sight right through the crack in the shutters of the window. In the dim light of the bedroom, she looked around, and located the bed. Douanna was there, sleeping peacefully, a thin cover pulled up to her shoulders. One of her arms was resting on the blanket, and her silvery scales glimmered in the low light.

Daphne focussed all her vision on the woman, and tried to enter her mind. She pushed her sight right up to the woman's closed eyes, but nothing happened. She concentrated with all her being, pushing her line-vision to its limits, trying to feel her way into Douanna's head. She was tiring, and was about to give up in frustration, when her vision went black, and she reeled in confusion.

She felt panic, and a strange, dislocating sense of being in someone else's mind. She could feel the woman breathing, and sensed her body and limbs as she slept.

Douanna? she whispered.

Nothing.

Douanna? she said a little louder.

Ahhh! Who's there? Am I dreaming?

No. Well, yes, you're asleep, but I'm really here.

Daphne? My dear, is that you?

Daphne half sobbed. *Yes.*

How cheeky! Douanna said. *You never told me you had the inner-vision.*

You know about that? I thought it was a secret.

Not a very well kept one, my dear, Douanna said. *Where are you?*

On the roof of the building across from your window.

Ha! Douanna laughed. *I always knew you were a resourceful girl. And what is it that I can do for you?*

I was hoping you might like to take me to Rahain, Daphne said. *We could be partners. I think my powers might be useful.*

Sounds a little risky, Daphne dear, Douanna replied. *Could be dangerous even. A long journey across the Plateau, and the Inner Sea, and then round the Grey Mountains to the cities of my people. Are you sure?*

I am.

Hmmm, Douanna considered. *One condition, my precocious young mage.*

Yes?

I'll need a cup of tea first.

AUTHOR'S NOTES

FEBRUARY 2020

This is where it all began. I wrote Trials and Retreat together, as a single book, back in early 2016.

In the first draft however, the Daphne and Killop chapters alternated, and that format was originally meant to be the first book in the Magelands series. However, after a lot of thought, I decided to disentangle the two stories, and lead with *The Queen's Executioner* for the series.

After some heavy re-writes and revisions, I felt that this was the right time to release the two stories, this time individually.

ABOUT THE AUTHOR

Christopher Mitchell is the author of the Magelands epic fantasy series.

For more information:
www.christophermitchellbooks.com
info@christophermitchellbooks.com